The Bookseller's Tale

Ann Swinfen was born in Akron, Ohio, on 5th October 1937, and died on 4th August 2018, in Broughty Ferry, Scotland. Educated in America and England, she was awarded degrees from Oxford, London and Dundee universities. Married to a fellow student in 1960, she brought up five children, while working variously as a computer journalist, a part-time lecturer in English, and a member of the Council of the Open University. Altogether she published one non-fiction book, *In Defence of Fantasy*, and twenty-three hugely successful, and mostly historical, novels, set in the 14th, 16th and 17th centuries.

Also by Ann Swinfen

Oxford Medieval Mysteries

ANN SWINFEN

the Bookseller's Tale

CANELO

First published in the United Kingdom in 2016 by Shakenoak Press

This edition published in the United Kingdom in 2022 by

Canelo
Unit 9, 5th Floor
Cargo Works, 1–2 Hatfields
London, SE1 9PG
United Kingdom

Print ISBN 978 1 80436 102 3
Ebook ISBN 978 1 80032 751 1

Look for more great books at www.canelo.co

Printed and bound in Great Britain by Clays Ltd, Elcograf S.p.A.

1

for David

Remembering Oxford

Chapter One

Oxford, Spring 1353

As for those of us who survived, every day is precious. To come awake in the morning – whether the sky is tranquil blue or thunderous grey – is an incomprehensible joy. I live! But such joyful thoughts are soon clouded by remembrance of those who have crossed that dark threshold, whose voices we shall never hear again, whose very faces are fading from our memory, slipping away like sad ghosts. Except, of course, when they have left living reminders.

'Papa!' Alysoun landed on my stomach, expelling all my breath, and proceeded to jump up and down, in case I might still have some air left in my lungs. 'May I have a puppy? Jonathan Baker has six, and he says if he cannot find homes for them, his father will drown them all in the Cherwell. You would not let the little puppies drown, Papa, would you?'

Her tone combined diplomacy with wheedling. Truly, there had been very few dogs in Oxford since the pestilence, when every single one that could be caught by the town authorities was slain, for fear of spreading the killing plague.

'I am sure,' I said, shoving her off and struggling to sit up, 'that Jonathan and John Baker will have no difficulty in finding homes for all their puppies.'

The bed was so vast, now that I occupied it alone.

Alysoun sat up, hugging her knees, and gazed at me appealingly, but remained leaning on my stomach. Sometimes I can scarcely bear to look at her, she is so like.

'What does your aunt say?' I asked, cowardly.

'She said I must ask you.'

Of course. All unpleasant decisions are referred to me. My sister decides everything else.

'And besides,' I said, 'it is hardly past dawn. Has Jonathan been here already?'

She clasped her hands together and looked at me piteously. Tears had welled up in her eyes. 'He must know *today*, else John Baker will drown them this very afternoon.'

'Off with you. Let me dress,' I said briskly. 'Then I will think on't.'

I already knew what my decision would be. Almost certainly, so did Alysoun.

She ran off, shouting. 'Rafe, Rafe, Papa says he'll think on't.'

I fumbled as I straightened my hose and tied my points. What would we do with a dog? Nay, a *puppy*? It would be underfoot. It would make puddles everywhere, to Margaret's fury. Almost certainly it would chew my supplies of parchment to rags, and if it were to find my precious books... Nay, it was impossible.

Margaret took one look at me as I entered the kitchen, her mouth pursed in disapproval as she thumped a mug of small ale down beside a plate of bread still warm from the oven. My sister will not buy baker's bread, for she swears they eke it out with chalk and chopped straw, even though this means she must prepare the dough every night before bed, then rise before dawn to bake it.

2

'Why do you give me that look?' I said, as I pulled out a stool and sat at the table. I took a long draught of the ale, pretending indifference, but in the face of her speaking silence, I could not help myself. 'What have I done?'

'It is not what you *have* done, it is what you are going to.'

She cut the thinnest possible slice of cheese and laid it next to my bread.

'I cannot have a puppy under my feet all day, tripping me up, making a dirty mess. It must needs be shut out of the shop, so I shall be left to care for it.'

'I have only said I will think on't.'

'Ha!'

She stomped out to the pantry. Even her footsteps spoke volumes. I began to break my fast. The bread, as always, was light-textured and nutty, but while she was out of the kitchen I reached over and cut myself more cheese.

'I saw that.'

I laughed. Margaret cannot sustain her annoyance for long.

'You would not begrudge me a morsel of cheese, Meg. I shall have a long day in the shop today, and this evening I must walk out to Yardley's farm for goose feathers. A man must keep up his strength.'

She pulled out another stool and sat down opposite me.

'Nicholas, I know it is difficult for you to refuse Alysoun anything. She grows more like Elizabeth every day. But she is *not* Elizabeth. And is a puppy the best thing for her?'

'She is tender hearted, and she grieves that John Baker will drown the puppies.'

Margaret sniffed. 'Unlikely. There's many folk in Oxford will be glad of a dog. Since the plague, thieves have had a fine time of it, with scarce a dog guarding any man's house.'

'And shall we not have a dog to guard our house?'

I was conscious of scoring a point, but Margaret waved my words away. 'In the meantime, there will be puddles on my floors.'

I glanced down at the slabs of golden local stone which formed the floors at street level of both house and shop. My father-in-law, their original builder, had a healthy fear of fire, when so much of his stock was vulnerable. Even the roof was one of the few town houses not to be thatched, but roofed with slates, like the colleges of the university. He had told me that he had made an exchange with Merton College, trading a fine copy of Aristotle's *Ethics* for enough of their tiles to roof this building.

Margaret kept the floors swept and scrubbed daily, so I could understand her concern.

'When we were children, I don't remember it taking long to train the dogs.'

'They spent most of their time outdoors on the farm. This creature will be a house dog.'

I reached across the table and took both of her hands in mine.

'I think she needs something to love, Meg.'

She looked down at our joined hands, then raised her face to me. There were unshed tears in her eyes.

'Aye, well, I suppose we all do. And we have already lost enough. Very well.'

I gave her hands a squeeze, then leaned across and kissed the top of her head, tightly swathed as usual in a spotless white wimple.

'I will tell her.'

I drained my mug and carried the last of my bread and cheese out into the garden, where I could hear the children's shouts. Alysoun was sitting astride a low branch of one of the apple trees, while Rafe danced about at the base of the trunk.

'Help me up, Aly. I can't reach!'

For a moment a flash of memory seized me – myself running after Margaret, crying, 'Wait for me!' But Margaret was five years my senior, while Alysoun and Rafe were but two years apart. It made a difference. And maidens grow up much more swiftly than lads. I can barely remember a time when Margaret did not seem to me to be one of the adults. When she was married off at fourteen I was nine, just three years older than Alysoun now. My sister and I had not lived in the same house again until four years ago, after the pestilence took my Elizabeth and Margaret's brute of a husband, the ill-named innkeeper Elias Makepeace.

In her heart, I knew that Margaret had found the death of her husband a release, after twelve years of drunken beatings, but then the plague had also taken her two children. She was brisk and kind to my children, but a haunted look came sometimes into her eyes when she looked at them. I could see her wondering how it might have been, had her sons still been with us, four years on.

For those of us who survived, there remained a lingering fear of ever allowing ourselves to love anyone again, so fragile is life, so terrifying the sudden loss. We walk on a cliff edge, averting our eyes from the precipitous drop on to the jagged rocks below.

'Well, Alysoun, shall we go to John Baker's and look at these puppies?'

She gave a squeal and threw herself off the branch. There was the sound of ripping cloth. Margaret would have something else to lay at my door. A cascade of petals followed Alysoun like an unseasonable snowfall, lingering in her hair. I let them lie.

'Me too,' Rafe begged, tugging at the hem of my cotte.

'Aye,' I said, 'you may come too. We must choose a puppy who will be right for all the family.'

We walked back through the kitchen, where Margaret studiously turned her back on us, then along the passageway with its doors to Margaret's stillroom and the storeroom where I kept my stock of parchment, ink, and quills. The whole front of the building on the ground floor was taken up by the shop, dim now, as I had not yet opened the shutters. Motes of dust danced in the thin shafts of light thrusting through the cracks, for the shop faced south and already the sun was bright.

I nearly fell over the small boy sitting hunched on the doorstep.

'Jonathan,' I said, 'what do you here?'

He stood up and scrubbed a hand across his face, leaving it smeared. His clothes were ragged, though his father was not poor. John Baker, like me, was a widower, but had no sister to keep house for him and mind his child.

'I was waiting to hear whether Alysoun might have a puppy, maister. My papa is going to drown them.'

'Nonsense,' I said briskly. 'How many are there?'

'Six.'

'I am sure you can find homes for them all. I am going to Yardley's farm today. I will ask there. And have you thought to ask at the mills? Your Jewel is a fine ratter. If her puppies are as good, any of the millers will be glad of one, to keep the rats from the grain.'

His face brightened at once. 'I'll go to Trill Mill and Blackfriars now.' He turned to run back up the High Street toward Carfax.

'There's Holywell Mill as well,' I called after him.

'Aye, but I know the miller at Trill's,' he shouted back over his shoulder. His bare feet slapped on the dried mud of the street.

Alysoun slipped her hand in mine. 'That was well thought on, Papa.'

I smiled down at her. 'The rats have become a plague of their own, and the millers lose much of their grain.'

The slaughter of Oxford's dogs and cats had been well intentioned, but the result had been an explosion in the town's population of rats, with few surviving predators to keep them down, only those whose owners – like John Baker – had kept them hidden away. He claimed he had done so in order to protect his flour from those same rats, but beneath his rough manner he was a good man, more soft-hearted than he would wish you to know, even if Margaret suspected the contents of his loaves. In his own way, he loved the dog Jewel, and I could not truly believe he would drown her puppies.

The bakehouse was across the High Street from our shop, but a little further west, three doors from Tackley's inn, where I had first lodged when I came to Oxford as a fourteen-year-old student. Both lay just outside our parish of St-Peter-in-the-East, falling within the neighbouring parish of St Mary the Virgin, the university church, an excellent location for a bakehouse. When we arrived, John had already lowered his counter flap, open to the street, and laid out loaves and buns. People buy their bread early, and the heady scent of fresh baking was drifting out into the High. There was a small crowd outside the bakehouse, so we waited until John had served his customers. He looked up and saw us.

'Good morrow, Nicholas. Have you come for bread?' He raised an ironic eyebrow as he leaned across the counter.

'Nay, I am persuaded by these children, yours and mine, that you are seeking homes for Jewel's puppies.'

'Aye. They needs must go. I cannot give houseroom to seven dogs. They're for the river today, any that do not find homes.'

'You do not mean that.'

'I do. With the pittance the colleges pay for their bread, I can barely keep myself and my son.'

It was an old grievance, and I had no wish to listen to a catalogue of his woes. 'Where are these puppies, then? I may take one of them.'

'Where's that son of mine? He can show you. I need to mind the shop.'

Alysoun slipped through the open door into the bakery. 'Jonathan is gone to see whether any of the millers will take a puppy.'

'That's well thought.'

'My papa thought of it.'

John grinned at me. 'Come you through, then. They are in the shed at the back. The children know the way. Take one if you want one.'

'Are they weaned?' I said, as I walked into the warm yeasty air of John's shop.

'Near enough. They've eaten some bread and broth. They can leave their dam.'

I thought it cruel to take the puppies from their mother if they were not fully weaned, but I was unsure whether John was serious in his intention to drown them.

The shop was also the bakehouse, with its sacks of different flours, from the finest white for gentlemen's wastel bread down to coarse mixed grains for maslin. The kneading troughs were scoured clean, for however untidy the rest of his dwelling, John must keep the bakehouse clean or be closed down by the town assessors. The ovens were still hot, and row upon row of loaves stood upon the shelves. John threw open the door at the back of the shop, the light catching the dusting of flour on his strong forearms. A baker develops muscles to rival those of a wrestler.

'Will you not keep one of the puppies yourself?' I said. 'To train up as a ratter?'

'Mayhap. I have not decided.'

We followed him along the passage to a small, untidy kitchen. The building was laid out much as our own, but lacked Margaret's firm hand. Like ours, the kitchen opened directly on to the garden.

'There.' John pointed to a shed halfway down the ill-kept garden. 'Take as many as you want.'

I saw Alysoun's eyes light up. 'One will be quite sufficient,' I said hastily. 'I have not decided whether I will take one at all, not until I have seen if they are healthy.'

'Papa!' Alysoun's face was tragic, but John merely grinned.

'Aye, they're strong and healthy. Jewel has nursed them well. 'Tis not her first litter, after all.'

'I know.'

The previous litter had been amongst the last of Oxford's dogs to be killed, thrown heedless into the Canditch with the other corpses of cats and dogs, and the occasional plague victim, who had died from home and tumbled in.

'Who's the sire?' I asked.

The baker shrugged. 'Who knows? She found a dog somewhere, or he found her. Some kind of spaniel, I'm thinking. You'll see.'

The shed door was partially ajar, sending a band of sunlight on to the heap of dogs inside. Jewel looked up at us and thumped her tail, but the puppies, curled up together, never opened their eyes. I saw at once what John meant. The puppies – all but one – had the long floppy ears of spaniels. The odd one looked mostly terrier, like their dam.

'If I keep one,' John said, pointing at the terrier pup, 'it will be that one. If the sire is some gentleman's hunting spaniel, the others will have the instinct to retrieve, not kill. I'll have a house full of live rats.'

I laughed. 'Best not say that to the millers.'

My suspicion had been right. John could not bring himself to drown the whole litter. We had all of us seen enough death to last a lifetime.

Alysoun had thrown herself down to kneel in the straw, and was stroking Jewel's head. 'We won't hurt your babies,' she whispered.

Rafe squatted down next to her and was regarding the puppies with awe, his finger in his mouth. I realised with a sharp stab that neither of them had ever seen a litter of puppies before. On our family farm, where Margaret and I had grown up, there had been at least one new litter every year.

'May I pick one up?' Alysoun looked over her shoulder at John.

'Of course, my maid. Which do you like best?'

'This one.' She lifted one of the smallest and cradled it under her chin. The puppy opened its eyes and yawned, showing its small milk teeth. Apart from a faint squeak when it was pulled out of the warm bundle of the litter, it seems not to mind being held.

'Isn't he beautiful, Papa?'

'Let me see.' I took the puppy from her. Despite its small size it was a good weight, the stomach well rounded. The fur was glossy and healthy, the eyes clear, the long ears free of mites.

'It's a girl, Alysoun. Did you want a boy?'

'Nay, I want this one! 'Tis no matter whether it be girl or boy.'

'Rafe,' I said, 'what do you think? Shall we have this one?'

As the youngest in the family, his opinion was rarely regarded. He reached out a hand and patted the puppy hesitantly. 'Aye,' he said.

'That is settled then.' I turned to John, who nodded.

'Take it, and my thanks. One less to drown.'

Alysoun turned a shocked face to him. 'You will wait until Jonathan speaks to the millers, will you not, Master Baker?'

'Aye, my maid.'

'And Papa will ask at Yardley's farm this afternoon.' She bent down and whispered to Jewel, who did not seem distressed that we were taking away one of her young.

'Off to Yardley's, are you?' John led us back to the shop, where customers were gathering again. 'Goose feathers?'

'Aye. I'll ask. They may need a dog. God go with 'ee, John. Time I opened the shop.'

I carried the puppy as we crossed the High Street, the children running ahead to open the door, shouting to Margaret.

My two scriveners were already in the shop, but showed no sign of starting work. I bit down my annoyance. They knew their tasks for the day and did not need me to repeat my instructions of the night before. Walter Blunt, the older man, had the grace to look somewhat guilty and began making much of laying out his writing materials and taking out the exemplar of the *Logica: Ut Dixit*, from which he must copy out two *peciae* today. Each section, each *pecia*, consisted of sixteen pages, and he should be able to complete the work within the day. He was writing on paper, producing a plain copy for students to rent. No fine penmanship or parchment was required.

Roger Pigot was another matter. Two years younger than I, he was as insolent as a bejant student of fourteen or fifteen. I would not have employed him, save for the fact that he had a very fine hand. He was working his way through a copy of a French tale of Robin Hood, writing on parchment and decorating the margins with flowing vines and flowers. He was no great artist, but he could design a pretty illuminated capital for the start of each section, good enough for the merchant's wife who had commissioned the work.

'Roger,' I said sharply, 'why are you idling about? Get you to work.'

Before he could return an impudent answer, I hurried through to the house with the children and the puppy, who was fully awake now and squirming in my hands. I set her down in the middle of the kitchen floor, where she looked about her with interest, then squatted down in a posture which was immediately recognisable. Before I could bundle her outside, a yellow puddle had spread out across the floor. The puppy stood up and sniffed it with interest.

'Alysoun,' I said, 'put her out in the garden at once. She has to learn that she must relieve herself there, not in your aunt's kitchen.'

I looked around helplessly for a rag to wipe the floor, but before I could find one, Margaret came in, passing Alysoun and giving the puppy a sour look.

'What did I tell you, Nicholas? Nay, not that cloth. I use that one to polish the knives and spoons.' She snatched away the cloth I had reached for. 'Away with you and mind your shop. I will deal with this.'

I turned and fled, feeling somewhat like a scolded puppy myself and relieved to be away from the drama of a sullied kitchen. In the shop I was master, but not always, I fear, in the house.

Walter had opened the shutters and was already at work, his quill moving rapidly over the rough paper, though he muttered under his breath from time to time as the tip caught. It could not be helped. I could not afford parchment for the *peciae* the students rented. And if the paper came back creased or torn, I had to fine them a farthing for minor damage, a ha'penny for worse.

Roger was still laying out a selection of quills and brushes, and went now to fetch the coloured inks he would use for decorations. The simpler ones I made myself, invading Margaret's stillroom to do so, but the more expensive, like the lapis blue, I bought in small quantities from the painter's merchant who supplied the local monasteries and friaries, as well as those colleges which employed their own illuminators. I had caught Roger the previous month trying to steal some of the precious blue, no doubt to sell, and he was under warning. Since then I had fixed a padlock to the storeroom door, which I now unlocked for him. He glowered at me through the heavy fringe of greasy hair which fell over his face, but I ignored him. I needed him to finish the French book so I could sell it and recover the cost of the particularly fine parchment on which it was being written.

Unlike almost all the other shops on the High Street, mine did not let down a shutter across the bottom of the window to form a counter into the street, on which to display items for sale. The goods I sold were much too delicate to expose to a dust-laden wind or to the risk of a sudden shower. However, once the shutters over the wide window in the shop front were opened, passersby could easily see the rack of secondhand books laid out on view, a safe distance inside. It was one of my obligations, having sworn the oath to become an official *stationarius* and *librarius* for the university, to display all secondhand books prominently. I was also restricted as to how much profit I might make on them. Moreover, the university fixed the rental price paid by students for the *peciae* of their essential study texts.

It was irksome, but the position of official bookseller to the university had the advantage of bringing in a regular income. As for any private commissions I undertook, like the French book, I could charge whatever I pleased. In the first years after the plague, when half the students and masters had perished, I often wondered whether we would have enough to live on, Margaret and the children and I. Even, I thought of returning to the family farm, but with my cousin Edmond now in possession, since the death of my father and elder brother, I put it off from day to day. Somehow, the university had survived. More students had arrived. A few masters, who had gone to teach in Paris or Bologna or Prague, returned to Oxford, as though those fearful years of plague had driven them to seek the comfort of their own country.

When Roger had finally settled to his work, I began to unpack a barrel of books which I had stored the previous day under the counter where I wrote my bills of sale and did my accounts. A widow from Banbury, who could not read, had brought her late husband's small library to me for valuation.

'They're no mortal use to me, Master Elyot,' she had said, wiping her eyes on the trailing hem of her sleeve, 'but my Edward set a great store by them. Learned to read with the monks of Abingdon, he did, like a proper cleric. Now I hope they will keep me and my daughter, for she had the pestilence and it has left her deaf. I'll not find a husband for her.'

The girl, standing shyly behind her mother, had been pretty once, but the scars left by illness marred her appearance now. Her face spoiled and her hearing gone, she might well fail to find a husband. When her mother died, how would she fare? Such afflicted souls have a poor time of it. Yet if she had a dowry – which these books could provide – some man might be glad of her, perhaps a widower like me, but left with a large brood of children and no sister to come to his aid. A second wife to care for his young ones might be forgiven her disfigurement. I would give the widow the best price I could for the books, but I must not lose money. I had my own family to support, and no income but this shop.

'When you finish that page, Walter,' I said, 'come and help me assess these books.'

He nodded, but did not raise his eyes from his writing.

Walter had worked for my father-in-law, Humphrey Hadley, for ten years before I married Elizabeth and joined the business, and he was as shrewd a judge of the value of a book as you could wish. When-Elizabeth's father died in the very first month of the plague, he bequeathed the property and the business to us, and we had been glad of Walter's assistance as we struggled to carry on through those black months. The plague was dwindling away as Elizabeth came near her time with Rafe and I dared to hope that we would all survive, but the birth had weakened her. Rafe was but two weeks old when she was struck down and died three days later. By then the horrors of the mass graves were over, and I was able to bury her decently in St Peter's churchyard. Without Walter in the dark days after her death, neither I nor the business could have continued.

I laid out the books in a row on the table, six of them, varying in quality. Walter came to stand beside me and immediately picked up one.

'This is a very fine bestiary, Master Elyot,' he said.

'Aye, I noticed it last night. It has been well read and the spine is just a very little worn, but otherwise it is in excellent condition.'

He turned over the pages. 'The colours are still very fresh.' He held the book open for me to see. The picture showed a strange animal with a horn growing from its forehead, a scaly hide, and cloven hooves. It was like no animal I had ever seen, either in the flesh or in a book, but it was exquisitely done, every blade of grass and daisy under the creature's feet picked out with care, a knowing gleam shining from its eye.

Roger abandoned his work and came to peer over Walter's shoulder. I did not send him back to his desk. Let him study the work of a real artist. Perhaps he would then be less arrogant about his own modest skills.

'I should be able to give her a good price for that,' I said, dipping a quill in my ink pot and scribbling figures on a scrap of paper. 'There is a Regent Master at Gloucester College who is interested in such books. I think he would pay well for it. The rest are not so valuable.'

I looked them over. Most were in fairly good condition, all except Boethius's *Arithmetic*, probably left from the owner's time as a schoolboy with the monks of Abingdon. Still, I would have no trouble selling that, for a modest price, to one of the young students newly arrived in Oxford. There was a collection of tales – Robin Hood again (shorter, and in English), Sir Bevis of Hampton, Arthur and Guinevere, Floris and Blauncheflur, Sir Galahad. Originally they had been separate small books, but at some time in the past (not recently, I thought) they had been bound together. This had necessitated trimming some of the pages to fit, which gave the book a somewhat ragged appearance, but such tales are also easy to sell. I would try the merchant's wife who had commissioned the French book.

There was a book of husbandry, another slim volume recounting the stories of classical heroes, and a useful volume of rhetoric topics, such as students use – I had one myself. I thought that the owner of these books had once had aspirations to become a scholar.

Between us, Walter and I arrived at what we reckoned was a fair price for the six books, and I wrote a message to the widow, which I would send with the next carter travelling to Banbury. Once she agreed to my offer I would contact the master at Gloucester College and the merchant's wife. The remaining four books would join the others on my secondhand shelf.

When the students emerged from their morning lectures, the shop became busy as they crowded in to buy writing materials. Two of the older students came to return *peciae* of Aristotle's *Metaphysics* and Boethius's *Music*. Both students had completed the fundamental course of the Trivium – Grammar, Logic, and Rhetoric – and were now studying the more advanced Quadrivium – Geometry, Music, Arithmetic and Astronomy, which also included additional reading in Philosophy. One of the students I knew quite well, William Farringdon, for he had once worked for me briefly and lodged at Hart Hall, where my friend Jordain Brinkylsworth was Warden. Jordain had told me only last week that he was worried about the lad, who seemed unusually distracted and inattentive in lectures, and lost his way in propounding his argument in the obligatory debates.

'A model student until now, Nicholas,' he said, 'but something is troubling him. He will not confide in me, but merely shakes his head and swears that nothing is amiss.'

I sometimes teased Jordain that he was as anxious as a mother hen over his charges, but I had seen that this time he was genuinely worried.

Looking closely at William Farringdon now, I saw that he was very pale and nervous, plucking at the neck of his shirt and glancing from time to time over his shoulder. However, if he would not admit his troubles to Jordain, he was not likely to tell me, a comparative stranger. There was a fresh ink blot on one of the pages of the *pecia* of the Boethius that he was returning, but I decided to ignore it. I saw him watching me from the corner of his eye as I inspected the document, and also saw his look of relief as I turned over the damaged page without comment.

Perhaps the lad had money troubles. It would not be surprising. Many Oxford students came from the families of small country gentry, who had suffered a great deal as a result of the pestilence, not only from deaths in their own families but from widespread deaths amongst the villeins and small tenant farmers who worked their land. Lacking the labour of the former and the rents of the latter, many of these families found themselves almost beggared. My own family was of yeoman stock, but we too had suffered financial loss.

I always closed the shop over the dinner hour, when the students would go back to their halls. It gave me the chance to eat my own dinner with my family, while my scriveners took themselves off to a tavern, usually Tackley's since it was nearest. It seemed the new puppy had won praise for performing liberally in the garden and had not yet sullied Margaret's clean floor a second time.

'And have you found a name for her yet?' I asked, after saying grace over our meal of mutton pottage.

'Rafe wanted Isolde, from that story you told us,' Alysoun said, 'but I told him it was too sad.'

Margaret raised her eyebrows at me.

'It was a very... *simple* version of the tale,' I reassured her.

Alysoun had heard of Tristram and Isolde from her older cousin, Edmond's daughter, the last time we had visited the farm, and had pestered me until I recounted a version suitable for children. Edmond's daughter was fifteen and a romantic.

'Aye.' I nodded. ''Tis a sad name. Have you thought on one yourself, Alysoun?'

'I can only think on boys' names for dogs – Valiant, Holdfast, Gripper.'

We all looked at the puppy, who was curled up near the hearth, despite the warmth of the spring day. I could have sworn her stomach was rounder than it had been. Perhaps Margaret had softened enough to give the mite some food. As if she felt our eyes on her, the puppy sat up suddenly, cocking her head to one side.

'I agree,' I said. 'She does not look like a Valiant or a Holdfast or a Gripper. Or even a Boarsdeath or a Stagkiller.'

They laughed as the puppy got to her feet and waddled over to us, with a look of enquiry on her face.

'Perhaps she is a Rowan,' I said, 'for although her coat is golden it has a reddish touch when the light catches it, like ripe rowan berries.'

The puppy sidled up to me and nuzzled against the back of my knee.

'Aye!' Alysoun was delighted. 'She knows her name already. Rowan it shall be.'

'Then the first thing you must teach her is to come to her name. Take her into the garden and reward her every time she comes when called. I expect your aunt has some ends of stale bread you may give her.'

'*After* you have eaten!' Margaret said severely.

—

The shop was quiet that afternoon, so I decided to walk out to Yardley's farm earlier than I had intended, leaving Walter in charge. He had almost finished the two *peciae* when I left, and Roger had written and nearly decorated three pages, which was a good day's work for him.

My route took me out of the East Gate by the end of the Canditch, then past a huddled row of cottages built just beyond the town wall, before I passed the hospital of St John. I crossed the Cherwell by the East Bridge, a trembling wooden structure that needed constant shoring up after the winter floods had come roaring down the river. It lay outside the town's jurisdiction and the maintenance of the bridge was a matter of constant dispute between the hospital and the other neighbouring landowners. Today it quaked under my feet and I wondered, not for the first time, how it withstood the traffic of beasts and carts coming in from the farms lying east of Oxford. The road led on, up over Shotover Hill and eventually to London, which I had visited just once on business for my father-in-law.

Today, however, I turned off along the narrow dirt track between hedges which led to Yardley's farm. On either side the last of the blossom lingered on the blackthorn, while the small wild crab apples and the bullaces were in full bloom. It felt like walking under a bridal arch. Elizabeth and I had stepped out from the door of St Peter's under branches of May blossom at this very season, seven years ago. My mother had come, but my father had refused to attend our wedding, holding it as a grievance against me that I had cast aside my years of schooling and the chance to rise, perhaps, as a cleric in the royal service, all to marry (as he put it) some shopkeeper's wench.

I could hear Yardley's farm before I reached it. Although Thomas Yardley had the usual milch cows, a pig or two, and a small flock of Cotswold sheep, his real love was poultry. I had never been there at dawn, but the roosters' greeting of the day must have been enough to wake folk halfway up the hill. No thief would ever dare attempt the farm, for his geese were as noisy as a pack of hounds and twice as vicious. I stood safely on the far side of the gate and shouted for Thomas.

He came ambling across the yard, impervious to the geese, who made no attempt to attack him, probably the only creature on two legs or four who was safe from them.

'Come for your goose feathers, Master Elyot? I've a sack put ready for you. Come you in-by.'

'Hmm,' I said, 'the geese?'

'Oh, aye.' He made a vague waving gesture which the geese seemed to understand, for they drew back a foot or so as I stepped cautiously through the gate. Thomas led me to the barn, where he had the feathers ready for me in a small sack.

'Have you no dog nowadays, Thomas?' I said, as I counted out the agreed money.

'Nay.' He spat on to the straw-strewn floor. 'Killed him, didn't they? Those constables from Oxford. They'd no right, out here. I'm no part of the town of Oxford.'

'Aye, it was bad. Should you not get another, now the plague is gone?'

'If it has gone.'

'It's to be hoped so.'

He shrugged. 'I could do with a good ratter. Them vermin get in the corn store, even in the house. One great brute tried to make off with a block of cheese, till I took a spade to 'un.'

'I know of some pups looking for homes. The dam is a prize ratter. Just what you need.'

Before I left the farm I had a promise to take back to John Baker, that Thomas would have one of the puppies, though as I closed the gate thankfully on the malevolent stare from goose eyes, I felt a twinge of sympathy for any dog who must learn to live with them. I set off briskly back to Oxford, coming out from under the blossoming hedgerow trees to be momentarily blinded by the brightness of the setting sun full in my face.

By the time I reached the East Bridge, I was seeing dancing black spots before my eyes from the glare of the sunlight, so I paused on the bridge and turned to look down at the cool waters sliding smooth and inviting beneath. I was hot from my walk and remembered the silky pleasure of jumping naked into the river here, off the bank stretching down from the hospital wall to the river. We were strictly forbidden to swim, of course, as students under the jurisdiction of the university, but have such rules ever stopped young lads from swimming on a hot day, when they are released from their lessons?

Was that someone in the river now? My eyes were still dazzled from the low-lying sun, and I shaded them to try to see better. Whoever he was, he was not so much swimming as floating. I felt a sudden chill. The youth was not swimming, for he was fully clad. And he was not swimming, for he was dead. And I knew him. It was the student from Hart Hall. William Farringdon.

Chapter Two

The boy's body stirred in the river current, a grotesque suggestion of living movement. It had caught for a moment amongst the reeds along the bank nearest St John's Hospital, but even as I watched, it began to free itself, turning slowly in the stream. I must act quickly, or it would be swept away, down to where the Cherwell joined the Thames, and then there would be nothing to stop it before it was borne away to London.

I ran to the town side of the bridge, threw down the sack of feathers, and pulled off my shoes. I looked around for something – a branch, anything – that I might use to catch hold of the body as it floated under the bridge, but there was no debris on the bank. There was nothing for it – I would have to wade out deep into the river fully dressed. The cold made me gasp as I slithered down the muddy bank and into the river. It had been a mild spring day, but it was evening now and the sun had not been strong enough to warm the water. I had hardly gone more than a few steps before my legs began to grow numb.

Perversely, the body swung out toward the deeper water in the centre of the river as it drifted under the bridge, so that I was forced to wade until the water was up to my waist. I made a lunge forward. If I missed, it would be gone before I could make a second grab. My hand met sodden cloth and I tightened my grip, though the body tugged, almost pulling me over. The current was stronger than I had suspected. When my foot slipped on mud, I nearly lost my hold and went under, but I managed to stagger back a few paces. My fingers were tangled in the cloth of William's hood, which had slipped off his head.

The hood was separate, not part of his cotte, and I was afraid it would come away in my hands. I heaved the body nearer, got my hands under the boy's armpits, and began to drag him toward the bank. I am reasonably strong, but he was a tall, well-built lad, and the sodden clothing added to the weight. Where was everyone? This was usually a busy road, but this evening it was deserted. I kept backing toward the bank, but I was losing my grip, when at last two of the lay brothers from the hospital appeared above me on the bridge, staring down in astonishment.

'Give me a hand here!' I gasped, for I was nearly out of breath.

At first they hardly seemed to understand, then they came reluctantly down from the bridge and round to the part of the bank I was trying to reach.

'Can you not help me?' I called angrily. 'I'm afraid of losing him.'

They looked at one another, then slowly began to kilt up the skirts of their habits, revealing two pairs of hairy legs. I was nearly at the bank now. One of the men took a few hesitant steps into the shallows, still wearing his sandals. The other seemed unwilling to venture even that far. Finally the first man took a cautious hold of William's left arm and shoulder, while I shifted my grip to the right. With inept assistance from the second man, we managed to drag the body up on to the grass, where it lay in a pool of water and slime.

'Who is it?' the more helpful of the lay brothers asked.

'He is a student, William Farringdon,' I said. 'A student at Hart Hall.'

'You know him?'

'He was in my shop just a few hours ago.'

'I know who you are,' the other man said. 'You have Humphrey Hadley's bookshop in the High.' He squinted at me suspiciously. 'What have you done to him?' He pointed with the toe of his sandal at the recumbent body.

'Done to him? I've done nothing,' I said, caught between annoyance and alarm. 'I was coming back from Yardley's farm when I saw him from the bridge.'

'But you know him.'

'I know most of the students, they are in and out of my shop all the time.'

I shivered. I was soaking wet almost to my chest, and it was nearly sunset. The small warmth of the day was seeping away. All I wanted to do was to go home and don dry clothes, but there were matters which must be seen to first.

'Poor lad,' the first man said. He was large and comfortable looking, and he turned a sad eye on the body lying in the grass. 'Suicide is a grievous sin. Why would he do such a thing?'

'We do not know that it was suicide,' I said firmly. Best to scotch such an assumption at once, or they would have the poor lad shovelled away in unhallowed earth without a qualm. 'He may have fallen in, and perhaps he could not swim. And who knows where he went in the river? Perhaps the bank was high and slippery, and he could not scramble out.'

'It must have been this side of Holywell Mill,' the other man said, still giving me that suspicious look.

'Aye, you are probably right,' I agreed.

Had William Farringdon killed himself? I remembered how worried and anxious he had appeared when I had seen him earlier. These boys, away from their families for the first time in their lives, sometimes were lost and frightened. I had had some bad moments myself. But William was not one of the very young students. He must have been eighteen, already four years or thereabouts into his university studies.

It was time to stop speculating and act.

'This must be reported to the parish constables,' I said. 'Will one of you go at once? He belongs to the parish of St-Peter-in-the-East.'

I directed my gaze firmly at the man who had helped me. I was not sure I quite trusted the other, who seemed to think that I had something to do with William's death.

'And you,' I said, turning to the other man, 'can you fetch some strong fellows and a hurdle or a door, so that we can carry him away from here? I will stay with him. We could take him to the hospital. 'Tis but a few steps.'

'I do not think John de Idbury, our Warden, will allow that,' the man said. 'This fellow is none of ours.'

So much for Christian charity, I thought.

'Then we will carry him to St Peter's,' I said, 'though it is a greater distance to bear such a heavy burden.'

They climbed up to the road and started on their way, the one walking briskly toward the East Gate, the other slowly and with backward looks, toward the nearby gate-house of St John's Hospital. I sat down on the grass beside the body, and forced my shoes on over my wet hose. What a waste of a young life, I thought. Jordain had thought highly of the lad, knowing that he was to stay on after he completed the Quadrivium, to continue to higher studies in Law or Philosophy or Medicine.

The body lay sprawled in an ungainly pose, so I stood up and tried to arrange him in a more seemly position. It was then that I saw what I had not noticed in the river. Indeed, the river had washed most of it away.

The breast of the boy's cotte bore a wide stain which could be but one thing. Blood.

–

By the time the one lay brother had returned with two strong servants from the hospital, carrying a wicker hurdle between them, and the other hurried back from the town with one of the parish constables, Edric Cromer, the light was fading. In the dim of twilight, William Farringdon's body was reduced to a tumble of flaccid limbs and heaped clothes reeking of dirty river water. I was reeking myself, and growing colder by the minute. While I had waited, I had examined the body more carefully. Tipping it on to its side, I had discovered more and larger traces of blood on the back of the cotte, where a slit in the cloth showed where a knife had penetrated. There was only the smallest of holes on the front, so the knife or dagger had been long enough to pass right through from his back, the tip just emerging from his chest. I decided to say nothing at present about what I had seen, in the presence of so many strangers.

As we carried William's body up from the bank to the road, we found a small crowd already gathered in front of the row of cottages, which faced the gate of the hospital on the other side of the road. I picked out one sharp-faced boy and beckoned him over.

'Do you know Hart Hall?' I said. 'At the far end of Hammer Hall Lane?'

'Aye, maister.'

'If you run there and ask for the Warden, and tell him to meet Master Elyot at St-Peter-in-the-East as soon as he can, then you shall have a silver ha'penny.'

'Aye, that I will, maister.' And he was off. The prospect of a silver ha'penny was even more enticing than the gruesome spectacle of watching a body being recovered from the Cherwell and carried into town.

I followed the men carrying the hurdle, squelching in my sodden hose, and beginning to grow very cold. At the last moment I remembered my sack of feathers and went back for them, silently cursing that I had chosen this evening to walk to Yardley's farm. Had I not been crossing the bridge when the body was washed toward it, I should have known nothing about it and would be at home now eating my supper and sending my children to bed. Now my family would be worried, not knowing what had become of me. And then I felt ashamed. For had I not been there, William would not have been found, except, perhaps, miles down river, by strangers.

We made a sad, bedraggled procession, in through the East Gate and along the High Street. The body left a dripping trail in the dry dust of the roadway, and I left my own dripping trail, following along in its wake. We reached St Edmund Hall, at the south end of Hammer Hall Lane, and turned the corner into that narrow alleyway, which zigzagged past the church and behind Queen's College, eventually reaching the town wall at the small postern, Smith Gate, near Hart Hall. Just beyond the boundary wall at the back of St Edmund Hall lay St Peter's churchyard, with the south door of the church at its far end. The west door opened directly on to the lane, but the constable fetched by the lay brother had sent word to the rector to open the south door for us.

Jordain's quickest route here would be along Hammer Hall Lane from the far end, but it was one to be avoided at night – and night was drawing in now. Beyond the church there was a cluster of poor cottages, leaning together, with a maze of narrow footpaths between them, so narrow you could not stretch out your arms at your side. It had always been one of the worst areas in Oxford, but the Death had wiped out all but a few of those who lived there. The last dregs of humanity had fled, leaving the cottages derelict and falling every year into greater decay. Now they had been taken over by thieves and vagabonds, and the worst of the pox-ridden prostitutes lodged there. Students were warned to stay well away from them, but not all of them listened. And no man who valued his purse or his life would walk that way after dark. The place was a disgrace to Oxford, but we were all slow at recovering after so much had been lost. Some day, perhaps, the town authorities would clean the place up, or simply knock the ramshackle hovels down. If William's body had been found there, it would not have surprised me.

We turned into the churchyard and followed the path to the south door of the church. It was a relief to see that the rector was already there, with the churchwarden, who held aloft a flaming torch, providing us with some light to see by, although it also gave the scene a somewhat macabre air. I heard running steps behind me and turned to see Jordain, his academic gown flying out like wings.

'You did not come by the lane, did you?' I said. 'After dark?'

'It is the shortest way. Besides, if this child is not afraid—'

'The child has nothing about him worth stealing,' I said.

Behind him, the boy held out a grubby hand. I felt in my purse and found a silver ha'penny.

'Now,' I said, 'if you run another errand, you shall have another.'

'Aye, maister?'

'Just along this side of the High, three houses past the gate of Queen's, there is the bookshop.'

'I know it.'

'Go there and tell Mistress Makepeace that her brother is delayed, but not to fret, he will be home soon. Can you remember that?'

'Bookshop. Mistress Makepeace. Brother delayed, but home soon. That'll be you, maister?'

'Aye, that's me.'

He nodded and ran off.

'Well?' Jordain said, eying the group which was being ushered into the church, 'What's to-do?' He peered at me, as we stood on the edge of the circle of light. 'Nicholas, *amicus meus*, have you been swimming?'

'Very nearly,' I said grimly. 'It's bad news, Jordain. William Farringdon. I found him in the Cherwell. He's dead.'

Jordain turned visibly pale and crossed himself, murmuring a soft prayer. His eyes were wide in dismay.

'I could have prevented! I knew something was amiss, but he would not say. Oh, why will the young fall into such despair? There's little in this life that cannot be mended in time. But suicide – that serves no end, and now he has imperilled his immortal soul.'

I took Jordain by the elbow and leaned close, so that I might whisper.

'Did I mention suicide? Do not assume it was suicide in front of these people. I have pointed out that it might have been an accident, that he slipped into the river and could not scramble out.'

He looked at me shrewdly. 'What is it that you are *not* saying, Nicholas?'

'Later.'

The boy was back, panting a little.

'I seen Mistress Makepeace, maister, and told her you got a soaking, but none the worse.'

I grimaced, I had not given him leave to tell Margaret that. It would be time enough for that particular drama once I reached home. If I ever did, this night.

'Here's your ha'penny.'

His hand closed over it swiftly, but he did not run home. Instead he began to sidle toward the door of the church. Jordain seized him by the back of his cotte.

'They will not want you in there, my lad. A poor fellow tumbled into the river and drowned. They'll lay him to rest quietly there while they lock the door. There will be nothing more doing tonight.'

'Aye,' I said. 'I thank you for running my errands, but off with you home to your mother now.'

I regretted my words as soon as I had spoken them, for so many of Oxford's children are motherless nowadays, but the boy gave no sign of distress. Slowly, glancing back from time to time, he made his way out of the churchyard.

'We'd best see how they fare,' I said. Jordain and I hurried after the others into the church.

The rector turned to us in relief. 'The constable says the boy should be left here for the present, but if he is guilty of *felo de se*… I am not sure…'

His words trailed away and he twisted his hands together. The constable, one of those doing duty for the parish this year, Edric Crowmer, a vintner with a shop not far from mine, was looking stubborn.

'I've nowhere else to put him, Master Elyot.' He turned to Jordain. 'They say he's one of your students, Master Brinkylsworth. From Hart Hall.'

'Aye, but I cannot take him there. It would be too distressing for the other students. Besides,' Jordain turned to the rector, 'there is no evidence that this is suicide. He must have fallen in. I do not think he could swim.'

The rector looked relieved, and wiped his forehead on his sleeve.

'Poor lad. Then he shall rest here.'

He turned to the servants from the hospital, who had laid the hurdle on the floor and looked as if they were anxious to get away as quickly as possible. In the more confined space of the church, the stench of the polluted river water was stronger than ever.

'This way.' The rector beckoned and we all followed him to the far west end of the north aisle. 'In this corner. It will be less disturbing when the parishioners come for Mass. I will fetch a cloth to cover him.'

With the body laid where he indicated, the servants and lay brothers hurried away to St John's Hospital, clearly relieved to be free of the unpleasant task that I had wished upon them. The rector brought an old and worn altar cloth and laid it carefully over William, then Jordain and I, the constable and the churchwarden, knelt with him to say a prayer for the dead.

When at last we were able to make our way back to the High, Jordain seized my arm and hurried me along past Queen's College nearly at a run.

'Your teeth are chattering like a flock of sparrows quarrelling,' he said. 'If the filth in the river doesn't kill you, the wet and the cold will.'

'Thank you for that,' I said, but my sarcasm was wasted in a fit of sneezing.

Mercifully, Margaret had not yet bolted the door and Jordain hustled me quickly through the shop and into the kitchen. Margaret sprang up from her wicker chair by the hearth with a face betraying a mixture of fear and anger.

'What have the two of you been about? You are no longer students! What mad caper is this?'

I crouched near the fire and began to pull off my sodden cotte, while Jordain attempted to pacify my sister.

'Nay, it was no caper, Margaret. A tragedy, rather.'

'What say you?' Fear conquered anger in her expression.

'One of my students has drowned in the Cherwell. Nicholas saw his body in the river as he was coming back from Yardley's farm. He had to go into the river to pull the body out.'

'*Had* to?' Anger was coming to the fore again. 'Why must it be you, Nicholas?'

'There was no one else about,' I said. 'He would have been swept away down to the Thames. It is one of Jordain's students, so I sent for him.'

I sat down on Margaret's chair and tried to remove my shoes, but they clung to my hose and I found that my hands were shaking so much that I could not grip them.

Margaret clicked her tongue in annoyance and knelt before the chair, easing my shoes off gently. I saw that there was a rip in the foot of my hose. I must have caught it on a stone in the river. Margaret had seen it as well, but made no comment.

34

'I'll fetch you dry clothes,' she said. 'Take everything off, mind. Everything. There is a towel in the coffer at the bottom of the stairs, Jordain.'

She hurried away and Jordain fetched the towel. When Margaret returned, I was wrapped in the towel and as close as I could get to the hearth without setting myself afire. She thrust the bundle of clothes at me, then turned her back modestly to lay out bowls and spoons on the table. She had seen me naked often enough as a child, but clearly wished to observe the proprieties before Jordain.

Once dressed, I no longer felt so deathly cold. Margaret had even brought my academic gown for additional warmth, though it seem incongruous to don it in the kitchen.

'There is a good leek soup keeping warm in the pot here,' Margaret said, thrusting me aside so that she could reach the hearth. 'And some cold bacon and bread. I daresay you are hungry as usual, Jordain.'

He grinned at her. 'I am always hungry for your cooking, Margaret.'

Jordain had been stick thin ever since we had first met as fourteen-year-old bejants, lodging at Tackley's during our early years at Oxford. However much he ate, he never grew any fatter, though I knew that meals at Hart Hall were poor fare at the best of times.

Margaret laid out an ample supper for us, and I spooned up the soup while it was almost too hot to eat. The warmth drove away the last of the shivering which had come upon me while I waited at the river side with William's body. As we ate, Margaret warmed some ale with a stick of cinnamon and a sprinkle of nutmeg, then sat down at the table to share it with us.

'And now,' she said, 'suppose you tell me the whole tale.'

'Aye,' Jordain said, 'I only know part myself, and Nicholas has been keeping something back.'

So I told them everything, from the time I had stopped on the East Bridge until I sent off the two lay brothers from St John's to fetch help. Then I paused.

'And?' Jordain said. 'This, I think, is where we discover what it is that you have not been telling me.'

I curved my hands around the pewter tankard which Margaret had just refilled, grateful for the comfort of the warm ale. I must tell Jordain what I had found, but was it right to involve Margaret? A sigh, unintended, escaped from me, and I began to cough.

'You shall have a poultice of nettles on your chest before you go to bed,' Margaret said.

To distract her from this unpleasant idea, I said suddenly, 'Where is the puppy?' I had just remembered it.

Margaret sniffed with disapproval. 'I said it must sleep in the pantry, so we shut it in there, but it howled without ceasing. Alysoun wept. Rafe joined in the howling. I could have no peace until I agreed to let them take the creature to their room for this one night only, since it must be missing its mother.'

I hid my smile. By now, I reckoned the puppy would be sharing Alysoun's bed, and tomorrow it would find its way there again.

'Puppy?' Jordain said, momentarily sidetracked, so I explained.

'I knew it would prove a nuisance,' Margaret said grimly. 'If there are any messes in the children's room in the morning, Alysoun shall clean them up herself and learn what it means to keep a dog in the house.'

'Quite right,' I said, nodding soberly.

'Nicholas,' Jordain said, 'you cannot avoid telling us whatever it is that you are hiding.'

I drew a deep breath and set down my ale. Margaret was a sensible woman, not like to faint or scream or turn sick. I would tell them both what I had discovered.

'William did not drown.' I said, 'either through accident or suicide. He was stabbed from behind. It was murder.'

Margaret gasped, but said nothing. Jordain looked sickened, but not surprised.

'I thought it must be some such,' he said, 'from your manner, and your anxiety to say nothing at the church.'

'The constable must be told, of course,' I said, 'and the proper authorities – the coroner, the university, the town officials. But it needs must be handled with care. There is no knowing if this is some town and gown quarrel or not. We do not want to start a riot, like those that have happened in the past. If the murderer is a university man, the case will come under the jurisdiction of the university, but if it is a townsman, well…'

'Aye. Trouble. There are too many killings in this town.'

'And there is the fact that I was the one to find the body. A graduate and a licensed bookseller, so that I have one foot in the university, but a shopkeeper with the other foot in the town. It has always been difficult to balance my loyalties fairly, so I try to avoid such disputes. And also—'

'Also?'

'One of those lay brothers from St John's, the lean one, with a nose quivering for scandal – he as good as accused me of causing William's death. By the time they saw me, I was dragging William to the bank, but I suppose to a suspicious mind it might have looked as though I was trying to drown him.'

Margaret pressed her hand against her mouth in alarm, but Jordain patted her shoulder.

'Once it is made known that the boy was stabbed, no one could suspect you of drowning him.'

'It will not be easily seen. Most of the blood was washed away by the river. However, there is a faint but wide stain on the breast of his cotte and a larger one on the back, where the slit in the cloth shows where the knife went in.'

'Cold water will wash out blood,' Margaret said, 'but it must be done before the blood dries, or it is much more difficult to remove every trace.'

We both looked at her.

'That means,' Jordain said slowly, 'that if William was stabbed next to the river and immediately thrown in, most of the blood would be washed away.'

I nodded. 'But if he was stabbed and the blood had partly dried *before* he went in the water, it would not wash away so thoroughly. But of course we do not know how long he was in the river, or where he went in.' I remembered what the lay brother had said. 'It must have been down river of Holywell Mill, or the body would likely have caught in the sluice or the wheel.'

Jordain nodded. 'How fast was the river today?'

'Fast. I nearly lost hold of the body. The snow lingered this winter, did it not? The last of the spring melt is still coming down from the Cotswolds.'

'So he must have gone in below the mill, and not very long before you crossed the bridge. How long would it take, from the mill to the East Bridge?'

I shook my head. 'We cannot tell. Even while I was watching, it caught for a time on some reeds near the hospital. That could have happened any number of times along the way, although that stretch of the river is fairly straight.'

'There is no good going over and over it now,' Margaret said. 'Listen! There are the midnight chimes. Time we were all abed. Some of us must rise before dawn.'

Jordain got to his feet. 'I must go. I have trespassed on your good will too long, Margaret.'

'You will go nowhere tonight,' she said firmly. 'If some cut-throat does not slay you, the Watch will arrest you for wandering the streets this late. You will spend the night here.'

'I should go back to the Hall.'

'Margaret is right,' I said. 'It is too dangerous to be abroad this late. I am sure your students will bolt the door, they are not fools.'

We none of us said, but it hovered in the air – since the Death there were many become desperate and lawless, men who might once have been honest workmen, fathers and husbands, young men with a future ahead of them. Why had God inflicted such punishment upon his children? Was there indeed a God? Why should a man try to live a godly Christian life, when all were struck down alike, sinful and innocent? Such men lived by violence now, and the world had become a dangerous place.

'There is a truckle bed in my chamber,' I said. 'You are welcome to that, and I will lend you a night shift.'

'Very well.' Jordain gave in readily, and smiled at us. 'I thank you both.'

On our way up the stairs which led to the rest of the house from a corner of the kitchen, I laid my finger to my lips. If the children woke, we would be even later reaching our beds. I pulled aside the curtain which closed off the small chamber the children shared, no more than an alcove, and peered in, holding my rushlight high. Rafe had abandoned his truckle bed and climbed in with Alysoun. The puppy lay curled up between them, cradled under Alysoun's arm. Jordain looked over my shoulder and grinned.

Once we were in my chamber with the door closed, he allowed himself a quiet chuckle. 'So that is the puppy. That little maid has you at her bidding, Nicholas.'

'There is no harm in her having a puppy.' I was defensive. 'It will guard the house and shop.'

'Not very easily from the child's bed.'

'This night only, as Margaret has said.'

I turned my back on him and pulled the wheeled truckle bed out from under my own. In the weeks after Elizabeth died, Alysoun had slept in it, with Rafe in the cradle beside her. My mother had wanted to take the children to live with her, in her cottage on the farm, but I would not allow them out of my sight.

'Here is a night shift for you.' I lifted one out of the coffer where I kept my clothes, all but my academic gown, which I now hung from a peg in the wall.

'I can sleep in my clothes.'

'No need to martyr yourself.' I tossed the shift over to him.

'I do understand, you know.' Jordain's voice was muffled as he pulled his cotte over his head.

'Understand what?'

'How it is with you. The children.' He looked for a moment uncomfortable, as if feeling he had said too much, then hurried on. 'That was no light decision you made, abandoning your future as a lawyer, perhaps even at court, to marry Elizabeth.'

I climbed into bed and clasped my arms about my knees.

'I could not live without her,' I said simply. 'To have taken holy orders and gone into the future alone, that would have been a kind of death.' I baulked at my own choice of words. 'We had three joyful years, which I shall never regret. And she gave me Alysoun and Rafe.'

'I should not have spoken,' he said, stretching out on the low bed. 'Forgive me.'

'If anyone has the right to speak of it, you have. I know you hoped we would carry on together through the university, but we have remained friends, despite following our different paths, have we not? And now, behold! You are a Regent Master of Arts, Warden of a Hall, one of the most popular lecturers in the university, and soon to be a doctor of Philosophy, while I am a jobbing bookseller and stationer.'

'Nevertheless,' he yawned hugely, 'I envy you those children.' He yawned again. 'What are we to do about the death of poor Farringdon? Some of my students have a knack for falling into trouble, but not he. Why should anyone want to kill him?'

'There is nothing we can do tonight.' I leaned over the stool beside my bed and snuffed out the rushlight. 'God give you rest, Jordain.'

'And you,' he murmured sleepily.

A certain shyness had prevented my kneeling to my evening prayers, but I said them now, remembering all those I had loved, wandering now in the dark land of Purgatory. I prayed for the safety of my children. And I prayed for William Farringdon, a boy on the threshold of manhood, snatched away unshriven by some murderer's hand.

–

There was no opportunity the following morning to discuss with Jordain what we should do. The children were excited to find that Cousin Jordain (as he called himself) had spent the night with us. Margaret was tired and cross, having had to rise after little sleep in order to bake the day's bread. The puppy rushed about barking, entering into the children's excitement, and must needs be hurried into the garden just in time to prevent another accident on Margaret's spotless floor.

'I cannot break my fast with you, Margaret,' Jordain said, 'though I thank you. I must away back to the Hall. Rumour flies on the wind, and Heaven alone knows what my lads will have heard already about this tragedy. I must reassure them, if I can.'

He looked from Margaret to me. The children were listening avidly. 'I will not mention that other matter Nicholas spoke of last night.'

We had both overslept. My scriveners had already arrived and I told Walter to open the shop while I hurriedly cut myself the usual bread and cheese.

'Take this with you, Jordain.' Margaret thrust a wedge of the cheese and the end of a new loaf into his hand. 'You may eat as you go.'

He kissed her goodbye, swung Rafe in the air, and patted Alysoun's cheek, then followed me through to the shop.

'I will come back as soon as I may. I have a lecture at seven o'the clock, but if I can I will be here straight afterwards. It is only a step away, in the Schools. I will see you then.'

He hurried off.

'Mother hen,' I murmured, but not loud enough for him to hear.

–

Oxford is a small place, though it be uneasily divided between town and gown. When something remarkable or untoward happens, news of it flies about – as Jordain said – seemingly on the wind. Perhaps the servants from St John's had gossiped in a tavern last night or this morning. Or the less amiable lay brother had put the word about. He seemed like a man with a long nose to sniff out trouble. I worried what evil suspicions he might be spreading about me. Once it was confirmed that William had been stabbed, he could hardly claim that I had drowned the boy, though I suppose a twisted mind might suppose that I had stabbed him and then dropped the knife in the river. Though surely any man of sense would question why I should then plunge into the river and insist on dragging the body out and informing the constable?

So I reasoned, but sadness at the boy's death and worry over unfounded rumours kept me from my work. All I managed to do was to arrange with a carter to take my valuation of the books to the widow in Banbury. Walter and Roger may have wondered at my distracted manner, but they worked on steadily, clearly not having heard about the events of the previous evening. Not, that is, until the constable Edric Crowmer came into the shop an hour or so after we had opened.

'Well, this is an unpleasant business, Master Elyot,' he said, clearly seeing no need to speak to me in private. 'If the boy killed himself, it will mean unconsecrated burial outside the town wall. Let us hope that it was an accident.'

I noticed that both Walter and Roger had stopped writing and were listening.

'Indeed,' I said noncommittally. I did not want to discuss the blood I had found on the boy's body, not now, in the middle of my shop. 'It will be for the inquest to make a decision. I understand from Master Brinkylsworth that the boy could not swim. There is no reason to suppose that he did not slip on a crumbling bank and fall in. The students sometimes go rabbiting in those fields on the other side of the Cherwell.'

This was irrelevant in the light of my discovery as to how William had met his death, but I was anxious that he should not be held guilty of the grievous sin of suicide.

'Aye, I have reported the matter to the coroners, and they are willing that the body should remain in St Peter's for the time being. They will call the inquest shortly.' Crowmer rubbed his chin. 'Rabbiting, you say? Would he have gone alone?'

I had no wish to enlarge on this theory, which I had invented on the spur of the moment, so I merely shrugged and turned aside to a group of students who came crowding in.

'You are early,' I said. 'Lectures surely cannot have finished yet.'

They looked shifty and pretended to examine a pot of quills set out on the counter. One, however, was bolder than the rest.

'Master Elyot, they are saying that you found the body in the river. Is it true?'

My scriveners had abandoned all pretence of work and stared at me open mouthed.

I cleared my throat. Probably I could not avoid this. I needs must say something.

'Aye. It was I who found poor William Farringdon in the river and managed to bring him to the bank. The matter is now in the hands of the coroners.'

I hoped that would silence them, but I was mistaken.

'William was worried about something.' Most of the students were younger than William, certainly still studying the Trivium, but the lad who now spoke was older. 'I am at St Edmund's, not Hart Hall, but I know William. We both attend Master Wycliffe's lectures on Ethics.'

'Do you know why he was worried? Could it have driven him to suicide?' Crowmer fixed the student with a stern look, so that he backed away.

'Nay,' he protested. 'William was very devout. He was to take full holy orders next year. He would never have killed himself. That is a monstrous suggestion!'

'You see?' I said to Crowmer. 'Tell me.' I turned to the student and spoke in a much milder tone than the constable. 'Have you any idea why he was worried?'

The student shook his head. 'He never said. Kept mostly to himself, did William, though he was a good scholar and would always help a fellow out.' He grinned. 'I struggle sometimes, and he pulled me out of many a hole.'

Then he paused and frowned. 'There was one day last week, though. When we came out of the Ethics lecture, on the way back to our halls for dinner, there were two men waiting for him. They took him aside, and I think he did not want to speak to them. He seemed afraid.'

'What were they like, these men?' I asked. 'From the university? From the town?'

I was not sure what I hoped he would answer. If the men who had accosted William were from the town, and were somehow involved in his murder, that meant trouble. On the other hand, did I hope they were university men? I could hardly wish for the university to be harbouring murderers.

The student frowned again. 'Difficult to say. I do not think they were university men. They did not wear academic dress, nor were they tonsured. But... somehow I do not think they were townsmen from Oxford.' He scratched the top of his head, where his own tonsure was growing back as ginger-coloured stubble.

'Not from Oxford?' I prompted. 'Why do you say so?'

'Well, they were quite prosperous looking. There are few prosperous in Oxford these days.'

I knew what he meant. Oxford, once a busy manufacturing town, had been in decline even before the pestilence had cut down half the population. Once famous for the weaving and fulling of high quality woollen cloth, and for skilled work in leather, it had lost its leading position to other towns. It was recovering slowly from the many deaths, but there was much poverty. The university had not always behaved well, either, buying up property cheaply, charging its tenants high rents, but paying niggardly fees for services provided by the town. John

Baker's complaints about the money paid for his bread echoed those of other tradesmen.

'You think they were strangers, these men?'

He shrugged. 'I cannot be sure. I had never seen them before. Perhaps they came from London,' he ended vaguely.

London, distant and foreign to these sheltered students.

'What is your name?' Crowmer asked abruptly and the student looked alarmed.

'Why do you want to know?'

'The coroners may want to know.'

The boy looked even more worried, but admitted that his name was Peter de Wallingford and he was a fifth year student at St Edmund Hall.

'Hey, you!' I said, grabbing one of the younger students who was thrusting something into the breast of his student gown. He had taken advantage of the distraction provided by Peter de Wallingford to steal a handful of my best quills.

'Put those back, or pay for them!'

Reluctantly he stuffed the quills back into the pot, bending one as he did so.

'You'll pay for the damage. That will be a farthing.'

Glowering at me, he handed over a bent coin which looked as if it had been snipped, even as poor in value as it was. I took the coin and clipped him over the ear, as he sidled past me toward the door. The other younger boys followed him. I turned to Peter.

'You should find better companions than those young louts,' I said. 'And should you not be at a lecture?'

He had the grace to look ashamed.

'Aye, well, if I hurry I will be in time for the seven o'the clock. I'm sorry, Master Elyot, they are not my friends. I came because I wanted to know what happened to William.'

'I think we would all like to know that,' I said. 'No doubt we shall know more after the inquest. Be off with you now.'

Crowmer followed him out of the shop and I watched them go: the student half running toward the Schools, the vintner making his stately way to his shop. When they had both vanished from view, I stood for several minutes, pondering what Peter had said, which bore out Jordain's opinion of the dead student. A bright, pious young man, planning to proceed to an advanced degree and to take holy orders. A future high in the church might have lain before him, a bishop's mitre, even a cardinal's hat. How could such a young man have become entangled in a web of evil which led to murder?

Chapter Three

It would be another hour before Jordain returned. I chided myself for wasting the morning, so I sat down to my accounts, a task I always postpone as long as I may. Money was owing to me from more than one of the colleges; it was time I sent them renewed bills for the books and writing materials I had supplied and for which I had not been paid.

I began with Merton College, whose debt was greatest and which should have no difficulty paying me. Like other tradesmen in the town I harboured some grievances against the colleges of the university on account of their miserly dealings and tardiness in settling their accounts. As a sometime member of the university, I seemed to be regarded as a man who should rise above such petty matters as cash in hand, but without the chinks I could neither feed my family nor purchase the materials that I sold. I would soon need to replenish my stock of fine parchment, for I had an order for a book of hours, to be copied from my own as soon as Roger finished the French book of Robin Hood. And the French book would need to be bound before I could deliver it to the merchant's wife, Mistress Lapley. Moreover the Carmelite Friary, out beyond Broken Hays, had put in a large order for parchment, paper, quills, and ink.

Concluding the bill for Merton with a humble request for payment, I signed it with a flourish, realising – to my considerable relief – that there was one simple task awaiting me which I could carry out however distracted I might be. I sealed the bill, stamping the wax with my ring with the onyx bezel. This was a ring which my father had given me when I graduated as a Bachelor of Arts. That was in the days before I fell into disgrace for abandoning my studies and marrying Elizabeth.

'Walter,' I said, 'as soon as you have finished copying that *pecia*, I want you to take this round to Merton. Do not leave it with the porter. Make sure you place it in the bursar's hands yourself, so there may be no pretence that it has gone astray.'

'Aye, Master Elyot.'

I could see that both Walter and Roger were eager to learn more about my discovery of William's body, but since the constable had left I had refused to speak more of it, merely saying that all would no doubt become clear at the inquest.

'I am going through to the kitchen to sort the goose feathers I fetched yesterday,' I said to Roger. 'If business becomes busy, you may call me.'

Sorting the feathers was always best done away from the shop, for the good flight feathers suitable for quills were always mixed with fine down and bits of straw and dust, which would fly about and settle amongst the books and the supplies of writing materials, which must be kept clean.

'Nay,' Margaret said, when I fetched the sack and prepared to open it in the kitchen. 'I have just finished scrubbing. I want none of your mess in here. You must take that into the garden.'

She pointed an accusing broom at the sack.

'You know that the slightest breeze will blow them about,' I objected.

'Then you must find somewhere else.'

I sighed. Sometimes Margaret lords it over my household worse than my mother used to, though my mother was a little more tolerant, living on a farm. Where could I go? I could not sully my storeroom any more than the shop. The stillroom was Margaret's domain. Even on a quiet spring morning the garden would be too windy. Besides, the children were out there playing with the new puppy. Picking up the sack I carried it upstairs to my bed chamber. Morosely, I thought I should be sneezing all night, after sorting the feathers there.

The coffer would need to serve as a table, so I dragged a stool over to it and began to pick out the flight feathers from the sack, setting the smaller feathers and the fine, soft down on to the end of my bed. Margaret would use them later to fill pillows and feather beds. As a by-product of my business, my family slept softer than many a lord. To avoid any disturbance of the air, I kept the shutters closed, but I could hear the children playing in the garden and smiled. The puppy might be one more mouth to feed, but it would more than repay the cost in happiness for the children.

Once I had emptied the sack, I bundled all the small feathers from the bed back into it and tied the neck shut. Not all the flight feathers were of the best quality, so I divided them into two piles. I sold the poorer ones cheap and untrimmed, for the students who could afford no better. Some of the better ones I would trim and shape, for a few of my customers preferred to buy quills ready to use, the others I would leave untrimmed. I have never understood how anyone can write with a quill shaped by someone else, for every writer's hand is different. Some like a broad tip, some a narrow. Some like a straight end, some a slope. The length of the slit controls the flow of ink. However, I could charge a little more for those quills that were ready to use.

I was just gathering up the good feathers when I heard Jordain talking to Margaret down in the kitchen. It must be past eight and his lecture finished. His foot was on the stair as I opened my chamber door.

'Stay!' I called. 'I am coming down.'

Jordain sat down at the table as I came into the kitchen, flushed as if he had been running. Over his shoulder he carried the worn leather satchel which he had brought when he came up to Oxford, stuffed then with all his worldly possessions. Now, I knew, it would contain books from which he would have cited passages during his lecture, and notes to which he never referred, since he was always carried away by his enthusiasm for his subjects, an enthusiasm which overrode any need for notes.

I had teased him about this from time to time.

'I feel more sure of myself if I have the notes with me,' he would say, patting the satchel as if it were a pet dog. 'Though I may never need to refer to them, it is a comfort to know that they are there.'

'Let me put these away,' I said, walking through to the storeroom, where I laid the feathers in the appropriate boxes until I could deal with them further. I put my head round the door to the shop, where Roger was painting in a tendril down the margin of a page.

Walter was just returning, wiping his face on his sleeve. The day must be growing warm.

'You gave the account to the bursar?' I asked.

'Aye, Master Elyot, and he swears he'll pay it before the week is out. Must have been overlooked. He says.'

We exchanged grins of disbelief.

'They know all about the drowning, over at Merton,' he said. 'The porter tried to question me about what you had seen and done, but I told him I knew nothing.'

'Aye, that's best.'

I withdrew to the kitchen and sat down facing Jordain. 'So?' I said.

'I spoke to my lads this morning, before they went off to lectures, but they could tell me nothing useful. William was quiet, always at his studies or in church. He generally attended Mass three times a week. The more I think on it, the more I am sure we can persuade the coroner he would not have killed himself. It must have been an accident.'

'Jordain?' I looked at him in surprise. 'I told you of the blood and the slash in the back of his cotte. Why are you talking now of an accident?'

He looked uncomfortable. 'Surely you must have been mistaken. It was already getting dark when you found him. The stains on his clothes were most likely from some rubbish in the river – you know what it is like. His clothes probably snagged on a branch and tore. Or on the timbers of the East Bridge, for the posts are rough and splintered. And I saw no sign of blood when we laid him out in the church.'

'You barely looked at him in St Peter's. And it was very dark inside, with nothing but the churchwarden's torch.'

He shook his head. 'It is better this way, Nicholas. A tragic accident, and an end to it. Best not to sully the poor lad's name and cause distress to his family with talk of murder.'

I tried to contain my astonishment at this change in Jordain's attitude.

'There is something else you need to know,' I said, 'that I only discovered this morning. William was seen with two strangers and seemed afraid of them.'

While he listened with his head bowed over his clasped hands, I repeated all that Peter de Wallingford had told me that morning. I could not understand why Jordain wanted to forget the evidence of stabbing, but maybe it arose from his desire to protect the students under his care.

He sighed. 'Perhaps we should look again at William's body, now that we have light to see by. Then we can be sure whether there really are the marks of violence on him.'

'Aye.' I jumped to my feet.

Margaret was just coming in from the garden, where she had spread out my clothes from the previous day to dry, having left them to soak overnight and scrubbed them clear of the river filth this morning.

'Jordain and I are going round to St Peter's,' I said. 'I'll not be long gone.'

'Have you not the shop to mind?'

'Walter can fetch me if I am needed.'

Leaving word with my scriveners, we hurried down the High and into Hammer Hall Lane. There were a few idlers lingering around the churchyard gate, but the churchwarden had taken the precaution of guarding it. He gave us a nod and allowed us into the churchyard.

'Rector locked the church last night,' he said. 'We must, nowadays, with that scum living along there.' He gestured up the alleyway to the cluster of ramshackle cottages. 'But he opened for Mass this morning and he's still there now, if you are wanting him.'

I mumbled something, hoping that the rector would not be offended if we began to examine William's body.

Light flooded into the church. Though not a large church, it had fine tall windows, some with stained glass which patterned the floor with pools of crimson, blue, and gold. The rector was on his knees before the altar, and although we entered as quietly as we could, he rose to his feet and shook the dust from his cassock.

'Ah, Master Elyot and Master Brinkylsworth, have you word as to what is to be done with the poor student? Am I to be permitted to bury him yet?'

'There must be an inquest,' I said gently. 'And we do not yet know the wishes of his family. They may want to bury him at home.'

Jordain nodded. 'I will write to his family today. But nothing can be done until after the inquest. We would like to look again at William, if you do not mind?'

'Nay, you must do as you wish.' The rector shuddered slightly and turned back to his prayers.

The body lay as we had left it the previous night, covered with the old altar cloth. No one seemed to have disturbed it, thanks to the locked church during the night and the vigilance of the churchwarden this morning. Jordain lifted the cloth carefully and laid it aside. We stood looking down at the body.

Someone must have closed his eyes. Perhaps the rector had done so last night while we were still in the church-yard.

'I know very little about these things,' I said, 'except what we were all forced to learn during the pestilence. Does not the body stiffen after a certain time?'

'Aye.' Jordain knelt down and peered at the front of William's cotte. Now that the cloth was dry, the stain seemed less visible, but it was still there.

'We need to turn him on his side,' I said, 'so we can look at his back.'

Jordain nodded and gritted his teeth. Between us we managed to roll the stiffened body on to its side.

'There, you see?' I pointed to the slit and the larger stain around it. The cloth which had been under the body was still damp.

Jordain pulled up the cotte and then the shirt, exposing the boy's naked back. Somehow it made him look even younger. The wound was narrow, but clearly visible and caked with blood. We lowered the body to the floor again and I spread the altar cloth carefully over it.

There were tears in Jordain's eyes.

'You are right,' he said.

'So you see,' I said, 'you must report this to the coroner, lest it be overlooked.'

A spasm of alarm passed over Jordain's face. 'But you were the one to find William's body!'

I shook my head. 'This is a university matter. He was your student at Hart Hall. And I am no longer part of the university. The matter must be dealt with by the university.'

'We do not know that.' Jordain frowned. 'The coroners are town, not gown. At any rate, they are Oxford county, laymen, no part of the university. And I cannot believe the killer came from the university. It must have been a townsman. It would not be the first time.'

Nor would it be the last, I thought, but did not speak the thought aloud. As long as there were wild young men in the town, and wild young students in the university, and as long as they all carried knives, there would be fights and there would be deaths.

'We cannot know who killed William,' I said, 'and it is not for us to discover.'

Even as I spoke, I felt guilty. William had not been the kind of student to become involved in a fight. Besides, he had been stabbed in the back, which did not suggest a fight, but an unexpected attack from behind. Someone must avenge his death, but neither Jordain nor I would know where to begin.

We stood there amongst the fresh green grass of the churchyard, with the birds singing from the yew trees. Perched on an overhanging branch from an apple tree on the other side of St Edmund's wall, a blackbird was giving joyous voice to the beauty of the morning.

'We cannot leave it thus,' Jordain said.

'What can we do?'

Jordain and I looked at each other in dismay.

'There is one thing we might do,' he suggested tentatively.

'Aye?'

'We could look in his room. See whether there is anything there to suggest what connection he might have with these two men he was seen with. He shares with two other students, but they will be attending lectures until they come back for dinner at eleven o'the clock.'

I nodded. 'Very well. It can do no harm. Though I hardly expect we shall find anything.'

We made our way out of the churchyard, past the churchwarden, who nodded to us, and the growing crowd of idlers, who stared at us curiously. Turning right up Hammer Hall Lane, then sharp left, we passed the crowded hovels from which an unpleasant stench arose.

They were dark and silent. None of their occupants would be abroad this early in the morning, for their trades belonged to the night. The lane ran along the back wall of Queen's College before turning sharp right.

There was a tavern and a shoemaker's shop here, past the college wall, and Hammer Hall and Shield Hall, as well as two lodging houses owned by townsmen, which sometimes took students who could not find accommodation in one of the halls. The university was beginning to frown on these town lodgings, considering that the students were safer – and better regulated – when they lived in approved halls, but the recent increase in numbers meant that there were not rooms enough.

A final left turn along under the northern portion of the town wall and we reached Hart Hall on the left, with Blackhall on the corner. Just beyond the end of the lane, where it met Catte Street, the narrow Smith Gate led through the wall, to where Oxford had spread out to the north past the old boundary of the town. A row of houses lay to both right and left along the Canditch. Although these houses had long plots behind, enough to grow food for a family, they cannot have been pleasant in hot weather when the ditch began to stink. The road north from Smith Gate led to Durham College and the Augustinian Priory, carefully sited far enough away from the ditch not to be troubled by the smell.

The whole area of Oxford around Catte Street and the west end of Hammer Hall Lane was occupied by student halls, for as well as those in the lane, there were Arthur Hall and Cat Hall round the corner in Catte Street, and in the Turl Stapledon Hall, beginning to call itself Exeter College, full of Devonshire men. But none of the halls were large, mostly being former houses, and the students lived three or four to a room. William Farringdon would not have had much privacy, though from what Jordain had been able to discover so far, his fellow students could throw no light on any reason why someone should wish to kill him.

Jordain threw open the door to Hart Hall and ushered me in. At some point earlier in the century, the hall had incorporated the adjacent building to the east, Micheld-hall, so the whole place was something of a coney warren, with narrow passages and steps up and down where the two old houses had been knocked together. Arthur Hall, separated from Hart Hall by a small passage at the back, also served as an annexe, with more student rooms. There were two large chambers on the ground floor of the main building, which provided space for lectures and study, and contained a small library of books, while the bed chambers were upstairs and also in the other buildings. Without Jordain to guide me, I always felt I should need to unroll a string to find my way out again, like Theseus in the labyrinth.

Jordain sniffed appreciatively. 'Adam is cooking something tasty for our dinner.'

I smiled. The cook was a large, slow-moving man who did his best with the limited ingredients Jordain was able to afford from the hall's small income. Meals here consisted of a great deal of day-old bread (bought cheaply), porridge, boiled cabbage, large helpings of stodgy pease pudding, and barley frumenty, flavoured and moistened with a very small amount of mutton broth.

I knew. I had eaten here. It was little wonder that Jordain appreciated Margaret's cooking.

'This way.' Jordain led me down the passage between the two teaching rooms to a narrow staircase which led steeply up to the bed chambers above.

'This was William's room,' he said, opening a door which groaned on its hinges, having sagged out of alignment.

Beyond the door was a room about the size of my own bed chamber, but seeming much smaller because of all the furniture crowded into it. Each of the three students had a narrow bed and a coffer, and these took up most of the floor. There was a table where they could write, with a bench and a couple of stools. Two shelves, leaning somewhat drunkenly to the side, held a few precious books and the piles of paper on which the students had copied out the study texts they borrowed from my shop.

'Which is William's coffer?' I asked.

'This one, nearest the window.' Jordain lifted the lid and propped it against the wall.

The coffer was only about half full. There were a few neatly folded garments, including a thick, hooded winter cloak, put away now the weather was warmer. Three pairs of hose, rolled up. A satchel similar to the one Jordain used, probably for carrying books and papers. In the candle box attached to one side there were, indeed, three candles – wax candles, not cheap rush lights. It also contained a dozen or so good quills, carefully trimmed, and some sealing wax. No books or papers, except for some careful notes on ethics in the satchel, probably taken from the lectures Peter de Wallingford had said they attended, given by John Wycliffe, a young Regent Master, a contemporary of Jordain and me.

Jordain lowered the coffer lid. 'Nothing unusual here.'

I peered under William's bed. Nothing there but a pair of winter boots.

'What about these books and papers?' I pointed to the two shelves.

We checked the books, one by one. They were all well-worn copies of the most popular student texts, which are bought and sold until they fall to pieces. Three contained William's name, the others belonged to the students with whom he shared the room.

'I suppose we should look at the papers,' Jordain said reluctantly. 'I must confess, Nicholas, I do not care for this. A man deserves his privacy, even men as young as these.'

'In the general way, I agree,' I said, 'but we are faced with the murder of an apparently blameless young man. I think it must be done.'

Sheet by sheet, we went through the stacks of papers. There were three piles, clearly one belonging to each student. The contents were much the same in all three – copies made from the *peciae* they rented from me, from which they could put together a copy of any study text they did not own in book form. Books being so expensive, few students could afford to buy them, except such worn old copies as these three possessed. Besides, I always found when I was a student that the copying of a book, section by section, for myself, helped to fix it in my mind better than simply reading it. So Necessity became a scholar's best teacher.

'These are William's papers,' Jordain said, indicating a stack written in a beautiful even hand. They might be merely for personal study, but they were in best scrivener's writing.

'Aye,' I said, 'I recognise his hand. Do you not remember? In the summer, two years ago, when Roger broke his wrist in some foolish game of football, I employed William for several weeks as a scrivener. He was a talented illuminator as well, with a clever sense of humour. I told him then that if he ever decided to leave the academic life I would give him a permanent job in my shop.'

'So you did. I had forgotten that. He makes the other lads' writing look like a tangle of spider's webs.'

We replaced the piles of paper where we had found them and looked around the room. There was little else to see. One academic gown hung from a peg in the door.

'That is William's,' Jordain said. 'He must have gone out yesterday without it.'

'So not on any university business,' I said. 'I wonder why he was there, somewhere between the East Bridge and Holywell Mill? I told the constable he was probably rabbitting, but of course I do not believe that.'

'The lads do sometimes go rabbitting for the pot,' Jordain said, 'but I do not think William would go off alone.'

'I keep coming back to what Peter said about the two men he saw with William. And that William seemed afraid.'

'Are you thinking he went to meet them?'

'Why should he?' I shook my head. 'If he was afraid of them? It makes no sense.'

I cast my eyes round the room again. Everything was just as one would expect in a student room, except that it was neater than most. I knew that Jordain kept a strict watch on the students under his care. He was almost as much of a domestic tyrant as my sister.

'There is one place we have not looked,' I said, walking over to William's bed. I lifted the somewhat lumpy pillow.

Underneath, carefully folded, was a night shift. It looked somehow particularly poignant, waiting for a wearer who would never return. Then I heaved up the straw mattress and rolled it back.

'Ah!' I said.

'What?'

'Something here.'

It was a small sheaf of parchment sheets. I lifted them up and let the mattress fall back. Sitting down on the bed, I examined them.

'Now this,' I said, 'is very strange.'

Jordain sat down next to me.

'What is it?'

'This is William's hand,' I said, 'his most careful and elegant hand. And look at the quality of his drawings! Not coloured in yet, only outlined. But then, we found no coloured inks, did we? He must have planned to finish when he had access to coloured inks, but where would he get them? From me?'

'But what *is* it, Nicholas?'

I did not answer him at first, but turned over the sheets carefully until I was sure. They were beautifully executed, all but the last, which was still unused. I had grieved for the boy before; now I grieved also for a lost artist.

I laid the parchment aside and clasped my hands about my knee.

'You remember that I was offered a place at Merton, to study for a doctorate in law?'

'Aye. Then gave it all up to marry Elizabeth.'

I did not need to be reminded.

'The Warden of Merton – Robert Trenge, it was then – showed me their collection of books, when they thought I would be joining them. It is remarkable, such a collection for a single college, and they hope to build a library to house them one day soon. Some of the books are very fine, including a remarkable Psalter, written and illuminated for an Irish king, some five hundred years ago. How they came by it, I cannot guess. You know that I have always loved books, even before I became a bookseller.'

He grinned. 'I know that you near enough starved yourself, that first year, so that you could buy your own book of hours from Master Hadley.'

'Aye.' I smiled sadly. 'That was when I first met Elizabeth. I was fourteen and she was twelve, already helping her father in the shop. Master Hadley promised to keep the book aside for me, and each week I gave him a little – sixpence or a penny – toward the cost. He would let me peep at it, and placed a ribbon to show how much of the book was mine.'

I shook myself. Now I still had the book, but had lost Elizabeth.

'Well, knowing my interest in illuminated texts, the Warden allowed me to look through their great treasure, the Irish book. I had never seen anything to match it, neither then nor since. Until now.'

I picked up the sheets I had found under William's mattress and held them out to Jordain.

'Until I saw these.'

'I don't understand.'

'These are copies. Very fine copies, but copies nonetheless, of the opening of that Irish Psalter. The text might have come from any Psalter, but the drawings are distinctive. Characteristically Irish. The boy was very talented indeed. Not only has he captured the antique writing. His drawings – even though they are but outlines – capture the flowing freedom of the originals. Once they had been coloured and gilded, they would have been magnificent.' I studied the drawings again. 'I wonder where he hoped to obtain gold leaf for the gilding? I keep it for the monastic scribes, but it is very costly.'

'I still do not understand.' Jordain reached out and touched one of the entwined capitals with the tip of his finger. 'If the original book is kept in the Merton collection, how could William have copied it? And why?'

'The "why" is not so difficult,' I said. 'Since he had the skill – and I know too that he loved books – why not make a copy for himself? But the "how"? That raises many questions. How was he able to see and copy the book? For although this is only the first part, it would have taken many hours. Did he persuade someone at Merton to admit him to their collection? Possibly. They can sometimes be persuaded to allow other scholars to read their books, and I know William was set to continue to a higher degree. Though their keeper of books would be unlikely to allow a student near such a treasure.'

'He was to be admitted to Merton as a junior Fellow this coming Michaelmas term,' Jordain said slowly. 'Like you.'

'Even so,' I said, 'very few are granted the chance to handle that particular book. It is kept in a locked box and only brought out rarely. It was an exceptional favour that I was shown it. I cannot imagine that William would have been given the opportunity.'

'But, as you say, you were shown it, at much the same age.'

'Aye, and the Fellow who cares for the books gave the Warden a scolding for it! Said I was too young to be allowed to touch anything so precious. He took it away from me and locked it in its box. The Warden himself was quite abashed. Robert Trenge died two years ago and the new Warden, William Durant, is far less welcoming to university men who do not belong to Merton. So how could William have had the book in front of him for many hours? Their custodian of books survived the Death. The same man, Philip Olney, still rules his literary domain. I have had a number of dealings with him since, in matters of business.'

'It makes no sense,' Jordain agreed. 'So what shall we do with these?' He pointed to the sheets, lying between us on William's bed.

'We should not leave them here, under the mattress. No doubt you will need to take in another student to occupy this room. I think we should remove these until we can discover just what William was doing.'

I looked around, wondering how I might carry the sheets but keep them safe.

'May I borrow William's satchel? You may have it back when you return his belongings to his family.'

Jordain lifted the satchel out of William's coffer and handed it to me. 'Do you want to leave these other notes here?'

'Nay. They are from Wycliffe's lectures, and it was after one of them that Peter saw William with the two men. I do not suppose there is anything... but I will read through them.'

We went soberly down the stairs again. I was turning over the puzzle in my mind, and I suppose Jordain was as well, for he said suddenly, 'Perhaps Merton wanted a copy made of the book, so that they might sell it. Or present it to some noble. Or even the king.'

I looked at him dubiously. 'If that were the case, would they not have brought it to me, or taken it to one of the monasteries? The Franciscans have an excellent copyist, Brother Severus. Why use a student, a boy of eighteen, whatever his skill?'

Jordain shrugged. 'Impossible to know.'

We had reached the front door. 'I have bejant students from Cat Hall coming for a disputation shortly,' Jordain said.

I nodded, my attention still occupied by this curious mystery we had uncovered. I turned in the open doorway. 'What I also find strange is this: William was not particularly well-to-do, was he?'

Jordain shook his head.

'Then where did he get the chinks to buy that parchment? It is of the highest possible quality. Very costly. And I do not think it came from my shop.'

'How can you tell?'

'Every batch of parchment has its own appearance – there are subtle differences in the feel and shade. You come to recognise them, working as I do. In particular with that very fine parchment. It did not come from my shop, I would swear to it. There are two other stationers in Oxford, but neither is licensed by the university, and neither deals in parchment of this quality. Where, I wonder, did William come by it?'

–

After I left Hart Hall, I hurried home as fast as I could go. I had been away from the shop far longer than I had intended, and I could only hope Walter and Roger had been able to deal with any customers who might have arrived in my absence. At least I would have returned before the usual crowd of students arrived after morning lectures.

As I passed the broken cottages I noticed a thin plume of smoke rising from the smoke hole in one of the roofs. None of these hovels had the luxury of a hearth with a chimney, such as we had. The crowd outside St Peter's gate had thinned a little, but there were still twenty or so standing about. I could not imagine what they were hoping to see. The churchwarden continued patiently standing guard, or rather sitting, for he had brought a stool from the church and planted it firmly inside the gate. I gave him a nod as I passed and hurried on to the High Street.

The shop was empty apart from the two scriveners, to my relief.

'I am sorry to have left you for so long,' I said. 'Have there been many customers?'

I saw them eying the unfamiliar satchel, but they did not comment on it.

'Some came just to poke their noses into other folks' business,' Walter said, with a wry grin. 'When they found you were not here and I pressed them as to what they might wish to buy, they made off again. The *librarius* from the Carmelite Friary came in to ask when their order would be sent. He said they were running very short of parchment and red ink.'

I nodded. I would need to make a trip out beyond the castle that afternoon, where the skinner who prepared my parchments had his workshop and soaking cages in one of the many side streams of the Thames. While I was there, I could ask him whether he had supplied the best quality to anyone other than myself.

'Mistress Lapley had been in,' Roger said. 'Demanding to know when her Robin Hood book will be ready. She thinks a man may snap his fingers and suddenly a book appears.' He gave an angry grimace. 'She does not understand the labour it needs to make a book.'

'Indeed, she does not,' I said soothingly. If Roger lost his temper, his work suffered. 'She has not been promised it for another ten days.'

'As for that,' Roger admitted, 'I should have it finished by dinner time, or soon after.'

'That is excellent news,' I said. 'If that is the case, I can take it to the book binders when I go for the parchment this afternoon. If they have not much work in hand, we may even present the lady with her book a few days early. And if the widow from Banbury is satisfied with my prices for her books, I shall offer Mistress Lapley the chance to buy the collection of tales before I display it in the shop.'

Walter laughed. 'That will please her. She always enjoys the chance to say that she has beaten any rival in gaining possession of a precious object.'

'Aye, that's true,' I said thoughtfully. His words made me think of William's copy of the Irish book. It would be someone of much more elevated tastes than Mistress Lapley who would want a beautiful copy of something so precious as that book. The cost of the copy, by the time it was written, illuminated, gilded, and bound in a jewelled, clasped cover, would be more than a year's income for one of our richest merchants. Or it would have been. Now that William was dead, the copy might never be completed.

Could this secret work of copying have any bearing on William's murder? It seemed incongruous. But that the work had been secret was evident, else he would never have kept the sheets hidden under his mattress. Certainly the other students at Hart Hall, even the two who shared his bed chamber, had known nothing about it, or they would have told Jordain.

And where had the work been carried out? He cannot have done the work in his chamber. In the room at Merton where the books were kept, then? Knowing, as I did, the ill-tempered and protective nature of Merton's *librarius*, I could not imagine William working there, yet he must have done, for the precious Irish Psalter would never have been allowed out of the room. There would be no time today to go to Merton, with the business I had out at the west of town, but I would go there tomorrow and see what I could discover. I would say nothing about our discovery under William's mattress, but try to find out whether the *librarius* knew the boy.

'I will just let Mistress Makepeace know that I have returned,' I told the scriveners, 'then I will have a look at your work, Roger. And I will bring in the new supply of cheap quills before the students arrive.'

I went through to the house, taking William's satchel with me and carrying it up to my bed chamber. I took out the pages he had written and looked at them again. The work was exquisite. The drawings – as far as I could remember – quite as fine as the originals, although of course the details of the painting might not have matched their quality when they were finished. Some of the originals had been so fine they seemed to have been painted not with a brush but with a single hair.

The lecture notes in the satchel were written on cheap paper and were probably of little interest, but I lifted them out and laid them beside the parchment on my bed, intending to look at them later. Then I noticed there was something else in the satchel. I drew it out.

It was a key. A heavy iron key. The key to a house door.

Chapter Four

After dinner I sat down with the original French book of Robin Hood which Roger had been copying and the pile of his manuscript pages, which I turned over carefully, one after the other. When he had first begun the task, I had required him to make a fresh copy of a few of the pages, but as he had continued his work had improved. He had a good hand, although perhaps not quite as elegant as William's had been in the pages we had found hidden under the mattress. It was in the illustrations that Roger lacked a certain freedom and originality, although he was a competent copyist. However, Mistress Lapley had said that she did not want the illuminations of the original to be copied; instead, Roger was to design something in the same style but unique to her own copy of the book. His work was adequate, if not exceptional, and I thought she would be satisfied.

'Very good,' I said, when I had finished, and I gave Roger a reassuring smile, for he was hovering over me like an expectant father awaiting the arrival of his firstborn.

'You have done very well. You shall have an extra quarter noble for the work.'

Walter raised his eyebrows, but said nothing. He was paid considerably more than Roger, in recognition of his years of experience and his duties in managing the shop whenever I was absent. He may have thought me over generous to Roger on this occasion, but he understood very well that the younger man had a difficult temperament and needed encouragement.

I took out my purse and handed Roger the small gold coin, which he took with mumbled thanks. I hoped that, with financial incentives and praise, he might not be tempted to steal my precious ink again.

'I shall be away for the rest of the day,' I told Walter as I wrapped Roger's copied pages carefully in a clean cloth and tied the package with tape. 'I shall take this first to the bookbinder, then call at Dafydd Hewlyn's for a fresh supply of best quality parchment for the Carmelites. On my way home I may need to call at Hart Hall, so I will leave it to you to close the shop.'

He nodded. 'What would you have Roger do for the rest of the day?'

I considered. 'He could prepare more student *peciae*. Nay, wait.' I had had an idea while I was eating dinner.

I felt in the barrel under the counter where I had stored the widow's books until I heard whether she accepted my offer.

'This collection of tales – Sir Bevis and the rest – I think we might make a book of our own to sell. You may copy the text, Roger, and I think we might create our own illustrations. This is a hodgepodge, made up of different hands and the work of different illuminators. What say you to an illustration at the start of each tale, full page, and an illuminated capital? If you make a start on the text and leave room for the pictures, the three of us can discuss later how best to illustrate each tale.'

Roger's normally sulky face lit up. He had never before been given the opportunity to make a book of his own rather than a copy, although he had had some freedom with Mistress Lapley's French book.

'Aye, Master Elyot! Which parchment shall I use?'

'Not the highest quality.' I lifted a stack down from one of the high shelves. 'We'll use this. It is good, but not too expensive. Duodecimo will be the right size, I think.'

Aware that Walter was looking somewhat glum, I grinned at him.

'Enough *peciae* for one day, I think, when you finish that one. Could you shape half the good quills I bought yesterday – was it only yesterday? Then I thought you could prepare some texts for horn books. Say half a dozen. I'll give you fresh red ink for the capitals. I see Roger has all but finished his. Tomorrow I will find you something more rewarding. You have slaved over the *peciae* long enough.'

He returned my smile, with a look of relief. Boredom can set in after days of copying *peciae*, and a bored scrivener is an inaccurate scrivener.

I fetched the flight feathers and the ink from the storeroom, then went through to the house to warn Margaret that I would be away for some time.

'Can we come too, Papa?' Alysoun asked. 'Master Baker has given me a collar and lead for Rowan and he says she must learn to walk with them.'

I shook my head. 'It is much too far for the puppy. She is only a baby yet, remember. I am going all the way out past the castle, the whole length of Oxford. Her short legs would soon tire.'

'I suppose.' She picked up the puppy, who had been leaning against her feet, half asleep.

'You could practise with the lead in the garden. That will be far enough for now. Did Jonathan persuade any of the millers to take a puppy?'

'Aye, both at Trill's Mill and the Dominicans' Black-friars Mill.'

'You may tell Master Baker that Thomas Yardley will take a puppy. So much has happened since I left the farm, I have forgotten to tell him.'

She counted up on her fingers. 'Us and two mills and the farm, that's four. Jonathan is sure his father will keep the terrier pup. We only need to find one more home, and they will all be saved!'

'There is still Holywell Mill.'

She wrinkled her nose. 'Jonathan does not like the miller there. He is afraid to ask.'

Holywell's miller had a reputation for beating any children he found stealing the apples from his orchard, so perhaps Jonathan had had an unpleasant encounter there. The boy ran wild much of the time.

'I may need to go out to Holywell myself soon,' I said. 'Ask John Baker if he will keep the last pup until I can ask there.'

'Thank you, Papa!' She embraced me about the knees and I dropped a kiss on the top of her red gold hair, which was in dire need of combing.

'I must go. I will see you at supper time.'

Alysoun followed me into the street and ran across to the bakery with the good news about the puppies. With Roger's parcel of pages in my stiffened satchel – designed to keep books and manuscripts from damage – I set off up the High. In my satchel I also carried the key I had found amongst William Farringdon's lecture notes. It had occurred to me that it might be nothing more than a key to Hart Hall. I did not think Jordain usually gave the students house keys, but William had been one of the most senior, perhaps entrusted to lock up in the evening.

As for telling Alysoun I might go out to Holywell, I fully intended to trace the route of the Cherwell from the mill to the East Bridge, as soon as I could, in the hope that it might throw some light on what had happened to William, but I could not go there today, since it lay in quite the opposite direction from the bookbinders' quarter.

The choir was rehearsing as I passed the university church of St Mary the Virgin, the high, pure voices of the boys soaring above the men's deeper tenors and basses. Then they would break off and repeat the same phrase again and again until the choirmaster was satisfied. I had sung as a boy in our parish church in the village, but after my voice broke I had never felt my voice good enough to sing in public. Besides, in Oxford there was an over abundance of men in holy orders to sing the services in the many churches and the chapels attached to some of the colleges. There were so many churches, you fell over them wherever you went, since Oxford was, in theory, a place of worship and religious study. That was to ignore the frequent outbreaks of violence and the ever increasing study of more secular subjects. My own parish of St Peter's was the largest in the town, the church originally an ancient Saxon foundation. Only St-Peter-le-Bailey approached its parish in size. Some, like that of St-Michael-at-the-North-Gate were very small indeed.

By the time I reached Carfax, I was quite hot, the weather having decided – for today, at least – that it really was spring. Here the four streets that joined the gates of old Saxon Oxford met at a crossroads: the High leading in from the East Gate, Fish Street from the South Gate, and Northgate Street from the north. Ahead of me Great Bailey should have led to the West Gate, but when the Normans built the Castle at the west end of the town they destroyed it. What was now called the West Gate resembled a postern, like little Smith Gate near Hart Hall.

I passed Swindlestock Tavern, standing right on Carfax, as I headed down Great Bailey. As usual there was a good deal of noise spilling out from it. One of the rowdiest drinking places in town, it had a reputation for trouble, though there was unlikely to be anything to fear from it during the afternoon. The road here sloped down, to what I suppose must once have been a quiet river valley long before the town was built. Our two rivers, the Thames and the Cherwell, form a maze of streams and tributaries all round the town, and the area beyond the Castle (which I reached by skirting the mound and going out through the small West Gate), has been likened to Venice. I have never been to Italy, but I am told that whole town consists of islands.

This waterlogged, marshy area west of Oxford is prone to flooding, but it suits a number of the businesses located here, which need water. Above all, for my purposes, the makers of parchment, who must leave their scoured skins for days on end in cages in the river, till they are washed clean and pure, and rendered soft by the action of the flowing water. Where there are parchment makers, there you will find bookbinders, and a number of book-binders had established themselves on an island here in the Thames, entirely surrounded by water, reached, unsur-prisingly, by Bookbinders Bridge. The road crossed to the far side of the island, leaving it in the west by the Small Bridge and continuing on to St Thomas's and Osney Abbey.

Once across Bookbinders Bridge on to the island, I turned left to the workshop of Henry Stalbroke. He was a small, frail-looking man, white-haired, with a pointed face and remarkable eyes, who might have been any age from fifty to eighty, for he was one of those who look like old men when they are boys, and like slightly withered boys when they are old men. My father-in-law had always dealt with him, and I had continued the partnership. Bookbinding is hard work, requiring strength as well as skill, but Henry Stalbroke's frail appearance was deceptive. He was a master of his craft and although he had two journeymen working under him, and four apprentices, he still did all the most exquisite work himself, creating covers of tooled and gilded leather which were unique works of art. As well as book binding, the workshop also made the inlaid and jewelled leather boxes to hold the most precious books. Not only was this the finest bookbinder's workshop in Oxford. Their work was also commissioned by the great abbeys and even the court. I hoped they would have time to take on the modest task of binding Mistress Lapley's French book.

'And how soon do you need the work completed, Nicholas?' Master Stalbroke asked.

'As soon as it can be managed,' I said. 'I have already expended a good deal of money on it, and it has occupied all Roger Pigot's time for several weeks.'

'I could not bind it myself until next month, but if you will entrust it to Thomas, he should be able to finish it by next week.'

Thomas Needham was his most senior journeyman and a competent workman. His binding would be quite fine enough for Mistress Lapley.

'Aye, let Thomas do the work,' I said.

We discussed which leather, out of the samples Master Stalbroke showed me, should be used for the binding, whether there should be clasps – not, I thought – and whether the edges of the pages should be tinted or gilded.

'Not gilded,' I said. 'It is not a work of devotion, but the lady would probably like a touch of crimson on the edges of the pages.'

We settled on the price, then I spent some time admiring the latest bindings, from two great bifolia Bibles (one for Osney, one for an abbey in Yorkshire) down to the little palm-sized books of hours, like my own most precious volume. I breathed deeply, drawing in the heady scent of newly polished leather, which I have found intoxicating ever since I fell in love with books as a boy, and I stroked the covers of the Bibles with admiring (not to say covetous) hands. Thomas unscrewed the press where a recently bound book had lain overnight, until the glue dried and the pages were flattened.

'Here's a pretty little book of hours, Master Elyot,' he said. He was smiling mischievously, and I wondered why, as he handed it to me.

I turned over the pages carefully. The tiny illuminations were exceptionally skilfully done, and I liked the lively antics of the squirrels and monkeys playing around the margins.

'This is an artist who knows how to depict animals,' I said, 'unlike some. He has observed them carefully.'

Master Stalbroke and Thomas both laughed.

'*She* has done so,' Master Stalbroke said. 'That is the work of a nun at Godstow.'

'Indeed!' I was surprised. Some nuns could write, a few even might call themselves scribes, but I had not previously encountered one with this level of artistic skill.

'A newcomer, I believe,' Master Stalbroke said, 'perhaps still a novice.'

'A rare artist, if she is so young.'

'They have both squirrels and a monkey as pets in the nunnery,' Thomas said, 'as well as dogs and cats, so she had models for her art.'

'Even so, it needs a special quality to be able to depict what you see as accurately as this.' I gave a wry grin. 'It has always been a regret of mine that I can barely draw an apple. To draw a monkey would be impossible.'

'To each of us the talents God has given us,' Master Stalbroke said.

Leaving Roger's pages with them, I set off for the parchment maker, Dafydd Hewlyn, whose premises were at the lowest tip of the island, where the two branches of the Thames joined together again and provided a good flow of water through his cages. I could smell Hewlyn's workshop from some distance away, for the raw materials of his craft were the newly flayed skins of calves, sheep, and goats, which with great patience and seemingly a kind of magic were turned into the creamy sheets from which all books are made. Because of the unpleasant nature of much of their craft, parchment makers are sometimes regarded with a kind of scorn, yet without them there would be no books, without books there would be no scholars. Indeed, there would be little to raise us above the level of talking beasts.

A wooden walkway lay between the buildings and the river, with posts at regular intervals, from which ropes disappeared into the water. From these, I knew, slatted wooden cages were suspended, in which the newly flayed skins were tied, one above the other with spaces between, so that the water could flow over both surfaces, washing away any remaining fragments of flesh or loose hairs left from the first preliminary scraping.

I opened the door and ventured into the main workshop, trying not to breathe too deeply, but even so the stench of the skins and the sharp smell of the lime caught at the back of my throat and made me cough. One of the apprentices was stirring the skins soaking in the lime and water bath, contained in one of the enormous stone dehairing tanks. He was standing on a stool and using a long pole like a giant broomstick. The other tank contained the skins which had been scraped and were receiving a second soaking to bleach them before the final dressing.

'Where is Master Hewlyn?' I asked another apprentice, who was tying down the netting over a cage of fresh skins before it went into the river.

'Out at the stretching frames,' he said, jerking his head toward the door in the side of the workshop.

I opened it and went through, glad to be out in the open air again. On a patch of ragged turf three stretching frames were set up, a large one for calf skins, the two smaller for sheep or goat skins. Strings were threaded through at crucial points all round the edges of the skins and drawn tightly outward to be tied to the wooden frames. From time to time, the strings would be pulled tighter, stretching the skins thinner and thinner. Dafydd's journeyman was carefully scraping the calf skin with a curved two-handled knife, shaped like a half moon, removing the last of the hair which had been loosened in the lime bath.

'Good day to 'ee, Dafydd,' I said.

The Welshman nodded to me as he picked up one of the smaller frames and headed to another shed, where the fine work on the skins was carried out. I followed him, but knew better than to offer to help him carry the frame. He was short and bowlegged, with a thatch of dark hair and a truculent expression, but he was a master parchment maker.

'What do 'ee want, then?' he asked, as he began untying the skin from the frame. I thought it was sheep skin, but it might have been goat. It was difficult to tell at this stage, but I could judge the difference in the finished parchments by the feel between my fingers.

Dafydd's English was perfect, since he had lived in Oxford for all his adult life, but he had never lost the sing-song inflection of his native land, his sentences soared and dipped like music, like the hills and valleys of Wales.

'I need to place a large order with you,' I said. 'A good supply of your finest quality, and some of the everyday.'

He nodded. 'You must wait a while then.'

I was accustomed to this. Although I was one of his best customers, he would always put the welfare of his skins ahead of the convenience of his clients. Having unstrung the skin from the frame and laid it flat on his wide table, he shouted for his journeyman to pin out another skin on to the empty frame. When the journeyman, as taciturn as his master, had carried it off, Dafydd picked up a pumice stone with a curved top which fitted neatly into his hand, and began smoothing the stretched skin with the flat lower surface of the stone. This was where the real skill came in. Rubbing too hard would tear the skin, and all the precious labour would be lost. Too faint-hearted an effort and the parchment would be left rough and uneven, useless for the preparation of books.

I hitched up a stool and sat down to watch. I never cease to wonder at the skill which can turn animal hide into creamy soft parchment, so thin that the light shines through it. I looked around me. The walls of the shed were lined with shelves. On some lay piles of prepared but uncut skins, and on others the final trimmed sheets, some for the great bifolia, like the ones I had seen in the bookbinder's workshop, down to the small fine sixteen-folds for the best quality small books. A separate shelf held the poorer sheets which were adequate for schoolboy texts.

When I judged that Dafydd was sufficiently content in his work, I ventured to ask the question which was my other reason for coming here today.

'Any strangers about lately?' I asked, making my voice as casual as possible. 'Strangers buying high quality parchment?'

He eyed me from under bushy black eyebrows, in which a few grey hairs flickered. 'Why do you want to know?' he said bluntly.

'I have come across some unfinished pages in odd circumstances,' I said, 'and they were not written on parchment I had supplied. I wondered where it might have come from. Too fine to be sold by the other stationers in Oxford, so perhaps someone bought it directly from you.'

I reached into my satchel for the single blank sheet from William's room and held it out to him. Dafydd laid down his pumice stone, dusted his hands on his apron, and took it from me. He carried it over to the open door and examined it, then handed it back before resuming the smoothing of the skin.

'Well?' I said.

'Aye, that is one of mine.'

My heart gave a small leap. Perhaps this would throw light on the tangled mystery of William's death.

'Who bought it, and when?'

He glowered at me. 'Why do you want to know?' He asked again.

I sighed. Dafydd Hewlyn could be both difficult and stubborn. I had thought it best to keep the discoveries Jordain and I had made to ourselves for the present, but it was clear Dafydd was not prepared to tell me more until I revealed at least some of those discoveries to him.

'I do not know whether word has reached you out here, but a student died in the Cherwell yesterday, and I was the one to find him. No one yet knows what happened. He lived at Hart Hall, and when the Warden and I looked in his room, we found some pages under his mattress. That is one of them.'

'That seems little enough reason for you to be coming all the way out here to ask about it.'

He had his eyes on his work, but I realised that he was paying sharp attention.

'We think – Master Brinkylsworth and I think – that the boy's death may not have been an accident. It seemed strange to us that he should have hidden the pages under his mattress. And as they were of this very fine quality, I suspected that they came from you. If the pages have anything to do with his death, we thought we should find out. I was coming here anyway, to order parchment from you and to take a book to be bound by Master Stalbroke.'

He shrugged. 'I suppose there is no harm in telling you. It must have been about three weeks gone. Aye, it would be three weeks. Two men came, said I'd been recommended by one of the college Fellows. They wanted a quarter ream of the best quality parchment, duodecimo, like that.' He pointed to the blank sheet, which I had laid on the edge of his table. 'It was an odd order, because I do not sell much of that size in that quality, except to the large abbeys. What were these pages you found?'

'They seemed to be for a Psalter,' I said.

One matter I was not going to reveal was that I knew *which* Psalter.

'Hmm, well that makes some sense, though not altogether. They said they were buying for Greyfriars in London, but why come all the way to Oxford, when they could buy in London? I'm not such an arrogant fool as to think I am the only man to make fine parchment. There will be plenty in London.'

'Were they friars?'

He gave a snort. 'Nothing like. Men of the world. I would have thought traders of some sort – not great merchants, small men – save that there was a certain shifty look about them. The sort you see at the great fairs, who are long gone before you find how faulty were the goods they sold you.'

'Then why did they not simply take the parchment back to London to sell? Instead of giving it to this student?'

'Aye, why not? Perhaps they thought they could have a cheap job of scribing done by a student, then sell the book for a high price in London. Or at one of the fairs, as I say. I do not believe they were buying for Greyfriars.'

'What were they like, these men? Can you describe them?'

He squinted and stopped smoothing for a moment. 'Both about your height, one a mite taller. Heavy built, both o'them. Especially the bigger man.'

'Age? Colouring?'

'My age, I'd say, somewhere short of fifty. One dark brown, one lighter, reddish. The reddish-haired one was pockmarked.' He frowned. 'The other had been in a fight some time and had his nose broken, it hadn't healed straight. A rough man, he looked. Violent.'

'Well, I thank you, Dafydd. I do not know whether any of this has a bearing on the boy's death, but it's as well to find out. By all accounts he was a decent lad.'

'Aye, well, we've seen too much death these last few years to want any more, especially of the young. Now, I must finish this today. Tell me what you have come to buy and I'll have one of the boys pack it up for you.'

I chose my supplies from the stock on his shelves and was soon heading back to Bookbinders Bridge, my satchel weighed down with the parchment. On the whole I was encouraged by what I had learned from Dafydd Hewlyn. Indeed, I had never known him so forthcoming and I suspected it was because he had not liked the two men from London. If they really were from London. What I must do was to question Peter de Wallingford more closely about the men he had seen with William. It was likely they were the same men, though I was not certain that would make matters any clearer.

—

It was evening by the time I had made my way back across Oxford, turning up Northgate Street after I came to Carfax, then following the town wall until I reached Hart Hall. Jordain was sitting at a table in one of the large rooms, struggling to read a student's poor handwriting by the light of a rush dip, which reminded me that William had possessed some good wax candles, rarely to be found in Hart Hall. Was that important?

I sat down opposite Jordain.

'I am afraid we have already supped,' he said, apologetically, 'but there may be some left.'

A smell of boiled cabbage hung in the air. Even had I wanted some, I was sure his hungry students would have eaten the lot. I shook my head.

'Margaret will have kept me something. I shall not stay long. I have been over to the bookbinder's and parchment maker's.'

I told him all that I had learned from Dafydd Hewlyn.

'It does sound,' Jordain said slowly, 'as though these might be the same two men seen by that student from St Edmund Hall. We need to question him closely. So Dafydd thinks these men bought parchment then persuaded – and I suppose paid – William to copy the Psalter for them. He thinks they might be the sort of untrustworthy traders who haunt the big fairs.'

'Aye. But Dafydd's idea does not quite make sense,' I said. 'For one thing, why would such men buy the very finest quality of parchment for such a fraud? Surely they would use a cheap sort, and pass it off, perhaps in a dim light. They would not waste their money on Dafydd's best.'

'True.'

'And besides, I did not tell Dafydd what book William was copying, merely that it looked like a Psalter, not that it was that ancient Irish treasure which Merton possesses. If these men were the fraudsters he supposes, they would not go to so much trouble. They would use some common Psalter.'

'Unless—'

'Unless what?'

'Suppose some rich nobleman coveted a copy of that particular book. Might he hire these men to arrange for a copy to be made? In that case, it needs must be written on the best parchment, for such a man would not tolerate anything less.'

'Aye.' I rubbed my chin and felt the bristles rasp. I had not shaved that day. 'It does not solve the most perplexing problem. How was William able to see and copy the original Irish book? I cannot imagine how these men could have obtained it. How would they even make their way into Merton?'

Jordain shook his head in bafflement. 'You have the right of it. Until we know the answer to that, we cannot understand what it was that William was involved in. Whatever it was, I do not like the sound of it, nor does it accord with all I know of the boy.'

'And even then,' I said, 'we cannot know how it relates to his murder. It must, somehow, for these men were about no honest affair. Dafydd was sure of it. And I would say he is a shrewd judge of character.'

'Well, I am glad you stopped to tell me what you discovered, but you must away home, or Margaret will be wanting to roast me before a slow fire.'

'There is something else,' I said.

I felt in my satchel underneath the package Dafydd's boy had made up for me, and drew out the key.

'When I looked through the notes which were in William's satchel, I found this at the bottom.' I handed it to him. 'It looks like a house key. Or I suppose it might be the key to a large strong box. It may mean nothing. Did you give William a door key for Hart Hall?'

Jordain turned the key over in his hands and shook his head. 'Nay, this is not our key, it is quite different. See.'

He drew up a key which hung by a thin chain from his belt. I knew that he carried it, but could not quite remember its shape. He laid the two keys side by side on the table. They were roughly the same size, about six inches long, but the shapes bore no resemblance to each other.

'Do you think it is a house key?' I said. 'I am not sure.'

'It certainly looks like one. But you are right, it might be something else. It could belong to a strong box or a locked coffer. Some of those are this large.'

'Perhaps it means nothing.' I dropped William's key into my scrip. 'It may be the key to his own home, though I do not know why he should have carried it off with him when he came to Oxford. Such keys as this – for it fits a complex lock – are not cheap.'

'Perhaps it *is* the key to his home.' Jordain sighed. 'I wrote to the boy's mother today. His father is lately dead. It is a task I hate. I thought after all the deaths in the pestilence that I should never need to do it again.'

'Was he an only child?'

'An only son. I believe there is a younger sister.'

'With the father dead and now William, they may find life hard. Do you know anything of their circumstances?'

He shook his head. 'Not very prosperous, I expect. Perhaps they needed money, which might explain why he would undertake a job of copying. William never spoke much about his past and his family, for he was looking to the future. Small gentry, I believe, or yeomen. Had he gone on to the promising future that lay ahead of him, he would have been able to support a widowed mother and sister, but now—'

'Every way you look at it, this is a bad business,' I said. 'Not just the murder, but whatever is behind it, and the hardships that lie in the future.'

I got up. ''Tis time I was away. Tomorrow we had best go to the coroners and tell them what we know.'

'Are they even in Oxford?'

I looked at him blankly. 'That I do not know. I will ask the constable.'

He saw me to the door. 'Do not go home by Hammer Hall Lane, not this late. It is quite dark.'

'Nay, never fear!' I laughed. 'I shall go down Catte Street to St Mary the Virgin. God give you good night, Jordain.'

'And you, Nicholas.'

Even Catte Street is narrow and dark at this time of night, although it has not the sinister reputation of the cluster of hovels at the far bend of Hammer Hall Lane. A few lights shone out from Cat Hall, and I could hear laughter and drunken singing, so it seemed the students there were having a riotous evening, unlike Jordain's students, who were so quiet they must have been studying or already abed. I quickened my steps, for I always tried to be at home when the children went to bed and I had not been there the previous evening. I had already failed in my promise to be home in time for their supper. Although Alysoun had not been much above two years old when her mother died, she had felt the loss. Sometimes I think she was afraid she would lose me as well, and would not always settle to sleep unless I was there to kiss her goodnight.

As Catte Street narrowed alongside St Mary's, my footsteps echoed between the hard-baked earth of the street and the wall of the church. I thought I could hear other footsteps behind me, but when I stopped and looked over my shoulder, I could see no one, although now I was beyond the light from Cat Hall it was very dark. I told myself I was imagining the sound. It was probably nothing more than a repeated echo between the close stone walls.

Nevertheless, I turned with relief into the wider High Street. There were a few taverns here, still displaying flaming torches before their doors, though no student should have been drinking there at this hour. The tavern-keepers were probably flouting the rules for townspeople as well, but since the pestilence such regulations had become slack. In a world where life seemed so fragile, even the strictest of town authorities were reluctant to clamp down on the few pleasures left in life.

I thought of what Jordain had said, about writing to William's mother. She must have believed that her son was safe, now that the time of pestilence was past. I had been too lost in my own grief at that time to pay much heed to Jordain, but it had also proved hard for him. The warden of Hart Hall had died about halfway through the plague, and Jordain had been appointed in his place, although he was but newly a Regent Master and only twenty years of age at the time. I knew that he had written to the families of all those students under his care who had died, but selfishly I had never given thought to the toll it must have taken on him. Little wonder that he had found the letter to Mistress Farringdon difficult to write. I wondered whether she could read, or whether she would be obliged to find someone to read it for her. Even receiving a letter would probably be a shock to her. Unless, poor woman, she thought it was a letter from her son.

I was glad to see that Margaret had left a rush light burning for me in the window of her room above the shop, with the shutters open, so that I was able to see to unlock the door of the shop. We never left it unlocked at night, for some of my stock was valuable and might prove a temptation to thieves. Once inside, I relocked the door and drew the bolts across. A light shone through from the house, so, as I suspected, Margaret had waited up for me. I laid my satchel on the counter and walked through to the kitchen.

I found her dozing in the wicker chair beside a dying fire. She had had little sleep the night before, and I felt guilty that I had kept her up for a second night. A plate was laid out on the table, with a slice of cold pease pudding, bread, a few early radishes from the garden, and a pot of custard. A jug of ale was covered with a cloth to keep the flies out.

I lifted a stool out from under the table as quietly as I could, but when I sat down, the legs scraped a little on the flagstones and Margaret gave a soft snort and a cough, and sat up.

'I did not think you would be so late, Nicholas,' she said reprovingly.

'It is not so very late,' I said, pouring myself some ale and cutting off a portion of the pease pudding. 'You are tired, after yesterday. It is a long walk to Bookbinders Island and back. And I needed to see Jordain before I came home.'

She rose from the chair and stretched. 'I am stiff. I must be getting old.'

She joined me at the table, pouring herself some ale and helping herself to one of my radishes.

'Thirty is not old,' I said, 'but you work too hard. Perhaps we should get a girl to help you.'

'We cannot afford a servant.'

'A young girl would not cost much above her keep.'

She shook her head. 'I've no need for an untrained servant girl under my feet, as well as two children and a puppy, I thank you, Nicholas! Besides, Alysoun should be learning to housekeep soon.'

I felt a stab of regret. 'Not yet,' I said. 'Let her remain a child a little longer. And I intend to continue with her lessons.'

'There is no need for a girl to be learned. I have learning enough myself to read and keep accounts, and that she may do already. There is no need for more. Why you think you should teach her Latin, I cannot imagine!'

She threw up her hands in despair, and I laughed.

'Elizabeth had some Latin. Alysoun may help me in the shop one day, as Elizabeth helped her father.'

'That will be for Rafe to do.'

'I hope that Rafe will attend the university. Already he makes good progress with his reading. In any case, we shall see. No need to decide yet.'

I began to eat my supper.

'At Master Stalbroke's today I saw a very beautiful book of hours. You would have admired it.' I grinned at her. 'It was made by a woman.'

'A woman!'

'Aye, a nun at Godstow. A beautiful hand and remarkable illuminations.'

'So that is what you have been doing all this while – admiring books written by women aping the occupations of men!'

'Nay, that was merely in passing. My purpose in going there was both for business and to try to discover more about this strange murder of the boy William Farringdon.'

I described to her just what I had done and heard on Bookbinders Island, and how Jordain and I had examined the key from William's satchel.

'This is a very unpleasant matter, Nicholas,' she said when I had finished. 'It may even be dangerous, if these men are the rogues Dafydd Hewlyn suspects them to be.

I think you and Jordain should leave the matter alone. Let the constables and the coroner, or the sheriff – whoever it is who deals with such things – let them discover what has happened. It is not for you to interfere.'

I was not quite sure why I felt so compelled to interfere, but I did my best to explain it to her.

'It was I who found William's body, Margaret, and Jordain was in a manner *in loco parentis*. I even employed William two summers ago, as you will remember. Moreover, we found those pages the boy had written, and I have identified the book he was copying, though how or why, I cannot say. Now it seems that the men who bought the parchment from Dafydd Hewlyn may well be the men seen with William. And he was afraid of them. Someone stabbed him to death. I cannot let it lie.'

'I remember him, when he worked here,' she conceded. 'He was a good polite boy. He would not take his lunch at the tavern with Walter and Roger, but brought a bit of stale bread or an apple to eat at his desk.'

'Aye, and you would bring him through to take his dinner with us.'

'They do not feed them properly at Hart Hall. They always look half starved.'

'They have no money.'

I saw that she was softening, now that she recalled the boy.

'Get you to bed, Meg.' I stood up. 'I am off myself. I will look in on the children as I go.'

'Aye, they missed you. I shall just cover the fire, then I shall away to my bed.'

As I climbed the stairs carrying a tallow candle, I realised how tired I was after my long walk and the heavy burden of parchment I had carried back with me. Lifting aside the curtain across the children's door, I saw that Rafe had tried to climb into bed with Alysoun and the puppy again, but was now hanging over the edge of the bed, about to slide on to the floor.

I set down my candle and picked him up. He muttered something and curled up in my arms like the puppy. I held him close for a moment. My son, who could so easily have followed his mother into the cold earth.

His bed was a tangle, but I straightened it as best I could with one hand, then tucked him in, drew up the feather bed around his shoulders, and kissed the tangle of his curls. They needed cutting. My children were like unshorn sheep.

As I picked up my candle I had a sudden sharp sense of that unknown woman, Mistress Farringdon, who must once have tucked her own young son into his bed and kissed him goodnight. And now her son lay in the cold and dark, alone in St Peter's church. I would pursue his killer, whatever the cost.

Chapter Five

The following morning I was in the shop early, before my two scriveners arrived, for I wanted to set out enough work to keep them occupied all day. My intention was to collect Jordain from the Schools when he finished lecturing at eight o'the clock, and persuade him to come with me to Holywell Mill. I wanted to follow the Cherwell down to the East Bridge. There might be nothing there to throw any light on what had happened to William, but I could not rest until I had investigated every yard of the river bank.

Roger had already made a start on preparing to create his book of tales, selecting enough sheets of matching parchment, preparing his quills and ink, and setting out a plan for the work on a scrap of waste paper. I smiled to myself. I was glad to see my suspicion that giving him the responsibility for the new book was already proving successful in encouraging him to take some pride in the work.

For Walter, I had a novel suggestion, and when the two men arrived, I put it to him.

'This is what I propose, Walter,' I began. 'I know that you have a great store of tales in your head. You have often amused Alysoun and Rafe with them, as well as Margaret and me. I do not know a better storyteller.'

Walter looked embarrassed and shifted on his stool. 'They are nobbut simple stories, Master Elyot. My mother – God rest her soul—' he crossed himself, 'she was a great one for telling us stories in the evenings, especially of a dark winter's night, when we had no light but the fire and it was early dark outside, but too early to be abed. She had no book learning.'

I nodded. Walter's father had also been a scrivener, although crippled by a stiffening of his hands in his middle years. His mother had been a country woman, a farmer's daughter, unlettered. Yet it is often amongst the unlettered that the old tales linger on, passed down from mother to child on such winter nights.

'While Roger is preparing a book of stories about such famous folk as King Arthur and Robin o'Wood,' I said, 'I would like you to write down some of these tales your mother used to tell you. Not about great heroes, but other folk – Puck, Hob-by-the-Fire, the Green Man, the Lady of the Whispering Pool – all those stories you used to tell us in your turn.'

There was no need for me to remind him how he had helped us through the dark days by drawing our minds away from the world that was dying around us. He had even lived with us for a time, having lost his own wife and child in the Death. The telling and hearing of the ancient stories had helped to keep us all from total despair.

Walter was looking at me in alarm. '*Write* the stories, Master Elyot? I am no poet!'

I laughed. 'I am not asking you to write them in verse, Walter. Write them down just as you would tell them. That cannot be so hard, surely?'

He shook his head. 'I do not know. I should probably find myself in a proper tangle. I'd be blotting and crossing out. It would never make a book.'

'Nay, I do not expect them to be perfect at once. Write them on paper first, and cross out as much as you need, but if you write them just as you would tell them, I think there will be little need for that. Then we can look at them together. When you are content, we will make a book of them. I would see your mother's stories saved, and since we live in a world of books, that is the best way to preserve them.'

He still looked very dubious, but he fetched a stack of the sort of paper we used for the *peciae*, and sat at his desk chewing the end of his quill.

'I cannot think what to write!' he said desperately.

'Imagine that you have Rafe on your knee and Alysoun is sitting on her stool, listening to every word. You are going to tell them the story of Hob-by-the-Fire.'

I tried to make it sound as though we were beside the kitchen fire in the evening, though it was difficult with the bright spring sunshine flooding in through the open window and the people of Oxford walking past in the street, but he closed his eyes, muttering to himself, then I heard the scratching of his quill as he began to write.

With both Walter and Roger occupied, I thought I should step along the road to Edric Crowmer's wine shop. It was time I reported to the constable some at least of the things Jordain and I had discovered about William, so that he could take word to the coroner. However, just as I opened the door to the street, the man himself appeared, hurrying along toward me with a self-important air.

'You are to come at once, Master Elyot,' he said. 'The inquest is called for this morning and you are distrained to appear, as finder of the body. You are already to be reprimanded for not summoning a hue and cry.'

'That is an ancient law,' I said, stung by his superior air. 'There is no point in summoning a hue and cry when a man is long dead and no sign of an attacker. You thought yourself that it was suicide.'

'The victim has now been viewed by the coroners,' he said pompously, 'and it has been ascertained that he was stabbed.'

So it would not be necessary for me to draw attention to the fact, I realised with some relief. I had begun to be worried because I had not reported it at once. I decided to keep silent on the matter, and would warn Jordain to do likewise.

'Where is the inquest to be held?' I asked.

'The coroners have ordered the hall of St Edmund's to be taken over. It will start when St Peter's bell strikes eight o'the clock. As usual, the four neighbouring parishes are summoned – St Peter's, St Mary the Virgin, All Saints, and, since he was found beyond the wall, St Frideswide's.'

Clearly Crowmer had been bustling about the other parishes, for he now wiped his sweaty face on his sleeve.

'You must present yourself to the coroners at once. And I must find Master Brinkylsworth, since the victim was a member of his hall and under his care.'

'He will be lecturing in the Schools until eight o'the clock,' I said.

'Then he must stop. I shall send a servant to fetch him out.'

Crowmer bustled off. Jordain would not be pleased to have his lecture curtailed, I thought, but there was nothing I could do about it, so I turned left and headed down the High to St Edmund's.

As I shouldered my way into the hall, I saw a number of familiar faces amongst the crowd, including some of the gawpers who had watched us carry the body up from the river bank to the road. Men from all four parishes would have been summoned to make a judgement on the manner of William's death – natural, mischance, suicide, or murder. As finder, I would need to declare the circumstances which had led to my discovery, and I hoped there would be no need for me to take any further part in the proceedings. In this avid crowd of townsmen, eager for anything sensational to be found against a member of the university, I felt uneasy for the boy, and for his family.

Suddenly I was convinced that I should say nothing about the pages hidden under William's mattress, or what I had learned from Dafydd Hewlyn. I looked around for Peter de Wallingford, thinking I should warn him to keep to himself for the present what he had told me about the men he had seen speaking to William, but there was no sign of him in the crowd. He was probably attending a lecture. Indeed the only member of St Edmunds' I could see was the Principal, looking anxious and somewhat angry at this occupation of his domain by the town.

People were still thrusting in behind me, and I saw Crowmer, with Jordan by the elbow looking flustered and annoyed. I began to work my way toward them. To my relief Crowmer, having captured his prey and delivered him to the inquest, was now conferring with more of the constables from the various parishes. I pulled Jordain into a corner and put my mouth close to his ear.

'I do not like the look of this crowd,' I murmured. 'They are off after the rumour of a university scandal, like scent hounds after a stag. If we want to protect William's name as much as is in our power, I think we should say nothing about what we have discovered. For the present, at least.'

'Aye,' he said, with some vehemence. 'Curse them! Do you know, that fellow Crowmer sent one of the servants of the Schools, a ruffian, to drag me away from my lecture without so much as a by-your-leave? I shall be a laughing stock.'

'Nay, I do not think so,' I said, wanting to calm him. 'Your students will understand, once they know the truth of it.'

'But now my whole course of lectures is disrupted,' he grumbled. 'I shall need to repeat this one, so how am I to finish before the end of term?'

This seemed to me to be of minor importance at the moment, but I merely gave a sympathetic smile.

'I am supposed to report myself to the coroners,' Crowmer said. 'I did not know there was more than one here.'

Jordain pointed to the front of the hall, where two elderly men in long gowns were speaking to St Edmund's Principal. 'I have been making enquiries earlier this morning. It seems we have *two* coroners active in Oxford. Do you suppose we have more sudden deaths than other towns? And they conduct their inquests together. They are William de Whatele – he is the tall man – and Richard de Eynesham, and it seems they know their business, for they have been in office this dozen years, at least.'

'In that case there is probably no need for any evidence we can provide. I'd best make myself known as the finder. It seems I am to be reprimanded for not raising the hue and cry.'

'But there was no one about, so you said. Not until those two lay brothers appeared. How could you have raised a hue and cry?'

I shrugged. 'Pettifogging lawyers will have their say.'

I presented myself to the two coroners with a bow, and explained that I was the finder of William Farringdon's body.

Richard de Eynesham, who was a small man, with shrewd eyes, said, 'And why did you not raise the hue and cry, Master Elyot?'

'There was not a soul about when I found the victim's body floating down the Cherwell,' I said. 'My main concern was to pull it from the river before it was swept away. It was only as I was nearly at the bank that the two lay servants from St John's Hospital appeared. Even then there was no one else to be seen. There was certainly no sign of any attacker who could be pursued. I sent at once for a constable and stayed with the body until I had it moved to safety. It was already growing dark.'

He frowned and gave a snort, which might have been of disbelief, but William de Whatele was calling the company to order and the boy's body was carried in. I supposed it must have remained in St Peter's until brought to the inquest, for it was still covered with the old altar cloth, which was now removed so that the jurors, eight from each of the four parishes, could examine it and state what evidence they could detect.

The coroners required me to recount in detail my finding of the body, and Jordain gave his opinion that William Farringdon was of good character and sound mind. In view of the clear evidence of stabbing, there was no longer any suggestion of suicide.

A surgeon from the parish of St Mary's gave his opinion that the victim had been struck by a thin-bladed knife some twelve inches long, and a blacksmith from All Saints declared that such a knife would have a value of one groat. This was recorded, so that, should the murderer ever be caught, he would be required to pay one groat to the Crown, which always had a financial interest in such cases.

The whole proceedings of the inquest were hurried through, and the jurors, after a brief discussion, gave their verdict that the victim had been unlawfully killed with a knife by some person unknown. Deprived of any exciting revelations, the onlookers, who had been standing throughout and crowded together with scarce room to move, began to drift away.

Near me one old man with a tailor's measure draped about his neck, turned to his neighbour in disgust. 'In the old days, there would not have been this haste to dispose of such a case. Was it town or gown? The coroners seem not to care who killed the student or why. Since the pestilence it seems no killing matters any more.'

'Aye,' his friend grunted, then added shrewdly, 'they'll not want folk to think 'twas one of our town lads, or the students will be after blood.'

'If 'twas one o' their own, they will cover it up, that's certain sure.'

Still muttering about the university's ability to hide the crimes of its members, they wandered out into the High Street, the brief excitement of their day over.

Jordain was talking to the rector of St Peter's, so I joined.

'The rector wonders whether he is to bury poor William in the churchyard. It will be some days before

I can hear from his mother what she would wish us to do.'

'And the weather—' the rector ventured delicately.

'Aye, it has grown warm these last few days,' Jordain said. He was looking tired and distressed. 'I suppose we must give William temporary burial at least. If you can have his body returned to the church for now, I will make arrangements for a coffin and for the funeral to take place tomorrow.'

With this agreed, they parted, and Jordain and I made our way out into the street.

'That was a shabby affair!' he burst out, when we were barely beyond the hearing of the coroners, who had followed us out.

I nodded. The whole business had seemed rushed and callous, as though William's body were some valueless object and not the mortal remains of a talented young man. I felt gloomy and sick.

'Before all this came up,' I said, 'I had planned to ask you whether you would come with me out to Holywell Mill. I want to examine the stretch of bank from there to the bridge.'

'Aye, I should be glad to get away from the town for a while,' he said. 'May I leave my lecture notes at your house?'

'Certainly.'

'I will see the carpenter in Ship Street, first, about making a coffin, then the sexton at St Peter's. It should not take me above an hour.'

'Come to the shop when you are done.'

'You know,' he said, as we walked back up the street, 'we cannot be sure which side of the river he went in.'

I stopped and looked at him. 'You have the right of it! For some reason I have been imagining it was the far side, where the students go rabbitting, but it might just as well have been the nearside.'

'Then we had better examine both.'

When Jordain returned, just over an hour later, we set off. I had told Margaret that I would not be back in time for dinner.

'The two of you should leave this matter well alone,' she said. 'It is no affair of yours. Let the constables and the coroners deal with it.'

I shook my head. 'As there is no trace of the attacker that they know of, they are inclined to regard the matter as closed. I think the coroners are weary after so many deaths and want to forget this one. As for the constables, what skills do they have to find William's killer? They are ordinary townsmen, appointed for a year, and, if many are like Edric Crowmer, they undertake the duties simply for the pleasure of bullying their fellows for breaking curfew or brawling or lying drunk in the street. It gives them importance for a twelvemonth. They will not trouble themselves with pursuing an unknown killer when the coroners themselves have dismissed the matter.'

She sighed, seeing that she could not persuade me to abandon the search for the truth about William's death.

'Very well, go if you must. I will make you up a parcel of food, since you will miss your dinner.'

As we set off, I carried a bag slung over my shoulder with the food she had provided, while Jordain hooked a flask of ale on to his belt.

'I think we should make our way up this side of the Cherwell first,' Jordain said. 'Starting at the bridge and following the bank upriver as far as the mill. Like you, I think William must have gone into the river below the mill, else his body would have been caught up in the sluice or the wheel.'

'I suppose it might have gone over the weir,' I said doubtfully.

'Do you not think someone would have seen it? Either the miller or his men? There are always people about during the day, working there. Or farmers delivering grain, or folk buying flour. Besides, I think if he had been tumbled over the weir, there would have been some sign of it about the body. Torn clothes, or bruising.'

'Do the dead bruise?' I said. 'I fear we are very ignorant, Jordain.'

'Aye, we are.'

We passed out through the East Gate and walked on past the row of small houses on the left before reaching the imposing front of St John's Hospital.

'We can cross the main channel of the Cherwell at the mill,' I said, 'but returning by the other bank we will need to cross some of the lesser branches. I remember one not far from the mill.'

'Aye. I think we can wade that one, but here near the bridge several come together. It's wide, isn't it? We'll need a boat. Or else we must retrace our steps.'

We had reached the near end of the bridge and I stopped suddenly.

'I have just thought. Suppose William's body did not come down the main channel, but one of the others? The maze of waterways here is nearly as bad as the Thames 'tother side of the castle.'

'Show me where you first saw him.'

We walked on to the bridge until we reached the spot where I had been standing when I spotted the body in the river. I leaned on the wooden railing, then jumped back as it groaned and bowed outward under my weight.

'This bridge is dangerous!' I said in disgust. 'The landowners responsible should be held to account.'

'They will do nothing until the whole thing collapses,' Jordain said with resignation. ''Tis pity it does not come under the jurisdiction of the town. Now, where was the body when you first saw it?'

'There.' I pointed to the bank on our left. 'Just as I watched, it drifted into that patch of reeds, about halfway along St John's wall.'

We both studied the reeds. A duck and drake were swimming nearby. As we watched, a procession of small yellow ducklings emerged one by one from amongst the reeds.

'There must be a nest there,' I said.

'Aye. But look, Nicholas. William's body could not have come down that branch of the Cherwell yonder.' He pointed to a wide side branch of the river to our right. 'They meet almost at the bridge. The body would not have floated backwards, against the current, to reach the reeds.'

'Nay, you have the right of it. So we may forget about that branch. There is still the other, just below the mill. I suppose he might have been thrown in there. That means we have much further to search, if we must follow up the banks of the branch as well as here. I do not know that we shall have time today.'

'We had best make a start, then.'

Jordain led the way back to the town end of the bridge, and we climbed down to the grassy slope which lay below St John's wall.

'It is as well the weather has been dry,' I said. 'I remember how slippery this used to be when we came swimming here.'

'And I remember when Tom Winter slid into the river that time, before he had taken his clothes off.'

We both laughed. Tom had found himself in trouble with the landlady of Tackley's, when he had come home dripping all over her newly scrubbed floor. She was not a motherly creature and cared more for the state of her floors than for the chill that Tom caught as a result of walking home in his sodden clothes. He did not die then, but later, during the pestilence.

The grass was dry enough now for us to make our way safely beside the hospital wall to where the ground opened up further along. This was an area of rough grass, where the town flock of sheep grazed. Some of the ewes lifted their heads and regarded us suspiciously, their legs planted firmly while they considered whether we were worth chasing. Their new lambs frolicked about, pretending alarm at the sight of us, until one or two of the bolder ones took a few steps toward us.

'It cannot have happened here,' I suggested. 'Too near St John's. Someone could easily have been looking out of a window. It must still have been daylight when he was stabbed.' Jordain agreed. 'And the town shepherd might have been about. See, he has a hut over there. In lambing season he must always be here, and those lambs are not long born.'

We continued, following the Cherwell north, the river on our right, a wide stretch of grazing land on our left, which ran all the way across to Longwall Street. Beyond that lay the southern end of the Canditch, in front of the town wall.

'This all still seems too open to me,' I said dubiously. 'Wherever William was attacked, it must have been in the daylight. He was in my shop just before the dinner hour, and he was in the river as I walked back from Yardley's farm. At that time of day, there are always people about, not only the shepherd back there with the lambs, but all along Longwall Street. Carts and packhorses going to and from the mill. People making their way further on, to St Cross's church. Or even those going round the town, instead of through it, to the Augustinian Friary or Durham College. You can see how busy it is now.'

Jordain nodded. 'I agree. Apart from a few bushes, it is all meadowland here. Nowhere for a stealthy attack. And surely it must have been stealthy, for him to have been stabbed in the back like that.'

I shuddered. 'Unless it was someone he knew, and he turned his back, all unsuspecting.'

Jordain rubbed his hand over his face and trudged on.

'You know, I can shorten the time even more. William came to dinner in hall after he had visited your shop. I heard him go out later, perhaps an hour later, but I thought nothing of it. They come and go as they please, as long as they are present for morning prayers and meals, and are withindoors by nightfall.'

'So it must have happened sometime after half past noon and before about five o'the clock, when I was crossing the bridge.'

'Less than that, even. For he must have walked from Hart Hall to somewhere near the mill, let us say. Then there would have been the time that it took for his body to drift down the river to the bridge. Between one o'the clock and four, would you say?'

'Aye, that sounds right.' I shut my eyes briefly, visualising the way William would have gone. 'He would go out through the Smith Gate, would he not? Then along Longwall Street until he came to the fork leading to St Cross on the left and the mill on the right. I think we have been wasting our time walking up this bank. He must have been heading for the other side of the river.'

Jordain quickened his steps. 'We should have realised that from the first. Come on, Nicholas. We need to cross the river.'

There was only one place where we could cross the Cherwell, without retracing our steps to the bridge, and that was by Holywell Mill. I remembered that I had told Alysoun I would ask the miller if he would take one of the puppies, but as we neared the mill, a large farm cart drawn by a yoke of oxen pulled up in front of it. The miller and one of his men began to help the farmer unload sacks of grain. They were clearly too occupied to be troubled by such a request, and besides, Jordain was hurrying toward the river.

The great water wheel was turning, driving the grinding stones within the mill, with such a clatter of machinery and such a roar of falling water that we could not speak. There was no bridge here, only a very narrow wooden walkway above the mill pool and over the sluice, so that the miller could reach the sluice gates. The miller was known for his hostility to those who used his walkway to cross the river, but had no power to stop the foot traffic. There was nowhere else to cross from one side of the Cherwell to the other unless you walked a good deal further upriver.

Once over the walkway, we stepped down into the water meadow which lay all down the east side of this branch of the Cherwell. Underfoot the ground felt spongy, still waterlogged from the winter rains which fill the river and overflow every year into this low-lying patch of ground. With the flood water now drained away, the meadow was a riot of colour, like the patched quilts Margaret made painstakingly from the scraps of worn clothing. Marsh marigolds opened their golden cups to the sun, lady orchids thrust up their tight-packed spears of pale purple flower heads, while the chequerboard bells of snake's head fritillaries bobbed in a breeze which blew unimpeded across this flat meadowland.

We turned to walk down river, on the far side of the Cherwell from the town. Apart from the mill, there was no building overlooking this bank of the river, and it was too far from Longwall Street to be observed. Moreover, willow trees grew here and there along the bank, their roots half in and half out of the water, the new leaves on their trailing branches a pale delicate yellow green. It was a quiet place, more lonely and deserted than I remembered. There were no sounds but the gurgle of the river and a constant hum of bees amongst the wild flowers of the meadow. A sudden flash of iridescent colour caught my eye as a kingfisher plunged from one of the willows into the river like a flighting arrow.

'I have not been here for years,' I said.

'Nor I. It cannot be here that the lads come for rabbits.'

'Nay. Too wet. They must go to the higher ground, further away from the river.'

We had hardly walked any distance when we met the main obstacle to our progress – another branch of this maze of waterways which make up the Cherwell, parting and joining and parting again. This branch of the river was almost as wide as the one we were following, though not nearly as deep, for it did not carry enough water to drive a mill.

'We must wade across, I suppose,' Jordain said.

'Aye.' I sat down on a clump of marsh grass and pulled off my shoes and hose. Jordain did the same. Then he drew up his knees and rested his chin on them.

'Do you think it is possible William could have gone into the river up there?' he said, waving a hand toward the upper part of the branch.

'It is certainly possible. I do not know how far it goes. I have never been that way. Do you think there is time to follow it today?'

He squinted at the sun and shook his head. 'Let us complete our examination of this bank today, and come back tomorrow if we find nothing.'

I nodded. 'Let's wade over to the other side, then eat this food Margaret has given us. I am tired of carrying it.'

We edged our way cautiously into the water, and both gasped at the cold. Although it only came a little above our knees, it was fast flowing and there were humps and hollows in the river bed which made it a treacherous crossing. Once on the far side, we sat on the grass and ate our food, while our legs dried. Margaret had given us a cold pie as well as the usual bread and cheese. The ale we drank straight from the flagon, passing it back and forth.

'I feel guilty,' Jordain said, lying back with his arm over his eyes. 'William killed here two days ago, and yet this seems like a holiday, as if we were boys again.'

'Aye,' I said. 'I feel the same. But we needed to come. I do not believe anyone else cares to look further into William's death.'

'I hope we may find something – *anything* – to tell us what he was doing with those pages, and whether it had anything to do with his death.'

I pulled on my hose and tied my points. 'Tomorrow I thought I might call at Merton. I can make it my excuse that I have come to collect the monies they owe me, then visit their *librarius*. Ask if I might look at the Irish Psalter.'

'He is not very friendly, you say.'

'He is not. But as a licensed stationer and bookseller for the university, I can express a natural interest.' I thrust my feet into my shoes.

Jordain was twisting around, tying the points at his back. 'But if we should want to come back here tomorrow—?'

'I will go to Merton in the morning, while you are at the Schools.'

'I have forgot. I have arranged the funeral for tomorrow afternoon.'

'Then we must return here the next day.'

It was as I picked up the bag which had held our food that I caught sight of something white, snagged on the protruding root of a bushy willow that grew just out of the water where the side branch met the Cherwell.

'Jordain, there is something...' I knelt on the bank and reached out. It was a fragment of white cloth, caught on a spike sticking out from the root. In freeing it I would have fallen headlong into the river, had Jordain not grabbed me by the belt and hauled me back.

'What is it?'

'Nothing but a piece of cloth. It is probably not important.' He reached out his hand for it.

'I noticed that there was a tear in William's shirt, but I cannot say whether this is a match.'

I stood up and studied the two sections of the river.

'Even if it is from his shirt, I am not sure that it tells us much. The body could have floated down either branch. See, there is a kind of eddy where they meet. The body could have been washed against that tree root from either direction and caught, then dragged free again. The river was flowing with some force when I was struggling to pull him ashore.'

'Aye.' He studied the piece of cloth, flattening it out on the palm of his hand. 'I cannot say. I must look again at his shirt. I am not sure the tear was as large as this. It may be nothing to do with William.'

'We have seen nothing between the mill and here,' I said, 'though it is no great distance. Could he have been stabbed so close to the mill? There would have been plenty of folk about in the afternoon.'

'I suppose there are some hidden spots behind the clumps of trees.' Jordain looked doubtful. 'But what I cannot see, is *why*? Why should someone stab a decent, studious boy like William, in broad daylight, and throw him in the river? It makes no sense.'

'That is not the only thing that makes no sense,' I said. 'Why was he here? Usually, he would have been at his studies, would he not? At that time in the afternoon? Why come here at all? Was he meeting someone? Someone who then drew a knife when his back was turned? Who would have such anger or fear or hatred of that boy to do such a thing?'

Jordain covered his face with his hands. 'I lie awake at night, turning those questions over and over in my mind, and I cannot fit together any answers.'

'Come,' I said. 'We will do no good lingering here. It is probably true that it cannot have happened between the mill and this spot. I think the first thing we must do is go back and see whether that scrap has indeed been torn from William's shirt. If it has not, it tells us nothing. If it has, then my guess is that he went into the river further up this side branch. There is no time to explore it today. Let us make our way back down the main channel to the bridge, but keep our eyes open in case there is anything else to be seen. Then, if that is part of William's shirt, we will come back tomorrow – nay the day after tomorrow – and study every inch of the way from here up to the head of this branch. I think it must flow across from that great bend in the river over to the east, at the foot of the rising ground.'

'You are right,' he said, folding up the damp piece of cloth and stowing it in his scrip. 'Let us make our way down to the bridge.'

We followed the east bank of the Cherwell from that point all the way downriver to the bridge, our eyes on the ground and the fringes of the water, but we found nothing unusual, save a child's worn shoe.

When the bridge rose before us, we were in something of a quandary, for at this point the other branch flowed in, the one we had rejected as we set out, so that we had come to what was, in reality, the tip of an island, with no way of reaching either the bridge ahead of us or the solid ground beyond either branch of the river.

'I do not care for the idea of walking all the way back to the mill again,' Jordain said. 'It is getting late.'

'If we follow this other branch upstream a little way,' I said, 'there is a fisherman who keeps a boat on the further bank. We can hail him, if he is there.'

We were in luck, which was as well, for we were both tired and discouraged. I knew the fisherman slightly and when I hallooed across the river he fetched us over in his coracle one at a time, landing us near the far end of the bridge. After bestowing profuse thanks on him, together with some coins, we made our way across the bridge and into Oxford as we had left it, by the East Gate.

'I must look at William's shirt before I do anything else,' Jordain said.

I nodded. 'Will his body still be in St Peter's?'

'Aye, though he may be coffined by now.'

'You mean we may have to open the coffin?' I shivered. It seemed sacrilegious to me.

'I suppose we may.' Jordain sounded grim, but he led me determinedly to the church.

As we expected, the coffin was there, laid on the steps before the altar and covered with the parish cerecloth.

'We cannot open the coffin without speaking to the rector,' I whispered, feeling more and more unhappy at the thought.

The rector was by the west door of the church, speaking to an old woman, so we waited nervously until she had left. Jordain explained about the torn cloth and our need to examine William's shirt.

'Oh, but you need not open the coffin!' The rector, who had initially looked shocked at the suggestion, now smiled with relief. 'The young man has been prepared for burial by my housekeeper and her sister, and sewn into a shroud. They will have his clothes back at the rectory. Come with me.'

He led us into the rectory kitchen, where the housekeeper and another woman were preparing supper. The women were puzzled at our request to see the clothes, but fetched the pile of neatly folded garments for us to examine.

'I was going to send them round to Hart Hall in the morning, maister,' the housekeeper said. 'There's wear in them yet, once the tear in the cotte is mended, though the poor lad's shirt is in a worse case.'

Jordain and I exchanged a glance, then he lifted the shirt – which had been washed and dried – on to the table. As soon as he unfolded it, we could all see the jagged tear. I held my breath as he took the fragment of cloth that we had found from his scrip and smoothed it out beside the shirt.

It fitted perfectly.

Chapter Six

Early the following morning, I presented myself at the gatehouse of Merton College. It occupied a large site south of Merton Street, the grounds reaching as far down as the town wall, which formed their southern boundary. The porter knew me well by sight, for Merton was a wealthy college and I had supplied it with a number of books in recent years. They were always in the market for anything fine or rare, although they would haggle over every last penny of the price. For some time they had talked of building a special library to house their collection, but the loss of Fellows during the pestilence, and the loss of income from their tenants at the same time, meant that nothing had come of these plans as yet. I also supplied the college with numerous articles of stationery. They were one of my largest customers, although not one of the best, since they were not prompt in paying.

Having sent Walter with a second bill several days ago, which had still not been paid, I considered that this was sufficient excuse to call on the bursar and politely request settlement. The porter nodded me through without question, and I made my way to the bursar's office, on the ground floor of the first quadrangle.

'Indeed, indeed, Master Elyot,' he said fussily, and with some annoyance. 'I have your money here. I intended to send it over to you today by one of the servants.'

He unlocked a strong box, requiring three keys, and drew out a fat purse, which he tipped out over his desk. I caught a half noble and two groats just as they rolled to the edge.

'It is all here,' he said, counting the coins out somewhat ostentatiously in front of me.

'Perfectly correct,' I said. 'If you will hand me the bill – the *second* copy of the bill – I will sign it to indicate that I have received your payment.'

He avoided my eye, and passed the bill to me, which I signed with an excessive flourish. I was never sure whether the delays were due to policy or neglect on his part, or whether he was instructed by the Warden to take as long as possible in settling the college's debts. Whatever the reason, it was a constant annoyance. Like many townsmen with small businesses, I found myself for ever needing to pay out immediately for any goods I bought, but having difficulty in extracting payment from my customers, especially when those customers were the colleges or the larger religious houses. However, I thanked him and stowed the purse inside my scrip, which was all I was carrying today, having no need of my manuscript satchel.

On leaving the bursar's office, I made my way across the quadrangle to the staircase leading up to the set of rooms which were used to house the college's collection of books until the proposed library could be built. As I expected, Phillip Olney, the Fellow of Merton who acted as their *librarius*, was there, seated at a desk, turning over the pages of a large volume and making notes on a sheet laid on the writing slope.

I was designated a *librarius* because I bought and sold books; Master Olney, because he was in charge of the college's books. It should have made for an amicable relationship, but that was not quite the case here. For some reason, small crabbed Olney always seemed to regard me with suspicion, as though I was designing to cheat him whenever I sold him a book. He would inspect every page of a proposed purchase, pressing his face close (he suffered from short sight), testing the binding, peering into the spine quite as if he expected to find a colony of worms nested there. I suppose the fact that I had abandoned the chance to become a Fellow of Merton in order to marry Elizabeth had forever tainted me in his eyes. I had betrayed the sacred life of the celibate and dedicated scholar for the earthy and secular pleasures of the married life. Certainly Master Basset, my former tutor, who had sponsored me for admission as a Fellow, had never forgiven me.

'Good day to you, Master Olney,' I said, attempting a pleasant tone as I took a seat (uninvited) on a bench opposite his desk.

He glowered at me. 'What do you want?'

It was an inauspicious beginning, but I gave him a cheerful smile. 'I have been offered a small library of books by a widow dwelling in Banbury,' I said. I did not mention that I had not yet received her agreement to my offer of a purchase price. 'Most of them would not be of interest to you, but amongst them there is a very fine bestiary. The calligraphy is of the very best. The illustrations are exceptionally fine. And the binding is imported Spanish calf skin, tinted maroon. Gilt edges. Virtually no wear and not a single blemish. It has been maintained with the greatest care.'

I still intended to approach the Fellow of Gloucester College, who had a particular interest in bestiaries, but there was no harm in setting up a little rivalry between two book collectors. I saw the gleam in Olney's eye.

'Have you brought it with you?' he said, softening a little.

'Nay, I came on business with the bursar, but then it occurred to me that the bestiary might interest you, so I thought I would call on you and mention it, while I was here.'

I had definitely caught his attention and he began to question me closely about the book. I answered in scrupulous detail, and watched his enthusiasm get the better of him, so that he became quite civil to me.

'Well,' I said at last, 'would you like me to bring the bestiary for you to inspect?'

Master Olney would never demean himself to visit my shop. I was obliged to carry any books which were of interest to him down to Merton for him to examine.

'Of course,' I added, guilelessly, as he hesitated, 'Master Caundish of Gloucester College will also be wanting to see it. As you know, he is assembling a special collection of bestiaries.'

I had not yet approached Master Caundish, not until I had the widow's agreement, but I knew he would seize upon the book with glee. And so did Master Olney.

'Aye,' he said, attempting, not very successfully, to hide his eagerness. 'You had best bring it for me to inspect. I doubt it will be of the quality we would want for Merton, not if it has been in a layman's possession.'

'I understand he was educated by the monks at Abingdon,' I said, 'and so halfway to becoming a scholar.'

I regretted the words as soon as I had spoken them, for in Olney's eyes, I too had been halfway to becoming a scholar. His face showed his distaste, but before he could say anything, I added, 'You need not worry about the condition, it is immaculate.'

'Then you had best bring it round this afternoon,' he said, with affected carelessness. 'I would not wish Merton to miss the chance of a bestiary, *if* it should prove to be all that you say it is.'

'I am afraid I must attend a funeral this afternoon,' I said. 'The student who was found in the Cherwell.'

He looked at me blankly. If he had even heard of William's death, it had made no impression on him. His world was made up entirely of the volumes in these two rooms.

'Tomorrow then,' he said.

'And I shall be out of Oxford tomorrow.' It was the only way I could think of to refer to my proposed visit to the upper reaches of the Cherwell with Jordain. 'I can bring it to you on Saturday, without fail.' I hoped that I would have heard from Banbury by then, for I could not sell the book to Merton until I had the widow's permission.

'And you will not show it to Master Caundish before that?'

'I promise that you shall have the first view of it, Master Olney.'

'Very well.' He stood up. It was a gesture of dismissal.

I turned toward the book shelves behind me, and made no move toward the door.

'Since I am here,' I said, as though it had just occurred to me, 'I wonder whether I might look at the Irish Psalter? I have had an order for a book of hours, copied from my own, and recently I saw a fine new example of one that Henry Stalbroke had just bound. It has started me thinking about the various arrangements in which they are set out, including within a Psaltery. I have not seen the Irish book for some years and wonder whether I might look at it now, as I am here?'

I looked toward the lowest shelf, which held nothing but the ornate box in which the book was housed, but I kept my hands to myself and did not reach out for it, much though I was tempted.

Master Olney hurried across to place himself between me and the box. He seemed flustered, and his face had flushed.

'Nay, you may not!' he said vehemently.

I stared at him in astonishment. You might have thought I proposed stealing it, or setting it afire. Seeing the look on my face, he began to bluster.

'The binding grows loose. It is so ancient. It has become fragile. Master Basset has instructed that it should not be handled until it has been repaired.'

I knew that my former sponsor had always taken a proprietorial interest in the Irish book, but I also remembered that when I had seen it, and handled it, the book had been in good condition. It had been written on the very highest quality parchment and the binding was as firm as the day it was made. That had been seven years ago, but it could not have deteriorated so much in so short a time, for it was only taken out of its box to be lovingly admired a few times a year. Together with the copied pages we had discovered under William's mattress, Olney's reaction made me instantly suspicious. I wished I might simply lift the box. Its weight would tell me at once whether the book was within.

'You will commission Henry Stalbroke to carry out the repairs?' I said, as though I believed him. 'He is surely the finest bookbinder in England.'

'Aye, I believe… that is what Master Basset has in mind. I do not think he has approached Stalbroke yet.'

'I see,' I said. 'Perhaps I might just see the binding, without handling the book? If you would be so kind as to open the box yourself?'

'Nay.' He began to edge me toward the door. 'It is not to be touched, or exposed to the air.'

I found myself at the top of the stairs, the door firmly closed behind me. Thoughtfully I began to descend them to the quadrangle. Even if the binding had become loose – which I did not for a moment believe – opening the box could not possibly have harmed the book, even as old as it was. My world was made up of books, and I knew just how robust that Psalter was, despite its age.

My purpose in coming to Merton had been twofold. Collecting the money owed to me and wooing Master Olney with the prospect of the bestiary had been merely the excuses. In the first place, I wanted to assure myself that the precious Irish Psalter was still safely in the custody of Merton's temperamental *librarius*. Second, I was anxious to ascertain that no harm had come to it through clandestine copying.

Having been unable to examine it, I could make no judgement on the second point. As for the first, I was very nearly certain that the priceless book was not safely in its elaborate box. The book, I was sure, was missing.

–

The funeral of William Farringdon, untimely dead by violence, was held that afternoon in his parish church of St-Peter-in-the-East. I had not thought that many would attend, but to my surprise the church was crowded. All his fellow students from Hart Hall were present, but also at least twice their number of students from other halls, including Peter de Wallingford from St Edmund's Hall. I recalled Peter had mentioned that William had often given him help, and from a few whispers I overheard as we were waiting for the service to begin, Peter was not the only student to have benefitted from William's generosity with his time and his learning.

Not only students were present. There were a number of townsmen – which I had not expected – although I suppose it was not surprising that the two coroners had come, as well as several constables, including Crowmer. Some other townsmen might well have come from mere curiosity, after that hasty and unsatisfactory inquest. However, I was surprised that at least a dozen senior members of the university had chosen to attend, amongst them four from Merton, the college that William would have joined in the autumn to pursue his advanced studies as a junior Fellow and scholar. One of the four was my former sponsor, Allard Basset. I kept well out of his line of vision, for encounters with him were invariably painful.

The rector entered, preceded by one of the church-wardens carrying the great gold cross and followed by the choir. I was certain that Jordain had paid for the funeral mass out of his own limited means, but I was taken aback that he had arranged for a full choral mass. It was sad that the boy's mother and sister could not attend, for it might have provided them with some small measure of comfort to see the number of mourners and the splendour of the service.

I have attended too many funerals in late years, and I no longer find anything uplifting in the service, although it is far less distressing than a few hasty mumbled prayers over a mass grave in time of plague. The music helped to lift the spirits a little, but even so I was exhausted after the two hours standing on the stone floor, in a church which seemed unseasonably cold. Or perhaps the cold came from within me.

When at last the service was over, six of William's fellow students lifted the coffin from its place before the altar, and we followed it out into the churchyard, where a sharp wind was scattering the last of the apple blossom from St Edmund's over the grass, like snow in May.

The sexton had dug the grave around at the back of the church, where the churchyard had recently been extended. The turf, which had been stacked neatly to one side, was dotted with the tiny blue flowers of forget-me-nots, a sharp reminder, to any who paid them heed, that the town authorities had shown an eagerness to forget and to bury the investigation of the boy's murder along with his body.

We gathered in an uneasy group around the damp hole, its sides gleaming moistly where the sexton's spade had sliced through the earth that morning. The student bearers, unaccustomed to the task, lowered the coffin awkwardly down into it. Jordain must also have paid for a coffin, for William's body was not lodged temporarily in the parish coffin before burial in nothing but a shroud. The rector began the final prayers and blessing for the dead, marking each phrase by sprinkling holy water over the coffin from a silver-handled aspergillum. Some of the students shifted uncomfortably from foot to foot, as though, having done their duty by their friend, they were anxious to escape from this place of sorrow and take up the reins of their young lives again.

I had managed to avoid Master Basset in the church and as we made our way to the churchyard, but now I suddenly found him opposite me across the open grave. He was not looking at me, but down at the coffin, with a strange look on his face, a mixture, so it seemed to me, of horror, distress, and fear. I suppose any man may feel fear when confronted by the death of one so much younger than himself, but this seemed more personal, although I could not have said why this crossed my mind.

As the rector concluded, closing his Bible and turning away. Master Basset looked up and caught sight of me staring at him. I averted my eyes quickly, but not before I had caught his look of hostility tempered with fear. I drew back into the crowd and followed the students out of the gate. Hostility was normal in Master Basset's reactions whenever he met me, which I did my best to make as infrequent as possible. But why should he show fear? Unless it arose from his sobering contemplation of the dead.

Usually when I came to St Peter's churchyard I would visit Elizabeth's grave, to say a prayer for her and whisper a few words to her about our children, but I would not venture near it amongst this great crowd. There was a burst of loud talking, interspersed with an occasional awkward laugh, the usual signs of relief after a funeral. I caught up with Jordain in the lane.

'Margaret has bid me tell you that you are very welcome to sup with us tonight,' I said.

He shook his head. 'I had best stay in with the lads tonight. They will be feeling William's loss all the more acutely after the funeral. Give Margaret my thanks.'

'I will do so.' As he turned away to follow his students back to Hart Hall, I laid my hand on his arm. 'Jordain, the cost of a choral mass must have been very great. Will you let me help?'

'Nay.' He smiled gently. 'I wanted to do it for the lad. The best way you can help is by continuing our search for anything which might lead to his killer.'

'I went to Merton this morning and asked to see the Irish Psalter, but Phillip Olney would not permit it. He claimed that it was in poor condition, too fragile to handle or even be seen. Yet when I last saw it, I swear to you that it was robust, in as sound a condition as a book made in our own lifetime. Olney seemed very wary and nervous.'

'Odd.'

'I do not think the book was there. The box that contains it was there, but he would not even let me look inside without touching. He fended me off and saw me out of the book room.'

'So you think—?'

'I am certain it is not there. But why? And whether Olney is complicit in removing it, I could not say. He claimed that Allard Basset had given orders that it was not to be touched until it was repaired. Basset has always taken a particular interest in the book, but Olney may simply have been trying to shift the responsibility on to someone else's shoulders. It may have naught to do with Basset.'

'If it is not in Merton, where can it be?'

'Wherever William was making his copy,' I said. 'It must have been somewhere private, a clean place to work, although he had only been writing the text and outlining the illuminations so far. He had not progressed to using coloured inks.'

'Well, it certainly was not done in Hart Hall,' he said. 'He could hide his pages under the mattress, but there was no sign of the book, and he could not have done the work there, under our noses.'

'Nay, he could not.'

'I wonder where he planned to buy his colours,' I mused. 'There are few places in Oxford. I am the only stationer to stock all the colours he would need, unless he bought from the paint-maker who supplies the abbeys. I buy lapis from him, but all his colours are expensive.'

'It seems these two men seen by Dafydd Hewlyn bought the parchment. Perhaps they also bought the colours.'

'Of course, you have the right of it, Jordain! I need to ask some questions. Are you still ready to come with me to follow that branch of the Cherwell up river tomorrow?'

'Aye, I will come. But now I must go back. The lads will be home by now. I should have no lecture tomorrow, but because I was interrupted for the inquest, I must give that lecture again. I will come to the shop when I have finished. Then we may go out to the Cherwell in the afternoon.'

I nodded my agreement. 'God go with you, then, Jordain,' I said.

'And with you.'

While we had been talking, I had walked halfway up Hammer Hall Lane with him. As I turned back and passed the church again, I saw that the churchyard was empty except for the sexton, who was slowly shovelling earth back into the grave. I shivered. If William's mother wanted his body sent home, it must needs be dug up again, not a pleasant prospect. It was as well Jordain had paid for a coffin.

As I walked slowly back home, I brooded over the whole strange affair. In the serious consideration of who had murdered William, one was apt to lose the other threads of the matter. Certainly it was clear that William had been secretly copying the ancient Irish Psalter. I was convinced he would never have done so on his own account. Someone must have persuaded him to do it. In any case, how would he have gained access to the book? We knew now that two men, strangers, whom Dafydd Hewlyn judged untrustworthy, had purchased the parchment William had been using. Therefore, they must have given it to him. Had they also, somehow, provided him with the Irish book?

The black ink he had used for the lettering had nothing unusual about it and could have been obtained anywhere, even from me. It would, however, be worth making enquiries to discover whether those same two men had been buying the coloured inks William would have needed to complete the illuminations. And he would also have needed gold foil for the gilding. As far as I could remember, there was a good deal of gilding in the original book. The colours also had been wonderful when I had seen them, as rich and bright as a stained glass window, not faded in any way by the years. To copy them accurately would have required inks of the highest quality. William would have enjoyed the work of completing the illustrations. I remembered how he had admired my own book of hours. It was comparatively modest, but very beautiful.

So much for the materials required, but *how* had William been able to copy from the book itself? The detailed precision of his outline drawings showed that he must have had the book open in front of him as he worked, they could not have been done from memory. I ran over in my mind my encounter with Phillip Olney that morning. He had always been a difficult, short-tempered man, but his behaviour when I had asked to see the Irish book had been decidedly peculiar. His hasty, unconvincing argument as to why I might not even *look* at the book was clearly spurious. Could *he* have asked William to copy the book? Nay, that made no sense. Olney was a true-blooded bibliophile. He would never have entrusted Merton's greatest literary treasure to a mere student. Did that mean it had been stolen, and he was terrified that the theft would be discovered? But it could not be concealed for ever. Master Basset, for one, would want to see it. I did not believe for a minute that he had told Olney no one was to touch the book until it was repaired.

If Olney hoped to conceal the disappearance of the book from Master Basset, he was deluding himself. But perhaps Basset already knew, and the two of them were trying to keep the fact from the Warden and the other Fellows?

I was still revolving all the possibilities in my mind when I reached the shop and went in, paying little heed to who was there. Two students, a monk who worked in the scriptorium of Osney, come to purchase parchment.

And, as if summoned up by my thoughts, Master Allard Basset.

He waited until all my other customers had left, pretending all the while to study the books displayed on my secondhand rack, none of which could have held any interest for him. He was a big man, impressive, I would judge, riding a fine stallion out to the hunt. I knew that he came of a noble family in Sussex, but not being the eldest son, his ambitions lay elsewhere. I thought he aimed for the wardenship of Merton, or another college. Or perhaps he would leave the academic world for a position in King

Edward's ever-growing royal service. He would not be contained by a mere Fellowship for ever.

As the shop emptied, he turned and confronted me, where I had taken refuge behind the counter. I had thought of retreating to the house and leaving Walter to attend to him, but that would have been the act of a coward. If he was determined to confront me, I must face him sooner or later. I wondered why he had not spoken to me at the funeral, but perhaps he preferred to have no audience, since he had now waited for the students and the monk to leave. Walter and Roger, however, were still present, making themselves as inconspicuous as possible, heads down, meekly writing.

Basset came close to the counter and leaned over it, till his face was barely a foot from mine.

'And just what do you mean by it?' he demanded angrily.

I gaped at him, for he seemed to be taking up the thread of a conversation that had never occurred.

'Mean by what, Master Basset?' I said, when I could persuade my voice to function.

I had never seen him like this. At one time I had near worshipped the man, for he was a famous scholar, corresponding with distinguished men in Prague, in Bologna, in Paris, the great universities of Europe. When I had first come to Oxford as a boy of fourteen, drunk with the excitement of books and learning, I had attended every one of Allard Basset's lectures, awed by his immense learning. Later, when he had taken me under his wing and encouraged my intellectual ambitions, I had been pathetically grateful, treasuring the books he loaned me, working until all hours by poor rushlight so that I might live up to his expectations. When he had undertaken to sponsor me for a Fellowship at Merton, I had believed my ambition could soar no higher.

Then I had met Elizabeth again. When I had seen her first, we were both children, but while I had been climbing the shaky ladder of academic achievement, she had been away, living for a time with her mother's parents in London. She returned, a beautiful young woman, in the fatal summer before I was to take up my place at Merton, and I was lost.

Allard Basset had never forgiven me.

Since then, he had displayed an anger both cold and cutting, treating me with contempt and scorn whenever we encountered one another – which was as rarely as I could possibly contrive. Now, however, he seemed incandescent with rage, and I was baffled.

'I do not understand you, Master Basset,' I said, withdrawing a step or two.

'I hear you dared to invade our book room and demanded to see the Irish Psalter. I will not have you sullying our greatest treasure with your *tradesman's* hands!'

Inadvertently I glanced down at my hands. As usual, they were somewhat ink stained, but otherwise perfectly clean. Very much like Basset's own hands, in fact.

'Your description of my visit to Merton,' I said levelly, having regained my poise, 'does not quite accord with the facts. I came first to collect overdue payment from your bursar. I then went to see Master Olney, in order to tell him about a bestiary I have acquired, that I thought might interest him. We had some discussion about it, and I promised to take it for him to inspect on Saturday. As I was leaving, I asked whether I might look at the Psalter. I have had some dealings with books of hours recently, and

I was interested to look at it again, at how the Hours were set out, not having seen it for some time.'

I was pleased that my voice sounded calm and normal, though I was aware that my heart was beating rapidly.

He drew a deep breath, as though he too were trying to steady his voice.

'The book is in a very fragile state, and must not be *touched* until we can arrange for its repair.'

'So Master Olney said. I was surprised. When I saw it, I recall that it was in very robust condition. How can it have fallen into such a state in so short a time?'

'Hardly a short time,' he said curtly. 'It is all of seven years.'

Aye, I thought. He would know exactly how long it was since I had the temerity to turn down his patronage and go my own wilful, secular way.

'Even so,' I said, 'it can hardly have received rough usage in the intervening years, being the treasure that it is. I hope you may find a craftsman skilled enough to carry out the repairs without harming the book. Henry Stalbroke is the best man in Oxford, probably in England.'

He opened his mouth as if he were about to say more, then closed it with a snap. His gown whirled about as he turned to leave, and Roger leapt from his desk to open the door for him. I watched him striding away up the High Street toward Magpie Lane. Even his back looked angry.

'You may close the shutters while you are about it, Roger,' I said, sinking on to my stool, feeling suddenly weak about the knees. 'It is a little early, but I think we will close for today.'

When Roger came back inside, both scriveners looked at me curiously.

'What did he mean by all that?' Walter asked, clearly speaking for both of them.

I shook my head. 'I cannot tell. Master Olney was in a strange mood this morning as well. They both declare the book is in a terrible state, which I find hard to believe.'

'Perhaps it is not worn with age,' Roger suggested, 'but someone has damaged it. Dropped it, perhaps, or broken the spine by forcing it backwards. And they are trying to hide the damage until they can see it repaired.'

'You may be right, Roger,' I said. 'But that book is always kept in a magnificent box, on a shelf by itself, in a room where Master Olney sits all day. I am sure he locks it up at night.'

'Perhaps one of them damaged it,' Walter said.

'Nay, I do not think so. Both of them love books more than people, and that book is their greatest treasure. If there were to be a fire, and that book was in the room with a baby, I know which one they would rescue.' I sighed. 'It baffles me, but it is their affair. Let me see what you have both done today. I have hardly been here. Let me light a candle.'

In order to give their work full attention, I lit a wax candle to provide a clear light. Roger had made good progress copying the Arthur and Guinevere tale, leaving a blank page for a large illustration and merely outlining the initial capital for each section, to be worked up later.

'This is excellent, Roger. Off with you now, and I will see you in the morning.'

He went off pleased with both the praise and the early end to the day. I preferred, however, to see what Walter had managed to write without Roger peering over our shoulders.

'I've done as you suggested, Master Elyot,' Walter said diffidently, 'and started with Hob-by-the-Fire. I fear 'tis a fine old mess at first, but I got more into the way of it as I went along.'

Clearly nervous, he handed me several sheets of paper. Indeed, there were many crossings-out and insertions on the first three pages, and some of the language here was stilted, but after that it flowed much more freely. We discussed the changes he might make to those early pages and he began to look less anxious as we worked.

'There,' I said at last, 'I think we have the start of an excellent tale here, and you should be able to finish it tomorrow, do you not think?'

He was leaning over with both arms braced on the counter, but looked up now and beamed at me. 'Aye, I think I have the trick of it now. To think, my mother's simple tales, made into a book!'

'It is not so strange,' I said. 'I expect those famous tales that Roger is copying started in the same way, told aloud by the fireside. It is just that they have become better known.'

I tapped his pages together and handed them to him.

'Now, Margaret will have supper ready soon. Come you in with me, and join us. It is quite a while since you have been to a family supper. And afterwards, perhaps Alysoun can persuade you to tell us another of your mother's tales.'

–

As our midday dinner had been a hurried affair, before I went off to the funeral, Margaret had prepared a more substantial supper than usual, roasting a joint of mutton on the iron turnspit before the fire. This was one of the new-fangled ones operated by weights, requiring neither kitchen boy nor turnspit dog to rotate it. She had declared that one would save her precious time in the kitchen if she need not be forever rotating the roast before the fire by hand, so I had had one made by a blacksmith in Fish Street. Walter was mighty impressed by it.

'Jordain would not come for supper,' I explained, 'for he felt his students needed him this day.' I did not enlarge on the reason why, for we had been doing our best to keep word of William's death from the children. Rafe might not remember him, but Alysoun certainly would, for he had made quite a pet of her.

'Instead, I have brought Walter,' I said. 'And I hope we may persuade him to sing for his supper by telling us a tale afterwards.'

'Oh, aye, Papa!' Alysoun exclaimed, grabbing Walter by the arm and swinging on it. 'But will he sing it?'

''Tis but a saying.' I smiled at her. 'I am sure he will tell it in the usual way.'

We sat down to our ample supper of mutton, beans, and cabbage, with batter cakes fried by dropping spoonfuls into the sizzling fat dripping from the meat. We do not usually eat meat for supper, but I was well ready for it after such a day. For some reason Margaret's cabbage does not have that mouldy, penetrating smell that seems to hang about all student halls. When Jordain and I lodged in the student rooms in the hall at the back of Tackley's Inn, both inn and hall were permeated with the smell every day.

'I helped Aunt Margaret to make the dried apple pie, Papa,' Alysoun said, bearing it with pride to the table. 'She says I have a good hand with the pastry.'

'Aye, it will do for now,' Margaret said, 'but you need not roll it out with such fierceness. You are not crushing cockroaches.'

Nevertheless, I could see that she looked pleased, but I hoped that this was not a strategic move to woo Alysoun away from her lessons.

'Can you fetch the cream, Rafe?' Margaret said. 'Be careful, now.'

Rafe went to the pantry, where the cream was kept on a cool stone shelf, and returned carrying the jug in both hands, his eyes fixed anxiously on his feet, for the puppy Rowan was skittering about, chasing a ball Alysoun had made for her out of red cloth stuffed with wool scraps.

When we were replete, Walter and I sat by the fire while Margaret and Alysoun cleared and washed the dishes, leaving them stacked to dry on the table. Rafe climbed on to Walter's lap, while Margaret brought her mending close by the fire, the better to see her stitches. It was the gown Alysoun had torn on the apple tree.

'Come, Alysoun,' I said, 'even though you can bake an apple pie, you are not too big to sit on my lap to hear a story.'

When she was comfortably perched, I rested my chin on the top of her head. Margaret, I saw, had attacked the tangled hair with a comb.

'So, what is it to be, Walter?' Margaret asked. 'Nicholas tells me you are to make a book of your stories.'

Walter looked embarrassed. 'He thinks they will make a book, Mistress Makepeace, but they are nothing but simple old stories.'

'They are *good* stories,' Alysoun said judiciously. 'Anyone would want to read them. Which one will you tell us?'

'I have been thinking on that. I do not think you have heard this one. I had forgotten it myself until something reminded me today.'

'What is it called?'

'It is the tale of Jestyn the Trickster. It is a short tale, for I think this little lad should soon be in his bed.'

Rafe groaned and protested, but Walter only smiled.

Once on a time, he began, *when the world was young and England had many kings, there lived a young man called Jestyn.*

'But how could there be many kings?' Alysoun objected. 'There is only one king, our King Edward the Third.'

'Don't interrupt, Alysoun,' I said.

'But I want to know.'

'In the old days, my maid,' Walter said, 'long before the Normans came, England was made up of many small kingdoms, and each had its own king. Our man Jestyn lived near here. His father had a farm over beyond the Cherwell, and he was the youngest of three sons.'

'Go on,' I said. 'And no more interruptions, Alysoun.'

Jestyn was a good lad and worked hard on his father's farm, but he had little to hope for in the future. His eldest brother would inherit the farm. The second brother was heir to his uncle. So what would become of Jestyn when their father died? He was clever with his hands, so he earned a little by carving small figures of the saints, which he would sell in Oxford market. Perhaps someday he would be able to earn enough to keep himself, but it would be a poor living.

Then one day in the market, a great procession passed by. The king was come to visit Osney Abbey, and he had with him his beautiful daughter. When Jestyn saw her, he knew at once that he wanted no other woman for his wife, but what hope did he have, a poor third son? He watched them pass, and from that day on, he knew no rest.

'What was she called, the king's daughter?' Alysoun asked, before I could stop her.

Walter pretended to think, closing his eyes and scratching his head. 'Why, I do believe she was called Alysoun!'

She gave me a self-satisfied smile, and threw her arm about my neck.

Now Jestyn could not rest until he learned more about Alysoun, the king's daughter, so everywhere he went, he asked about her. And he learned that the king, who was a devout man, but also somewhat greedy, greatly desired a golden statue of the Virgin, which belonged to Osney Abbey. The abbot had refused all his offers to buy the statue, but the king had not given up hope. He had declared that if any man could obtain the statue for him, that man should have his daughter's hand in marriage.

Jestyn was greatly excited by this and over the supper table one night he made the mistake of telling his father and brothers of the king's promise.

'Then I shall have the princess,' his eldest brother said. He was a big, swaggering fellow, used to getting his own way. 'I shall buy the statue. The monks will not dare to stand against me.'

The next day he went to the abbey and offered the monks the whole of his father's farm in exchange for the statue. But the monks refused him. When his father heard what he had tried to do, he cuffed him about the ears.

'I shall have the princess,' said the second brother. He was small and wiry, quite unlike the eldest one, and he was a sly fellow. 'If they will not sell the statue, then I shall steal it.'

It was lucky for him that his father did not overhear.

The next night he climbed over the abbey wall and slipped into the chapel. The statue stood on the altar, and as he reached out to grab it, a great black dog, the guardian of the statue, rose up and seized him by the seat of his hose. He managed to tear himself away and threw himself over the wall, but he came back with the seat of his hose quite torn away!

Alysoun giggled, but stuffed her fist in her mouth when she saw Margaret's frown.

'His mama would scold him,' said Rafe, and gave a great yawn.

'Aye, she would,' Walter said, smiling.

How strange, I thought, that Rafe should say that, never having known his own mother. He must have learned it from Alysoun, or one of their friends.

'Go on, Walter,' Margaret said. She bit off her thread and laid her sewing aside. 'What did Jestyn, the third son, do?'

'Ah, well, you see, Jestyn was much cleverer than his brothers.'

Walter settled the sleepy Rafe more comfortably and continued.

Jestyn decided to visit the abbey and view this amazing statue. Indeed, he went to Mass there every day for a week and studied that statue until he knew every line of it, then he set to, and carved a copy so like that you could never have told them apart.

'But the statue in the abbey was made of gold,' Alysoun objected.

Walter merely nodded.

Jestyn had saved a little money from the carvings he sold at the market, and he took all his money to the stationer who sold gold leaf.

Walter bowed to me.

It took every penny he had, but he bought enough gold leaf to cover the statue, and when he had done it, you would have said it was the very statue that stood on the altar. The problem was, he now had to exchange his statue for the real one. Once again, he attended Mass there every day, and he almost despaired. It seemed all his labour would be in vain, for although he carried his statue with him in his scrip, he had never a chance to exchange them. He prayed hard to the Virgin, for he thought she would favour his marriage to the princess, despite the trick he was about to play. It seems she heard his prayers, for one day during Mass, fire broke out in the abbey kitchen. In the confusion, Jestyn exchanged the statues.

Alysoun's arm had been tightening round my neck, but now she relaxed and gave a contented sigh.

The next morning, Jestyn set out for the king's castle. He had no horse to ride, so he had to walk all the way, and he was dusty and footsore when he arrived. At first the servants would not let him in to see the king, but at last he prevailed. When the king saw the statue, he leapt from his throne and embraced Jestyn. 'You shall have my daughter and half my kingdom!' he declared. And that was just what happened.

'But,' Alysoun said doubtfully, 'you said he was a good man. I don't think he was a good man if he cheated the abbey like that.'

'It's not quite the end of the story,' Walter said, easing his arm where Rafe had slumped against it, asleep.

Jestyn and the princess Alysoun were married, and he was kind to his father and brothers, now he was grown rich and powerful, but he was troubled about the wooden statue covered with gold foil that now stood on the altar at Osney. It cost him many a night's sleep. However, the king died not six months after the wedding, and the first thing Jestyn did after his death was to mount his fine horse and ride to the abbey with the real statue. He confessed everything to the abbot, who set him a penance, but it was not a severe one, for he was mighty pleased to have the statue again. When Jestyn returned to the castle with the statue he had made, he told Alysoun all that he had done to win her, and how he had returned the real statue to the abbey. He thought she would be angry, but she only smiled and kissed him.

'They cannot be very clever, these monks,' she said, 'for the weight of the statues is quite different. Any woman who lifted the statue to dust it could have told them that this one is made of wood.'

Jestyn laughed, for he knew that his wife spoke the truth, and that she was indeed cleverer than all the monks of Osney put together. Nevertheless, to the end of his days he believed that the Virgin had helped him to win Alysoun, by pulling the wool over the monks' eyes.

Alysoun yawned. 'That is a good story. I am glad Jestyn married Alysoun, but I am also glad that the monks got their statue back. Is it still there?'

'That I do not know,' Walter said. 'I have not been to Osney Abbey, and it did happen a very long time ago.'

'There are many treasures in the abbey,' I said. 'Quite likely it is still there. That will be a good tale for your book, Walter. And now, princess Alysoun, it is time you went to bed.'

'Carry me!' she said imperiously. 'I am a princess!'

Walter laughed. 'I will bring Rafe.'

When the children were safely abed, I drew the curtain across their doorway, but not before I had seen from the corner of my eye a puppy-shaped shadow slipping into the room behind me.

'I'll be away home, then,' Walter said, when we reached the kitchen. 'I thank you for an excellent supper, mistress.'

'And I thank you for an excellent tale, Walter,' Margaret said. 'It was good to see you at our table again.'

I saw Walter through the shop to the door, locking and bolting it after him. Back in the kitchen I sat for an hour or so with Margaret before I went exhausted to bed, but oddly, I could not sleep for a long time. When I did, Walter's story haunted my dreams and when I woke I had the unsatisfactory sense that it had tried to tell me something.

Chapter Seven

That Friday morning the shop was unusually busy, leaving me little opportunity to think about William's murder or the seeming disappearance of the Irish Psalter. I was pleased, however, when the carter returned from Banbury with the news that the widow had accepted my offer for her husband's books. She would be glad, he said, of the money soon.

'Her husband was a decent fellow,' he said, 'Goodman Preston, holding a tenant farm just outside the town, but he was a dreamer. The last few years he has let the farm slide, and once Goodwife Preston has paid the heriot due to the lord — their best pair of oxen! — she will have little enough. The farm must go back to her overlord, for she has no sons to work it.'

'What will she do?' I asked. I felt somewhat guilty that I had not offered more for the books, but as it was I did not expect to make much profit from them. Perhaps if I could squeeze a little more out of Merton for the bestiary, I could send Widow Preston the extra.

'She and her daughter are both skilled lacemakers,' the carter said. 'She has taken a cottage in the town and will sell at the market. I daresay she will earn enough to keep them both, but until she has stock to sell, they must eat and pay rent.'

'I will ride over there on Monday,' I said, 'and take the money myself.'

He had hardly gone when Mistress Lapley also called in, wanting to know when her copy of the French book would be ready.

'It is with the binders, Mistress Lapley,' I reassured her, 'and they have promised to have it ready sometime next week. I will send Roger to you with it as soon as it is in my hands.'

She had been coming into the shop at least twice a week since she had first commissioned the work, to Roger's annoyance, and I saw him now making a face behind her back. I hoped also to sell her the bound set of mismatched tales, but I would not show it to her until Roger had finished making our own better book from it, which I might hope to offer to a wealthier customer.

After that, a crowd of students arrived, coming from their lectures, some returning their rented *peciae*, some choosing others to take away and copy. The summer disputations were but a few weeks away, and as the time drew nearer it always proved a spur to their studies. I had not realised it was so near the dinner hour when Jordain arrived, breathless and dishevelled.

'I am sorry, Nicholas,' he burst out, when he was barely through the door. 'I cannot come with you this afternoon.'

I took him by the elbow and steered him through into the kitchen. Margaret was stirring something in a pot over the fire, Alysoun was laying out plates on the table, and Rafe was rolling about on the floor with the puppy, who was washing his face earnestly.

'Come through into the garden,' I said.

We took the path that lay between the vegetable plot and the herb garden, and took a seat on the bench under one of the pear trees. Opposite us the quince was in full bloom. Last year it had borne little fruit, but by the signs the harvest would be bountiful this autumn.

'What's amiss?' I said, for he looked distressed.

He took off his academic cap and ran his fingers through the thick curls which surrounded his tonsure. His hair was dark with sweat.

'Has something untoward happened?'

'Nay, nay, I am making too much of it.' He clapped his cap on to the back of his head, where it perched precariously. 'A lad from the Cross Inn caught me as I was leaving the Schools. It seems William's mother and sister arrive in Oxford today. They sent ahead to the inn, to be sure of a room. They will be here sometime this afternoon, so of course I must be here to receive them.'

'Aye, you must. But it is only – what? – three days since you wrote to Mistress Farringdon. They are very quickly come.'

'Their home is but over the border in Berkshire, no great distance.' He gave me a troubled look. 'I wish now that I had delayed William's funeral another day.'

'You were not to know. They will understand. Do you want me to come with you to meet them?'

'Nay, there is no need. It is best if you carry on with our original plan. We need to know whether there is any sign that William ever went up that other branch of the Cherwell. I will see them settled at the Cross Inn, then take them to visit William's grave. Mistress Farringdon must tell me what she wishes to do, whether to take William's body home, or leave it here in Oxford.'

'I will make the trip as swiftly as I may,' I said, 'though I have no idea how far along that portion of the river extends. As soon as I am back in Oxford I will find you. Will you be at Hart Hall?'

'Aye, if I have finished my business with William's poor mother, though I cannot say how long it will take. We may still be at St Peter's.'

'I will find you,' I said firmly, 'never concern yourself with that. Now, take some dinner with us before you go off to await them.'

He shook his head. 'I have no appetite. I dread this meeting with the boy's mother. She would have believed that he was safe in my care.'

'You cannot be held responsible for his death, Jordain. He was not a child. I married at about his age.'

'Nevertheless, he was under my care.'

There was no persuading him otherwise, and I knew better than to press him. He hurried away to await mother and sister at the Cross Inn, and I went in to dinner with my family.

—

There was no need to go the long way round, this time, by the East Bridge and up the west side of the Cherwell. Once I had eaten my dinner and seen Walter and Roger settled for the afternoon, I headed up Carte Street to the small Smith Gate, then over the Canditch, and right along Longwall Street. Sometimes this first portion of the road that follows the curve outside the town wall is known as Holywell Street, for at the point where the wall and the road turn sharp south, two branches lead ahead. The one on the left goes to the church of St Cross, a daughter chapel of St Peter's, while that on the right leads directly to Holywell Mill.

The whole area around both church and mill is known as Holywell, for close by the church there is a well of pure, sweet water, sacred to St Winifred and St Margaret. Its water is known to be efficacious in the case of skin diseases and other ills. Even some with leprosy have been cured. I had drunk from it myself as a young student, when I had a persistent cough, and it had cured me, so I could vouch for its healing powers. I had read my ancient history, and I knew that this ancient well must once have been sacred to some pagan god or goddess. Whoever the presiding deity might be now, pagan or Christian, the water is surely blessed.

I took the right hand way to the mill, stepping aside on to the verge almost at once as a farmer's cart came from the opposite direction, having delivered a load of grain for grinding. Here and there along the dirt track, clusters of birds flew up at my approach, starlings with their dagger beaks and plumage as fine as eastern silks, plucky little sparrows, defiant in the face of the larger birds. Somehow I always regard the sparrow as a very English bird. They were all feasting on scattered grain that had spilled from the many carts which passed this way. As I neared the mill, I nodded to a wiry villein trudging toward me, bowed under a heavy sack of flour, sent by a master no doubt too mean to spare a horse or a mule for the task. He returned my nod, but wore a surly look.

'Hard work on a hot afternoon,' I said sympathetically.

He grunted, and swung the sack to the ground, then straightened and pressed his fists into the small of his back.

'Aye, with so many dead, maister treats us that are left like treadmill beasts. We'll not endure much more.'

It was not the first time I had heard such sentiments. Landowners were hard pressed since the Death to find labour enough to work their land, and many a man whose ancestors had been tied to the same manor for generations was running away from his villein service.

'It's hard,' I said, 'but do you not have bed and lodging, at least? There's many a vagrant or outlaw would be glad of that.'

He made a scornful noise. 'No need to become either. I'll be making my way into town one day soon, and stay my year and a day.'

'You will still need a trade,' I said cautiously. This was a dangerous conversation, and I would be well out of it as soon as possible.

'Oh, I've skills enough,' he said carelessly. 'I can turn my hand to most things.'

He would need more than that, I thought, to find himself a position as a craftsman, but did not pursue the matter.

'Well, I wish you a better future, friend,' I said. 'God go with 'ee.'

'And with 'ee, maister.' With a grunt he heaved the sack on to his back again, and set off down the road.

As I neared the mill I realised that the miller must not be grinding at the moment, for the only sound was the rushing of the river over the weir. The great wheel stood silent and still, but the wood gleamed wetly and sparkling drops fell from the timbers. It must just have ceased turning. Remembering my promise to Alysoun, I put my head through the door, briefly blinded by the darkness within after the sun and glimmer of the water outside.

'Goodman Wooton!' I called. 'Art at home?'

The burly figure of the miller loomed out of the shadows beyond the chute which delivered the ground flour into sacks here on the lowest floor of the mill.

'Aye?' he said, none too welcoming, for it was clear I brought him no business.

I stepped inside and broached the matter of a puppy, born of a good ratting dam. With Goodman Wooton it was as well not to waste words or he would merely walk away.

He shrugged. 'I might take it, I might not. I'd fare better with a dog grown, not a new weaned pup. John Baker in the High Street, you say? He buys of me, though not all of his flour, I'll be bound. And his son is a young devil.'

This, I thought, was hardly fair to Jonathan, but there was no purpose to engaging in a dispute with the miller. And I knew very well that John bought only his coarsest flour here, the mixed grain for maslin bread. The finer qualities he bought from Blackfriars.

I had done my best, and I had not expected an eager agreement from Miller Wooton.

'Aye, well,' I said. 'I thought to mention it, since I was passing. There is just the one pup left.'

'Runt of the litter, is it?'

'Nay, I think we have the runt, but for all that she's a sturdy little dog, and brave. All of the litter are strong and well grown. The mother is a champion ratter.'

I would leave it at that. If Miller Wooton did not want the last puppy, I was sure another home could be found for it. As I turned to leave, a thought occurred to me.

'Had you heard about the student fished out of the river below here on Monday?'

He was already busy tying a fresh sack to the end of the chute and had his back to me.

'I heard.'

'It was a lad called William Farringdon. Did you ever see him out this way? Did you see him on Monday, say between dinner and four o'the clock?'

He did not bother to turn round.

'There's always students and other folk making free with my walkway to cross the river,' he said sourly. 'I've no way to stop them. As long as they don't interfere with the weir gate or the machinery, I pay them no heed. And I don't know this student.'

He finished tying the sack and walked over to the great lever that released the water wheel to turn. There was a creak and groan of timber, then the whole mill building began to vibrate as the wheel started to move. The interlocking gears crashed together, and from overhead came the tooth-jarring grate of the mill wheels grinding together. The miller began to climb the ladder to the upper floors, and it was clear I would get no more out of him.

It was slightly less noisy outside, but the flimsy walkway juddered under my feet from the movement of the great wheel driven by the force of the river. I made my way cautiously across to the far bank. But for that neat incision in William's back, I could well believe that he had merely lost his balance here on the walkway and tumbled in.

The ground in the meadow was still spongy with water absorbed during the winter floods, and although it had been sunny, even hot, earlier in the day, clouds were beginning to gather, passing over the sun from time to time and setting shadows racing across the meadow grass, leaching the wild flowers of colour. I shivered. I had not thought to bring a cloak, never expecting rain, but I feared I might suffer a sousing before I was done. The scent of warm grass rose around me as I brushed through it, intensified by that expectant feel in the air, which sharpens all smells before a storm. The outlines of the willows on the river's edge were clear cut, like ink lines on parchment.

When I reached the branch where Jordain and I had found the piece torn from William's shirt, I hesitated. There was no certainty that his body had been washed down this tributary of the river. It could have come from either direction. The sky was growing more threatening by the minute. If I turned back now, I might just reach home before the storm broke. If I went on, I would be drenched. There was no longer any doubt of that. I was tempted, but having come so far, I decided to go on. If I did not finish what I had set out to do, I would simply have to come back another day. And Jordain was counting on me. I went on.

At least I would spare myself the unpleasantness of wading across the river. I would make my way up the near side. It was narrow enough that I could see the other bank. If there was anything worth investigating I could always wade over further up. But as I trudged on, I could see nothing to suggest that William had been here.

The walking was easy for the most part. As I drew further away from the main channel the ground rose very slightly and was a little drier, which made for surer footing. Even so, the whole area of water meadows was still very flat, and I knew that much of it flooded in winter. Some distance ahead of me I caught flashes of water where yet another main channel of the river ran roughly north to south, like the one on which Holywell Mill stood. The whole of the Cherwell was a veritable maze, like a tangle skein of yarn. The branch I was following probably flowed from over there, joining the two channels. I recalled that there was another mill on that far channel, the King's Mill, to which the farms in those parts, like Yardley's, were required to send their grain for grinding.

I had nearly reached this other, larger, channel of the river, which I reckoned was the furthest point from which the body could have floated, when I noticed a small building half hidden in a clump of willows on the bank I was following. As I came nearer, I saw that it was yet another mill, but a very small one, and no longer in use, for several of the paddles of the wheel were broken and hung awry, giving it a skewed, desolate appearance. The building itself seemed sound, timber built and thatched, but was clearly deserted, for ivy and bindweed grew across the only window on the side facing me.

It must have been some forlorn attempt in the past to harness the moderate power of this portion of the river, but it could never have driven anything more than small grindstones. There was no track leading to it from this direction, though perhaps there might be on the far side. I tried to remember what lay over there. The King's Mill stood a short way up river, and it was easily reached from the road on the far side which led from the country end of the East Bridge to the village of Marston. Perhaps there was a track from the King's Mill to this small mill, but why should anyone want to come here, instead of to the larger mill? Unless, of course, they wanted to avoid paying the substantial fees the royal mill demanded. That might explain both the mill's origins and its abandonment. A brief attempt to outwit the king's commissioners, soon closed down.

Perhaps it would be worth taking a closer look at the building. There was no door on this side, only the broken wheel thrust into the river and the choked window. I circled round the clump of willows, behind the mill, and came to the upriver side. I noticed now that, whereas the grass along the bank I had been following showed no sign of having been flattened by passing feet, there was a clearly worn path through the meadow grass heading from this side of the building directly back toward Holywell Mill. I could just see the roof of the mill above the trees on this side of the miller's walkway. So someone – or several people – were in the habit of walking directly here, cutting across the meadow, not following the bank down to the junction with the branch, then along the branch to here, the longer way that I had come. I thought I saw movement amongst the willows by Holywell Mill. It might be students on their way to the coney burrows further up, or it might be the miller himself about some task. It was too far away to be sure.

Rounding the corner of the building I found, as I expected, the door to the mill, firmly closed, and also two windows, whose shutters on this side, unlike the other, had been cleared of the curtain of climbers. These had been recently cut back, by all the signs, for the thicker branches of ivy showed fresh cuts, and there was a heap of withering foliage at the foot of the wall. Someone, therefore, was using the mill, though not for milling. It might be a disgruntled villein, like the one I had met, run away from his master. Though such men usually tried to buy their freedom by taking up residence in a town. Or perhaps outlaws or footpads were using it. There were many masterless men roaming the countryside since the Death. In which case I would be wise to leave well alone.

Yet having come so far, it seemed cowardly to turn my back and simply walk away. Besides, the first drops of rain were beginning to fall. It did not seem that anyone was about the place, for there was not a sound to be heard from inside, nothing but the meadow birds calling, and the stridulation of grasshoppers in the long grass. I could take shelter here until the shower passed, for I could not believe it would last long. Few of these spring showers do so. There was already a small fragment of blue sky beginning to show upwind.

Despite the derelict appearance of the old mill, it boasted a stout door, and when I tried it, I found it would not open. I thought at first that it was merely warped with age, sticking to the frame, although it seemed sound enough. I lifted the latch again and heaved with my shoulder against the boards. It remained immovable. There was a lock below the latch, which I had ignored at first, thinking no one would bother to lock an abandoned mill, which was clearly no longer of practical use. Nor would it make a comfortable dwelling for any but the most desperate, out in this desolate, damp place. In winter the ground floor would probably be flooded.

I stood back, frustrated and annoyed. I had had a long walk, with nothing to show for it, and very shortly I was going to get a soaking. I was on the point of abandoning the place, debating whether I should return the way I had come or cross the other channel of the river at King's Mill and seek shelter from the storm at Yardley's farm. As I turned away from the building, my scrip swung heavily against my hip, and I remembered suddenly that it still contained the key I had found at the bottom of William's satchel. Could it possibly be the key to this door? Perhaps it was not so unlikely. I had come searching for any sign that William might have been thrown into the river here. I had seen no trace. But here was a building on the bank of the river and on a direct path from Holywell Mill. Here was a locked door. And here was a key.

I took the key from my scrip, weighed it for a moment in my hand. It was the right size. I slid it into the lock and turned. The lock was well oiled. It turned smoothly with a firm click as the key engaged each of the levers. I pressed the latch and the door opened with a slight creak of the hinges.

My heart began to beat a little faster as I withdrew the key from the lock and dropped it back into my scrip. William, it seemed, had been here. At last I had found something which linked him with this part of the river. Whatever had happened, his body must have gone into the river here. Had he been stabbed because he had disturbed some ruffians who were hiding out in the old mill? I had better take care. As I took a hesitant step forward, I left the door wide open behind me, in case I had to run for my own life.

But, wait! That would not do. If William had been killed for disturbing the nest of some rogues, why had he possessed a key to the mill? Even more confusing, if he had a key and had come all the way out here, why had the key been left behind in his room at Hart Hall? Unless someone else had a key, so that William would not have needed his. And that could only mean that he was meeting someone here.

My eyes had adjusted to the dimmer light within the building. If the shutters on the two windows to either side of the door were opened, there would be a fair amount of light, especially in the morning, since they faced roughly east. Though William, surely, could not have come here in the mornings, since he was required to attend lectures. One shutter hung askew from a broken hinge and allowed some light to enter. More flowed from the open door, but the gathering storm had over-clouded the sun.

The room was not very large, about the size of my own bed chamber, and much of the space was taken up with the usual clutter of mill machinery. It was, however, surprisingly clean. The floor had been swept. A new broom leaned against the bottom of the chute. There were no cobwebs in the corners or draped across the window frames. Any enterprising spider would have chosen such a favourable spot, so even the windows had been cleaned recently. As well as the mill equipment, there was a table, pushed against the wall below one of the windows, as if to catch the light, and the ordinary sort of three-legged turned stool you will find anywhere.

I could see that there were a few objects on the table, so I went nearer, to make them out better.

And I stopped dead, for I recognised one of the items at once. It was an ink well, of rather unusual design. It was made of pewter, in the form of two scallop shells, clasping the cylinder which held the ink. The lid was in the form of a smaller scallop shell, which could be clipped down over the ink reservoir so that the whole could be carried about without the risk of spilling the contents.

It belonged to William.

'It was my grandfather's,' William had told me one day when I admired it. He brought it with him every day when he worked for me.

'He bought it in Santiago de Compostela, where he went on pilgrimage as a young man. When he was dying, he gave it to me. He had never used it, just bought it because the scallop shells reminded him of his pilgrimage.

He said that if I was bent on being a scholar, it was the very thing I needed.'

I could hear his voice telling me the story as I picked it up. It was half full. Making sure the lid was secured, I dropped it into my scrip, where it rang, metal against metal, as it collided with the key. This, above all, was evidence that William had been here.

The other things on the desk were equally revealing. There were two candles in cheap wooden candlesticks. The candles were of the same size and the same colour of wax as the ones we had seen in his coffer in Hart Hall, where Jordain was forced to strain his eyes by rushlight. There was a half dozen of quills, neatly trimmed. And there was an ample supply of parchment, probably most of the quarter ream which had been purchased from Dafydd Hewlyn. I picked up one sheet to examine it. I had not Dafydd's expert eye, but it looked the same to me. I folded it and added it to my scrip. I would ask Dafydd to look at it, to be sure.

This, then, must be the place where William had come to copy the Irish Psalter in private and without anyone's knowledge. A key to give him access to the old mill. Expensive candles to provide light for the fine work, especially for copying the illuminations. Quills trimmed to the angle he favoured. The highest quality parchment which surely matched what we had found under his mattress. Finally, and irrefutably his, the scallop shell ink well.

One thing only was missing. Where was the Psalter itself?

He must have had it here. How he had obtained it was another matter. But where was it now? We had certainly not found it anywhere in his room at Hart Hall. He could not have taken it home, for he had not been there since

Christmas, and everything pointed to recent activity here. I also had a strong suspicion that it was not safely lodged in its box in Merton's book room.

For a moment I had a horrifying thought. Suppose William had been holding the book when he had been surprised by his murderer, who must surely be some vagrant who wanted this place for himself. Perhaps he had been stabbed and thrown in the river still holding the book. In that case, waterlogged, it would now lie on the bed of the Cherwell, rapidly disintegrating and feeding the fishes. It would mean not only the death of a promising young man, whatever skulduggery he had been engaged in here, but also the loss of one of Merton's, one of Oxford's, rarest treasures.

I did my best to push the thought away, though my inner eye conjured up an image of those illuminated pages waving in the river like water weed, flakes of gold foil spinning in the sunlight down the stream like some irides-cent insect, tempting the jaws of a passing trout. Nay, the book must be here somewhere. I had not properly examined the whole room.

The table was a simple structure, four legs and a top. No drawers. I moved the stool aside and looked under it. There was nowhere there that anything could be hidden. Upside down, the stool revealed nothing but the under-side of its seat. I began a careful investigation of the mill machinery. I ran my arm up the chute as far as I could reach, but encountered nothing but a film of old flour, which I dusted off on the hem of my cotte. The mech-anism which had once operated the wheel provided no hiding place. I stood in the middle of the floor and turned slowly round. The book could not have been hidden on the upper level, for the ladder was worm-rotted and lying discarded on the floor.

The only other possible place was a pile of old sacks lying in the corner. I could not believe William would have risked putting the ancient, priceless book anywhere so damaging, but for the sake of thoroughness, I had best look.

The sacks smelled of mould and mice. And mice had been making good use of them, tearing away pieces to make their nests. Easy enough, for the old sacking disintegrated in my hands as I lifted it to look underneath. There was nothing but mouse droppings. Whoever had cleaned the room had missed this corner. It was a pile of filthy rubbish, and there was no sign of the book there.

I was still kneeling by the sacks, trying to scrub my hands clean on my cotte, with little success, when I thought I heard a rustle in the dead foliage that lay outside beneath the windows. Probably more of the mice, or even a rat, for such might still linger around an old mill even after all the grain was gone. Half rising, I had a sudden sense, a change in the light, a stirring in the air – there was someone there.

If I had not already been moving, the blow would have cracked my skull. As it was, the right side of my head seemed to explode with pain. I had only a sideways glimpse of my attacker before I fell, with my face in the rotting sacks and the dark closing over me.

–

I have no idea how long I lay in darkness. Gradually I became aware of intense pain in my head, and a lesser pain in my stomach. I was half suffocated by the filthy sacks, but it seemed almost too much trouble to lift my face or even turn my head. There was a noise beyond the drumming of pain in my head. At first I could not be sure what it was, but with an immense effort to gather my wits together, I remembered that I was in the derelict mill. I identified the sound as rain beating against the broken shutters and rustling in the thatch of the roof like an army of mice. The occasional groan I took to be the timbers of the old waterwheel straining in the flow of the river and not noises escaping from my own involuntary lips, although when I tried to heave myself up I did groan aloud, and thought the better of trying to move.

The pain in my stomach worried me. Had I been stabbed, like William? I have little knowledge of these matters, but I had heard it said that sometimes a stabbed man can hardly feel – until it is too late – the thrust of a slender dagger which will let out his life's blood. I rolled on to my side, which was less sickening than trying to get up, and felt around my stomach, to check whether there was any blood. My hand came away clean, but I had touched something hard. My wits were still moving slowly, but when I felt again, I subsided on to the sacks with a feeble laugh. As I had fallen over, my scrip had swung forward. All this time I had been lying with the sharp edge of a pewter scallop shell pressing into my stomach.

Filled with relief, I decided the best thing I could do was just to lie here, perhaps have a little sleep. Then my head might feel better and I could stand up without feeling as though the world was tipping sideways. I shut my eyes. Sleep would be good. Later I would make the effort to go home. But before I could make myself comfortable amongst the mouse droppings, a voice in my dulled brain said, 'Why haven't they tipped you in the river?'

That brought me awake.

If the man or men who had killed William were also those who had attacked me, they had a convenient means of disposing of bodies. I struggled on to my knees, and promptly vomited, which made the pile of sacks even less inviting. I tried to grasp the brief glimpse I had had from the corner of my eye just as the blow felled me. A man with reddish hair. I had heard that somewhere before. Had Dafydd not said that one of the men who bought his parchment had red hair? But two men had come to him, and, if they were the same, Peter de Wallingford had seen two men talking to William. I had not seen two men, but that was no assurance that two men had not been here.

They might still be here, still intending to tip me into the river. Stunned as I was, I could easily drown. In which case, it did not seem like a sensible plan to wait around for this to happen. I turned my head carefully, biting down on my lips to avoid a cry of pain. There was no one within my limited range of sight. I levered myself to my feet and grabbed the side of the grain chute as the floor dipped and tried to throw me down again. Still holding on for support, I eased myself round until I could see the whole room. The storm rolling overhead had cast a pall over the light, but the door still stood open. In the relative gloom I could not make out anyone but myself in the mill. Weak-kneed, I shuffled over to the table. Apart from the wooden candlesticks, one knocked over and lying on its side, the table was bare. The candles, the quills, and the parchment were gone.

I wondered whether they – or *he* – had noticed that the ink well was not there. And had they – or *he* – been puzzled by the fact that the door was unlocked? I still had no idea whether the man who had struck me was alone. If he was, that might explain why I had been left here and not dumped in the river. He might have thought that the blow had been enough to kill me, and without another to assist him, it was not worthwhile bothering to carry me to the river. If the men were about in Oxford, they must have heard that William's body had been quickly found and an inquest summoned. My body, left to rot in this abandoned place, might not be found for months. The thought caused my stomach to heave.

Outside, the rain was pelting down, a full-blown spring deluge. Surely the men, or man, would not wait about, out there in the rain? Of course, there would be some shelter under the willows, but not much, for they were not yet in full leaf. To go or stay? I was still weak and shaken, but if I waited, two men might come back for me. I was no match for them in my present state, and I carried no weapon but the workaday knife I used at mealtimes or for slitting paper in the shop when needed. If I ventured forth I would soon be soaked to my very skin, but that was better than waiting for the storm to pass over, with the men returning.

I sidled to the door, still supporting myself with a hand against the wall, and peered cautiously out, like a nervous hedgehog uncurling. There was nothing to see but rain, in wavering grey sheets blotting out the view of everything more than a few yards away. I could not see the King's Mill now, but I had only to follow this narrow branch of the river until it reached the other channel, then turn left and follow its bank to the mill. I hoped I could manage to walk that far. It had not seemed much of a distance when

I had first reached the derelict mill, but now my legs were as unreliable as those of a babe just learning to walk.

When I reached the King's Mill – I would not allow myself to think of failing – then I could decide what to do. I might borrow a horse, if I was capable of staying in the saddle in my present state. Or I might continue on to Yardley's farm and seek Thomas's help. Nothing would be accomplished by delaying any further. Leaving the door ajar, as my attacker had done, I began cautiously to pick my way along the bank in the direction of the bigger channel.

I wondered that he had not locked me in. He was not to know that I had a key and must have thought I had found the door unlocked. Locking me in would have made it more difficult for me to escape, if I were still alive. The windows were small, but I might just have managed to squeeze through. If I were dead, why then it would make it even more unlikely that my body would be found. Clearly they had finished with the mill, for everything of importance had been cleared away, though I still could not imagine what had become of the Psalter.

With the rain obscuring everything, I had no idea how near I was drawing to the junction of the rivers. My shoes squelched in the long grass, rivulets dripped off my hair, and my clothes were as sodden as if I had indeed been thrown in the river. I still felt as weak as a newborn lamb, tottering along, but the slash of the cold, wind-borne rain in my face revived my brain a little.

After what seemed an interminable time, I reached the larger channel of the Cherwell. It was probably not as far as it felt, but the rain and the fact that I could not see my way made it seem longer. Thankfully I turned left on a firm footpath, and even as I did so I realised that the rain was slackening at last. Gradually my surroundings came into view, as if the solid wall of rain had been a thick mist which was now dispersing, and I saw ahead of me my goal, the King's Mill.

Being a royal mill, this was a substantial property, with a comfortable house attached for the miller and his family, since he was a king's servant of some standing. There was a solid bridge crossing the river, not a tremulous walkway, for which I was grateful. I did not think I could have trusted my legs to take me across Miller Wooton's perilous structure, although they were beginning to feel a little less like green twigs and more like solid limbs capable of holding me upright.

Both the main mill building and the miller's house stood on the far side of the river, so I crossed and knocked on the door of the house, since the wheel was turning at the mill, making it almost impossible for me to make myself heard there.

The miller's wife, Mistress Harvey, answered the door herself. I had met both the miller and his wife before, since he was lettered and devout, characteristics not common amongst men of his trade. He had bought a book of hours from me the previous year, so that he and his wife could follow them faithfully at home. All their children had survived the Death, which they put down to their unshakeable faith. I had known many who were equally devout, including my Elizabeth, whose faith had not saved them, but I did not question their sincerity.

'Master Elyot!' Mistress Harvey exclaimed, throwing up her hands in horror at the sight of me. 'What has come to you! Have you been in the river? And your head – the blood!'

Oddly, once I had ascertained that I had not been stabbed in the stomach, I had not felt my head for blood, only aware of the throbbing pain. I touched it now, and my fingers came away sticky, though much must have been washed away by the rain.

'Come away in,' she cried, taking me by the elbow and leading me down a screen passage and into what was clearly her parlour.

'Nay,' I protested, 'I am in no fit state. Take me to the kitchen.'

She clicked her tongue, but saw the sense in that.

When we reached the kitchen, I found myself irresistibly drawn to the hearth. Until now I had not realised that I was shivering so much that my teeth rattled together like dice in a gaming box. Certainly the storm had turned a warm spring day much colder, but I think the blow on the head had unbalanced my humours, so that I felt as cold as a winter's dawn.

Mistress Harvey asked no more questions, but set her kitchen boy to heating water and filling a tub for me beside the fire, while she shooed her maid servant before her out of the kitchen. As she closed the door I heard her telling the girl to run and fetch her master.

'He must leave the journeyman in charge. Here's Master Elyot, the Oxford bookseller, in such a state—'

The door cut off the rest of her sentence, but I did not care. I was stripping off my clothes and sinking into the warm water. I think if the kitchen boy had not roused me, I would have fallen asleep there. He had come back with some of his master's clothes I was bidden to put on, and his mistress would be back shortly to dress my injury.

Master Harvey was a bigger man than I, very broad in the shoulders and chest, due to all that heaving of sacks of grain and flour, but I was glad to don the dry clothes however loosely they hung on me.

Both miller and wife came hurrying into the kitchen when the boy opened the door, and made much of me, Master Harvey pressing a beaker of wine into my hand, while his wife brought salves and dressings for my head.

'I never meant to cause you so much trouble,' I said apologetically. 'I came only to ask if I might borrow a horse to take me home. I fear I might find it hard to walk so far.'

'With that dint on the head,' Master Harvey said, 'I doubt you should ride. I'll drive you there in the cart.' He helped himself to some wine. No doubt he needed fortifying after the sight of me.

'Lean your head over a little,' Mistress Harvey said. 'I fear I must cut away a little of your hair here.'

'How bad is it?' I asked.

'A nasty blow,' she said, proceeding to salve and bind my head with calm practicality. 'It caught the top of your ear, and that is where most of the bleeding is. It could have been much worse.'

'Aye. I think he sought to kill me.'

They were too polite to ask what had happened to me, but it seemed only right, in view of their kindness, that I should give them some explanation. I reminded them of the death of William Farringdon earlier in the week, and said that I and the Warden of his hall suspected that he might have been thrown in the river somewhere along the branch which led from a little below King's Mill to the channel of the Cherwell which flowed parallel to the Oxford town wall.

'And indeed I found things belonging to William in an old abandoned mill there,' I said, 'just before I was struck from behind.'

I kept to myself any mention of the Psalter, or what William had been doing there.

'I know the place,' Hugh Harvey said. 'It was in my father's time some fellow set up a mill there, but it never lasted but a few years.'

'Aye, 'tis falling apart.'

'And did you not see the rogue who did this?' Mistress Harvey asked, bundling away her linen and salves, having swathed my head in what felt like an unnecessarily large bandage.

'Only the merest glimpse,' I said. 'I think he had red hair.'

Miller Harvey shook his head. 'I've seen no foxy heads about here.'

I did not say that I thought he had come from the opposite direction.

'There is no need for you to drive me to Oxford,' I said, getting to my feet. 'If I could borrow a horse or a mule?' But even as I spoke, I swayed and had to grab the table for support.

'Hugh!' Mistress Harvey said, picking up my beaker and sniffing it. 'You did not give Master Elyot wine!'

'He needs strengthening,' her husband protested.

'Not with wine. Not after a blow on the head. Master Elyot, you are in no fit state to ride. Hugh will take you in the cart. The journeyman will finish the day's work at the mill. But will you not take supper with us first?'

'You are very kind, mistress,' I said, 'but my sister will be worried. I will send back these clothes tomorrow.'

'I have made up yours into a bundle,' she said. 'Please give my respects to Mistress Makepeace.'

As we made our way toward the door, I saw a row of young faces peering down at us from the top of the stairs, and raised my hand to the Harvey children. All were watching, open-mouthed, save the eldest boy, who came leading the horse and cart from the barn. The miller gave me a hand up into the back of the cart, where I made myself comfortable, with my bundle of wet clothes, amongst half a load of straw and a pair of sacks of flour.

'Do not think you are taking me out of the way,' the miller said cheerfully. 'I have those sacks to deliver to St John's, and your shop is not much further along.'

'I'm grateful for your kindness, nonetheless,' I said.

He climbed up to the front of the cart and chirruped to his horse. Before we were halfway to the bridge, I was asleep, cradled in straw and flour.

Chapter Eight

I woke from a troubled half-sleep, half-waking night-mare, when the cart stopped at the gatehouse to St John's Hospital. Miller Harvey was talking to the porter at the lodge, then there was the squeal of hinges as the main gate was dragged open to admit the cart. As we drove into the outer court, I sat up and tried to brush the fragments of straw off my borrowed clothes, for I had no wish to look like a wandering beggar here, where I was known. The cart passed through into a further courtyard and stopped. The sacks of flour would be unloaded here, so I stood up and tried to heave them to the rear of the cart, but I was still too weakened to shift the first more than a few feet when Harvey swung himself up into the cart and took it from me.

'Leave that, Master Elyot,' he said with a grin. 'If you start that wound of yours bleeding again I shall have my wife after my skin.'

He slung the sacks easily down to someone waiting below, while I scrambled to the front of the cart. I did not want to arrive under the noses of my neighbours like another sack in the body of the cart. His delivery made, the miller climbed up beside me, turned his horse, and urged him ahead out of the gates. We passed both men and women as we went, for this was a mixed house, caring for the sick and needy, though I had heard that relations between the two sides were not always as harmonious as they should be amongst men and women of the cloth.

'Not far to go now,' Harvey said, as the gates closed behind us, leaving only the small wicket open.

We turned right, past the cottages and through the East Gate. The storm had turned the road to a quagmire, so that people drew back as we passed, to avoid the mud thrown up by our wheels. When we stopped outside my shop, I saw that Walter had already closed the shutters. I had lost all sense of time and the storm had darkened the day early. Even now, although the storm clouds had passed, the sky was dull. It must be considerably later than I had expected to return home. I climbed down carefully, carrying my bundle of wet clothes.

'I give you thanks, Master Harvey, for all your kindness, yours and your wife's. Will you step inside for a bite of supper?'

'Nay, I thank you.' He pushed up his hat with the butt end of his whip, which he seemed to carry merely for show. 'I'll away back home before the East Gate is shut.'

With that he turned the cart, with some difficulty for the mud dragged at the wheels, and set off back the way we had come.

I must see Margaret first, then I had better look for Jordain, who would be wondering what had become of me. By now he would surely have finished showing William's mother and sister the grave in St Peter's churchyard. He would escort them back to the Cross Inn and might sit with them for a time, but he must now be back at Hart Hall. Suddenly it seemed a long way to walk.

When I came into the kitchen, the murmur of talk, which I could hear as soon as I entered the shop, stopped abruptly.

'Nicholas!' Margaret sprang to her feet, a mixture of alarm and annoyance on her face. 'What have you been doing? Why are you turbaned like an infidel?'

'Someone took a swipe at me,' I said, sinking into the chair she had vacated. I did not quite trust myself to stay upright on a backless stool. 'Mistress Harvey at the King's Mill dressed it for me and I think she has used an overabundance of bandaging.' I felt the side of my head gingerly. There was indeed a great deal of linen about my head.

The children were staring at me open-mouthed, and I saw that Walter was still here. Like my sister he had also risen from his seat.

'King's Mill?' he said in bewilderment, as well he might.

'Aye, it was the nearest place to go, after I was struck.'

'And why are you wearing those ridiculous clothes?' Now that she was assured I had come to no serious harm, Margaret's voice had become exasperated.

'I took a soaking in the storm. These are Miller Harvey's clothes. Mine are here.' I pointed to the bundle I had dropped at my feet.

She snatched it up and began to shake out the sorry mess of my clothes.

'I won't ask *why* you did not take shelter from the storm, or *why* you have been all the way over to the King's Mill.'

I understood very clearly what that meant. Wearily, I passed a hand over my face.

'Is there any supper?' I asked meekly. 'I have no idea what hour it is. I was quite out of my wits for a time. After the blow.'

Her gaze softened a little. 'We were about to sup. Walter stayed, for we were not sure what had become of you. Had you not returned for supper, he would have come looking for you, for he knew we were worried.'

In the past, I think she would not have worried if I was absent a little beyond my hour, but these were lawless times.

'That was good of you, Walter, but after we eat, there is an errand you might do for me. I had promised to see Jordain Brinkylsworth when I returned, but I am not certain of making my way to Hart Hall and back. I am still somewhat uncertain on my legs.'

'Gladly, Master Elyot,' he said.

Margaret was spreading my wet garments out to dry near the fire, moving the puppy firmly aside when she tried to help by sitting on my cotte.

'And did you walk all the way home from the King's Mill?' she said.

'Nay, Miller Harvey drove me in his cart. He was delivering flour to St John's.'

I said no more about where I had been, or what I had found, until we had eaten a supper of leek soup and bread, which steadied my empty stomach. Margaret put the children to bed, and by the time she returned to the kitchen I had made up my mind not only to tell her everything, but also to take Walter into my confidence. He was a man of good sense and discretion, and he would need to give Jordain a clear account of the afternoon's events.

'Jordain and I decided that William's body might not have floated down the river from Holywell Mill, but from a side branch which links our channel of the Cherwell with that over where the King's Mill stands. You know how the river winds about and splits and rejoins, all through those water meadows. We found a piece of his shirt snagged on a willow root, just at the junction. There was no time to walk up that way on Wednesday, so that is where I went today. Jordain must stay to see William's mother and sister, so I went alone.'

I told them about the derelict mill and what I had found inside.

'This ink well belonged to William,' I said, taking it out of my scrip and setting it on the table.

Walter picked it up. 'I remember it,' he said. 'He used it when he was here.'

The sheet of parchment I laid down as well, and recounted all that I had learned from Dafydd Hewlyn.

'I am also certain this is the same batch.'

Walter fingered it. 'Fine quality.'

'Aye. Expensive.'

In order to account for all of this, I had to explain how we had discovered that William had been copying the precious Irish Psalter which belonged to Merton, and Walter whistled softly, a look of alarm on his face.

'But how did he come by that?'

'I do not know. Nor do I know where it is.'

I explained how I had been kneeling, searching under the sacking, when I was suddenly struck from behind.

'By the time I came to myself, candles, quills, and parchment all were gone. So, it seemed, was the man who attacked me. It was the worst of the storm then, but I thought it wise not to wait about for him to return, so I made my way to the King's Mill. And got a thorough soaking.'

'He believed he had killed you,' Margaret said flatly.

'Mayhap. I do not know. He cannot have missed the ink well, or he would have searched me. Nor realised I had a key. Even if there were nothing else, the key links William to the mill. Who killed him, or why, I cannot tell, but I believe that is where his body was thrown into the river.'

When I had finished, neither of them said anything for some minutes. Eventually, Walter shook his head in bafflement.

'I do not understand why the lad was doing this. Someone must have put him up to it. But why? If a copy of the book was wanted, we could have made one, here in the shop, open and fair.'

'If Merton permitted,' I said.

'Aye, they might not have agreed. You say that it is kept safe in a special box in one of the college book rooms, and locked away at night. How could it be stolen?'

'And if it was stolen,' Margaret pointed out, 'would not Philip Olney have started a hue and cry? His most precious darling gone? Worse than a murder!'

'That also baffles me,' I said. 'How the book was taken. Where it is now, and why Olney is concealing the fact. Or so I suspect.'

'Has no wish to see himself held responsible for the loss,' Walter said shrewdly. 'More than his Fellowship is worth, I'd say.'

'You are probably right. In any case, I promised to tell Jordain how I fared, and there is all this now to tell him. If you are willing to walk up to Hart Hall, Walter, it would be a relief to my mind if Jordain knew all.'

Walter stood up. 'I'll gladly go, Master Elyot. And I thank you for trusting me with this. If I can help you discover who killed William, I will do all I can. He was a fine lad, and whatever tangle he got himself into, his death is a terrible waste.'

'It is that,' I said. 'Take the ink well with you to show Jordain. I will keep the parchment, for I must collect Mistress Lapley's book from Henry Stalbroke next week and I can show it to Dafydd Hewlyn at the same time.'

He went off at once, and as soon as he was gone, Margaret insisted on examining my head wound.

'Let me first change into clothes that do not hang loose on me like these,' I said, getting up a little unsteadily and heading for the stairs.

When I returned to the kitchen, she had set out a bowl of warm water and her own salves, although once she had unwound me from my Saracen turban she admitted that Mistress Harvey had done well enough.

My wound salved again, but bound less plentifully in linen, I sank back in the chair by the fire and allowed my eyes to close. After Margaret's good soup I no longer felt so weak, but the blow had made me very sleepy. I think I must have dozed again before Walter returned.

I woke to the sound of several voices, and saw that Jordain had come with Walter.

'Partly to assure myself that you are not dead,' he said, with a grim smile. 'It seems you are lucky the fellow did not draw a knife on you as he did on William.'

'It may not have been the same man as killed William,' I said, trying to struggle to my feet, until I was pushed down again by Jordain's firm hand on my shoulder.

'You think there are two murderers lurking about this old mill?'

'Well, Dafydd spoke of two men, and so did the lad from St Edmund's Hall. It was nothing but a momentary glance, but I think there was only one there today.'

'And you say he is the red haired one?'

'Truly, Jordain, I think so, but it was no more than a glimpse from the corner of my eye.' I rubbed my hand over my face. My head was beginning to pound again, and I could not see quite as clearly as I should like.

'He should be abed,' Margaret said.

'Soon.' I lifted a hand to halt her, because she was rising to hustle Walter and Jordain away.

'Tell me first, Jordain, how matters went with Mistress Farringdon and her daughter. Had they anything to say that might help us in all this tangle?'

He looked thoughtful. 'Perhaps. Aye and nay.'

'Don't play the scholastic with me,' I said, 'I am too weary.'

'Forgive me, I am not trying to be obscure.' He pulled up a stool and sat down beside me, stretching his hands out to the fire. 'Who would believe we have been hot for the last few days? Out there it feels as though February has returned. Sometimes I think our low-lying town caught in this web of water is not good for our health.'

Walter had retired to a far corner of the room and looked as though he was about to leave.

'Come by the fire, man,' I said impatiently. 'You are part of all our schemes and our bafflement now.'

Walter brought over another stool and perched on it. Rowan, who had been stretched out with her rounded puppy stomach warming by the fire, sidled over and sat on his feet. He bent down and ran her silky ears through his fingers.

'I am not sure that what William's mother told me has any bearing on why William was killed,' Jordain said. 'He was last home with his family at Christmastide, but it was a sad season for them. His father was already failing and died before Twelfth Night. I knew very little about the family, for William never talked much about them, but it seems that his father commanded a division of light cavalry at Crecy and distinguished himself there and was sore wounded. The king himself granted him a pension of a hundred pounds a year, so the family was able to live quite comfortably, and send William to Oxford, which had always been his ambition. They held a farm of the Earl of Leicester, which William's elder brother worked on his father's behalf, until he died of the pestilence, and his young wife too, leaving an infant girl.'

'And how was the farm managed after the brother's death?' I asked.

'William had just started at Oxford then, but proposed coming home. His father said that he would employ a steward instead. William should continue with his studies. In time he would make a better life for all the family than ever he would do on the farm, in which he had no interest.'

'What became of the girl child?' Margaret asked.

'Her grandmother, William's mother, took her in. She is left behind with a neighbour at present. The other girl, William's sister, is here with her mother. I would judge her to be about thirteen or fourteen.'

'But,' I said – and despite the ache in my head I could put my finger on the nub of the problem – 'when the father died, the pension died with him.'

'Aye. The rent on the farm and the steward's wages were paid up to Lady Day, but in the weeks since then the mother and the two girls have stayed on in the farm by grace of the lord. He wants them out now. The steward has left. The new tenant is in a hurry to take up the tenancy.

They have nowhere to go, and by the look of her, I believe the mother is not well.'

'Money,' I said. 'They needed money. William was now the head of the family and he would feel responsible for them.'

Jordain nodded. 'His mother had written to him, explaining what had happened, and he wrote back, about a month ago, telling her not to worry, he would find a way to send her money.'

'So,' Walter ventured, 'he agreed to make this copy of the book, to raise money for his family.'

'It would seem so. Though who is behind it, and how they knew William needed money, we are no nearer to discovering.'

'Poor lad,' Margaret said softly. 'Why did he not come to one of us? We could have helped, at least a little. Nicholas could have given him work.'

'Even the university might have helped,' Jordain said bleakly. 'There are funds which can be advanced to students, even though they may need to be paid back in the end. He would have been qualified to teach, come the autumn, and earned his fees. Only a few months to wait. I failed him. He did not feel he could confide in me.'

'Perhaps he was too proud,' I said. 'The young can be sensitive and secret in their pride, particularly boys who must take on the care of their families. You should not blame yourself.'

But he would do so.

'So,' Margaret said, 'we can perhaps understand why William undertook work which was certainly somewhat underhand, and perhaps criminal, but we are no nearer finding these men who killed him, and almost certainly also attacked Nicholas.'

'Nor do we know what has become of the book,' I said.

'If we find the men, we may find the book.' Jordain did not sound hopeful.

'Aye.' I could not keep the doubt out of my own voice. 'Somehow I feel that would be too simple. And in any case, we must find the men first. Two men, about my height, nearing fifty. One with red hair, one with a broken nose. There are probably dozens such in Oxford.'

'One thing we have not done,' Jordain said, 'is to question the lad from St Edmund's. Were they the same two men that he saw?'

'If not,' I said gloomily, 'then it all becomes a great deal more confused.'

There was little more we could do that night. In the morning, before coming to the shop, Walter would call at St Edmund's Hall and leave a message for Peter de Wallingford, asking him to come and see me as soon as he might. Jordain had promised to call on William's mother again at the Cross Inn, and would wait there until I joined them.

I gave a sudden groan. 'I have just remembered. I told Philip Olney that I would take the bestiary from the Widow Preston for him to examine tomorrow. I am in no mood to haggle with him over the price.'

'He still believes himself too grand to come to the shop?' Jordain asked.

'Either that or he does not like to leave his books unguarded so long. I think sometimes he is not quite sane where they are concerned.'

'Little good it has done him,' Margaret said grimly, 'if the most valuable has been stolen from under his nose.'

'Very true.' I sighed. 'I suppose I must go to Merton, but I shall wait until after dinner, which will leave me time to come to Mistress Farringdon in the morning. And, Margaret,' I turned to her, 'we must find some way to return Hugh Harvey's garments to him.'

'I will see to it,' she said.

With these matters settled, Jordain and Walter set off home, and I made my way to my bed chamber. I hardly had time to exchange my clothes for a nightshirt before I crawled with relief into my bed. I was still mumbling a prayer of thanksgiving for having escaped worse injury than a blow to the head when I fell asleep.

–

In the morning my head was less sore, and I persuaded Margaret to relieve me of the bandage, for I had no wish to be seen in either Merton or the Cross Inn looking like a casualty from a battlefield. Besides that, it had occurred to me that my assailant might have struck out blindly in the dim light of the old mill as the storm gathered. He might not even be aware of my identity. Walking about Oxford with a heavily bandaged head, I would draw attention to myself. I preferred the man not to have an opportunity to improve on his previous day's work.

Margaret made a face when I asked to be free of the bandaging.

'You bled a good deal,' she objected.

'Aye, but it was mostly from my ear. The blow to my head mainly caused bruising, not bleeding. 'Tis fortunate I have a thick skull.'

'That you do have,' she said grimly, unwinding the bandage, but for all her scolding doing it gently.

'I shall wear my academic cap with the flaps down,' I said. 'That will hide my bloodied ear. Have you thought how we may return the miller's clothes?'

'We women rise before dawn, not like you slug-abed men. I have already spoken to Mary Coomber at the dairy. This is her day for walking out to Yardley's for eggs. She has already taken the bundle of clothes and will leave them with Thomas. He will see that Mistress Harvey has them. If she has not been to the farm in the next few days, he will send his boy to the King's Mill with them. It is all settled.'

Relieved that one matter was at least in hand, I went to open the shop. Walter arrived, having already left my message at St Edmund's Hall, and indeed close on his heels Peter de Wallingford hurried in, somewhat breathless.

'I have a lecture at six, Master Elyot, but I was given a message that you needed to see me quickly.'

'This will not take long,' I said. 'Master Brinkylsworth and I thought you might be able to describe more fully the men you saw with William after you attended Master Wycliffe's lecture. Can you cast your mind back, and tell me what you saw?'

'I will try my best.' He closed his eyes, the better to concentrate. 'They were quite old, older than you.'

To a lad of this age, a man of five and twenty is old.

'Can you place their ages more specifically?'

'Well,' he opened his eyes, and smiled with the easy confidence of youth. 'My father is eight and forty, and I suppose they would be about the same age. Still had their hair. Though one – the dark one – had some grey in it.'

'So one was dark.' Not very helpful, but a start. 'And the other?'

'Oh, the other was as red as a squirrel. With a small beard.' This was more promising, although Dafydd had not mentioned a beard.

'A beard?'

'Aye, just one of those small pointed ones. Not a full beard. I was not close enough to see clearly, but I think he had the scars of the pox. Perhaps he grew the beard to hide some of them.'

The scars accorded with Dafydd's description. 'What manner of men were they? Rich? Poor? Well-dressed?'

'I think I told you I thought they might be from London. It was their clothes made me think that. They were not university men, you could never imagine that. But I did not think they were Oxford townsmen. They were – different.'

He shrugged.

'This may be important, Peter. Try to remember why you thought they were different.'

'Well, they wore long robes, for one thing. No one in Oxford wears a long robe these days, except merchants and officials, or some for special occasions. Everyone is too poor and works too hard. But their robes were not of the best cloth. I have an uncle who is a member of the Drapers' Livery in London, and I do know a little about cloth. These robes were showy from a distance, but poor quality when you looked close.'

That fitted with Dafydd's impression of men who worked the fairs, passing off shoddy goods for fine quality.

Peter's hand was on the latch of the door. 'I must go. The lecture will be starting.'

'One more thing.' I did not want to prompt him, so I chose my words carefully. 'Was there anything else notable about these men, apart from their robes, showy but shoddy, and one man's red hair?'

He was halfway through the door, but he turned with a grin. 'Aye, reckon the foxy head was the cleverer. He had a keen eye. The other man, bigger, with dark hair, I'd say he was a fighter. Sometime in the past his nose had been broken.'

He was gone before I had even let out my breath. They must be the same men, even though Dafydd had not mentioned a small beard. I had not seen enough of my assailant to notice whether he had such a beard. But nevertheless, I was certain now. We were not hunting for four men, but for two. The men Peter had seen with William and the men who had purchased the parchment were the same. And I was sure my assailant was the red head. If Peter's assessment was correct, that the dark-haired man was a fighter, perhaps he was the one who wielded a long, thin knife.

None of this made clear why these men should have wanted to kill William. If they were employing him – either for themselves or for someone else – why would they kill him? They needed him alive, at least until the task was complete. Something had clearly gone awry with their scheme, whatever it was.

I set off up the High Street, turning the matter over in my mind. Someone had commissioned a copy of the Irish book, for it was clear that these two ruffians were not acting on their own. The more I thought on it, the more I felt Dafydd's suggestion was wrong. Men like this would not gamble so much expense on a chance sale at a fair. They would only have undertaken the scheme if there was already a customer in mind, *ergo*, as our logic masters would say, there must be a man of some wealth behind it all, a man with a desperate desire for such a book.

I have known bibliophiles who would sell their family inheritance to lay hands on a book they coveted, though I had never yet met one who would countenance murder in the getting. Perhaps the buyer had *not* countenanced it and the dark man, the man of violence, had struck out at William without authorisation. In which case, our two rogues must find themselves at a pretty pass now. Having lost their scrivener, and even that portion of the book which he had copied, they would be forced to find another to take William's place, and begin again.

That would explain why the red-headed man had gone to the derelict mill where William had worked, in order to retrieve the expensive parchment. It would have been difficult to account for its loss, as well as the loss of their scribe. It must have been a shock to him, finding me there, searching the place. No wonder he had struck out, no doubt in a panic. He must have been carrying a stout staff, but it was my good fortune that he was not a man who wielded a knife so expertly.

The book must be concealed elsewhere. If Jordain and I were to catch up with them, we must try to think as they would think. If they had the book and they had the parchment, they would now be looking for a talented scribe and illuminator. At some point, also, they would need to obtain inks and paints and gold foil, although it would seem, from the pages we had found under William's mattress, that the plan was to finish the lettering first, and to paint the illuminations last, before binding. And that, too, was a consideration. Would they risk taking the manuscript to Henry Stalbroke? If the intention was to mimic the original binding, they would need an exceptionally skilled binder.

Where would they look for a new scrivener? We still did not know how they had found William, with both the skill and the need for money. Of all towns in England, Oxford was second only to London in the abundance of skilled scribes. Indeed, I ventured to think that though we might have fewer, we probably had greater talent amongst us. I am a fair scribe myself, and so are my men. Two other booksellers in town had competent men. Then there were all the religious houses in and around Oxford – Osney, St Frideswide's, Rewley, the Carmelites, Franciscans, Dominicans, Augustinians. And although the mendicant orders were meant to have no worldly possessions, books were an exception, especially here, where their members were being sent in increasing numbers to receive a sound education. Even the colleges had their scriveners, not only the law clerks for their charters and their day-to-day business, managing property both movable and immovable.

There was a vast array of talent here in Oxford, but it might be difficult for our rogues to reach the right sort of man, with the skills they required, in need of money, and the willingness to keep his counsel.

As I reached Carfax and turned right up Northgate Street, a gaggle of youths burst from the door of the Swindlestock Tavern. They were only mildly drunk, but drunk they were for so early in the morning. Dressed in the everyday clothes of their secular peers – short, very short, cottes and brightly coloured hose – their tonsures revealed them as students, though in one or two cases the tonsure was disappearing under new growth. It was common knowledge that when students went home for the summer, they allowed their hair to grow back, just as they returned to the sports of their fathers, hunting and hawking. Indeed one of these boys had a great mastiff on a chain, which was pulling him along. No doubt who was master of that pair. The university constantly brings out new regulations, banning the keeping of animals by students, but to little avail. When I was a student, there was a fellow came from Germany with a bear cub. I wonder what became of him? Another had a snake, but it was killed by a mastiff not unlike the one now surging in my direction.

I quickened my steps to avoid an unpleasant confront-ation, and entered the yard of the Cross Inn.

The innkeeper pointed me to a small back parlour, away from the main room where the inn's guests gathered. Jordain was there, seated at a table with a thin, worried woman, perhaps in her early forties, and a delicate young girl, not quite in her full bloom yet. Both had eyes red and swollen with weeping. There was a jug of wine and beakers on the table, all untouched. Jordain presented me to them.

'I cannot say how sorry I am for your loss,' I said, taking a seat next to Jordain and opposite mother and daughter. 'I do not need to tell you what a fine young man William was. He worked for me in my bookshop for a few weeks, two years ago.'

The woman nodded. 'I thank you for your kindness, Master Elyot. William had spoken of you. He said that if he did not succeed in becoming a scholar, he could think of no better trade than that of a bookseller.' She was keeping admirable control of herself, but she could not hide the trembling in her voice. I understood why Jordain thought she was ill. It was not recent grief only that had hollowed her face so that the cheekbones stood out sharply under her skin, and dark shadows had ringed her eyes. The girl – it seemed her name was Juliana – said nothing, but tears welled up in her eyes and fell silently. From time to time she wiped them away with the trailing hem of her sleeve.

This was even worse than I had dreaded, and I wondered why I had agreed to come. There was nothing I could do to ease their grief, and I felt that the presence of Jordain and me must simply increase it. However, I was here now, so I had best make the most of it.

'Jordain has already told you about this strange business of the Psalter?' I said. 'Had William said anything to you about it?'

Mistress Farringdon shook her head. 'Nothing at all. Only, in his last letter he said I was not to worry, that he would send money so that we could take a cottage and have enough to live on. I did not understand how this could be, unless he meant he would be working for you again, or beginning his teaching in the university, though that would not be for another six months. When I wrote back, I asked him how he would find the money, but he never replied.'

She swallowed painfully. I poured wine for her and handed her the beaker. She took it obediently and drank a little. I thought it might give her a little strength in this ordeal.

'We think he had undertaken the work to earn some money for his family,' I said, 'quite understandably.'

Jordain and I had agreed that we would not mention the fact that copying Merton's book, certainly without permission, was a kind of theft. Tragic enough that they should suffer William's loss, without besmirching his name, but Mistress Farringdon was no fool.

'These men he was working for, you think they killed him? They were scoundrels, I think, although you are not saying so.'

Jordain sighed. 'Mistress, we do not know. Very little is clear. Why they should kill him is a mystery, but we can think of no one else.'

'We are not even sure who they are,' I said, 'but we are perhaps a little closer to finding them. We have a good description.' This was a little more than the truth, but I found the despair in her eyes nigh unbearable.

'Master Jordain tells us that you too were attacked, Master Elyot,' she said. 'And badly hurt.'

'Nay,' I said. 'Not seriously. Just a sore head. I'll soon mend. So, you can throw no further light on this work of William's?'

She shook her head. 'I am sorry.'

'I did not ask Jordain when I saw him last night.' I cleared my throat. This was a delicate matter. 'Do you wish to take William's body home with you? Or leave him here at St Peter's?' She smiled so sadly it wrenched my heart. 'He loved Oxford,' she said. 'From a small boy, all he ever wanted was to become a scholar here. Let him rest in Oxford.'

Jordain and I exchanged glances. 'I think we should leave you now, Mistress Farringdon,' he said. 'Why do you not take a few days to rest, after your hurried and unhappy journey? I have arranged for Hart Hall to pay for your lodging at the inn. We would like you to have time for a little quietness here.'

She tried to protest, but Jordain can be very stubborn when he makes up his mind to it. Hart Hall would pay, indeed! The money for the inn, like the cost of the funeral mass, would come out of Jordain's own pocket, but I supported him.

'I think this is an excellent plan, Mistress Farringdon. Would you permit my sister to call on you? It might be of help to have a woman friend here in the town.'

I saw that she looked relieved. Margaret would be just the support she needed, and could offer the kind of comfort that would be unacceptable coming from us. As we rose to take our leave, the girl Juliana spoke for the first time, looking at me with dark blue eyes still enlarged with tears.

'Master Elyot, you should speak to our cousin Emma. She and William were always close, at least until she came here.'

I looked at her blankly, then turned to her mother for an explanation. She looked uncomfortable, and a faint blush coloured her cheeks.

'My sister's girl by her first husband,' she explained. 'Emma Thorgold. When Emma's father died – six years ago, it would be – my sister married again. Her new husband already had five children of his own, and he needed someone to care for them and keep house for him.'

She said this with some bitterness, and I understood the kind of marriage it would have been. These things happen.

'Her stepfather never had much use for Emma, and she spent time with us when she could. She's of an age with William. Then last summer my sister died of a stillbirth, the only child of this second marriage, and in truth she was past safe childbearing.'

'The week after her death,' Juliana broke in resentfully, 'her stepfather sent Emma away to be a nun at Godstow.

She cried and cried. She did not want to be shut away from the world, in a nunnery. It was a hateful thing to do.'

'Hush, child,' her mother said. 'Though it was unkind, and against her wishes, I am sure the nuns are good women and will look after her. She is a novice there now.'

'When William was home at Christmas,' Juliana said, 'he told us he was able to see her. He used to visit once a week. It is not so very strict a house, and the novices are allowed visits from family. We are the only family Emma has.'

'Sister Benedicta she is called now,' Mistress Farringdon.

'Benedicta! Not very blessed,' Juliana said stubbornly. 'William might have told her something about this scheme he was a part of. She was like a sister to us both.' She turned toward her mother. 'And not *that* kind of sister, however holy.'

Having found her voice, the child had grown quite voluble. 'I thank you for that,' I said, smiling at her. 'We will certainly visit Sister Benedicta, if we are permitted.'

'Emma.'

'I think we must use the name the abbess has given her.'

With that, we took our leave, promising to visit them the next day and conduct them to Sunday Mass at St Peter's, where special prayers were to be said for William. I would send Margaret to see them in the afternoon.

As we made our way back toward Carfax, Jordain said, 'Poor creatures. I hate even having to mention this whole matter in which William was caught up.'

'I am sure they have told us all they know. No need to mention it again unless we are able to bring the men responsible to justice.'

'You have the right of it. And I cannot see that a trip out to Godstow would serve any purpose. Even if we were allowed to see this novice, Sister Benedicta, she cannot have anything to tell us.'

'Probably not,' I agreed. I grieved for the girl, forced into a monastic life for which she had no vocation. At least I had first chosen the celibate scholar's life of my own volition, and when I found that my life lay elsewhere, I was able to break free. Once imprisoned behind the convent walls, no such choice would be available for Emma Thorgold.

Jordain and I parted at the junction of the High and Catte Street, he to his dinner of boiled cabbage, but I, so I hoped, to rather better fare. When I reached the shop, which Walter was about to close, at midday, as usual on a Saturday, he had news for me.

'Master Caundish from Gloucester College has been here,' he said, 'asking about the bestiary.'

'How has he got word of that?' I was surprised. 'I have mentioned it to no one except Master Olney at Merton.'

'Perhaps he boasted that he was to have first refusal. He would enjoy gloating over Master Caundish.'

'Aye, he would. Or perhaps the widow from Banbury had mentioned it to someone who knew that Master Caundish collects bestiaries. What did you tell him?'

'I would not let him see it.' Walter grinned. 'He might have snatched it and run off. I said he must come back on Monday and speak to you about it.'

'Well done.' I grinned back. 'Now I shall have even more to bargain with, when I see Master Olney this after-noon.'

Chapter Nine

After dinner, Alysoun and Rafe asked that they might run across the street, taking Rowan with them, to pay a visit to John Baker's puppies again before the millers from Blackfriars and Trill Mill came to make their choice later in the afternoon. Thomas Yardley had sent word that he could not come until next week.

'Tell Master Baker that I had no success with Miller Wooton at Holywell Mill,' I told Alysoun. 'He must seek another home for the last pup.'

'Perhaps Cousin Jordain would like to have him?' Alysoun said winningly.

I laughed. 'Cousin Jordain is hard pressed to feed those students of his. I do not think he has any to spare for a growing puppy. We will put our heads together soon, and think who might be glad of a dog. Will John keep the terrier-like one, do you think?'

'Oh, aye, he says so.' She beamed and took my hand. 'Thank you, Papa.'

'For what, my pet?'

'For helping us find homes. I could not bear to think of them drowned.'

'Nor I. Wanton killing is evil in the eyes of God,' I said. 'Never forget that.'

The time would come when I would have to tell her the full story of William's death, but I prayed it might not be soon. Let her keep the unblemished innocence of childhood a little longer.

· When they had run off, I found Margaret in the garden, feeding our small flock of hens, and explained that William's mother and sister would be staying a few more days in Oxford.

'I thought perhaps Mistress Farringdon would be glad of a woman friend,' I said. 'This is a fearful time for her, not only losing her son by the hand of a murderer, when he was caught up in some suspicious affair, but also finding herself on the brink of a very uncertain future. She knows no one in Oxford, apart from Jordain and me. I thought, if you would not mind—?'

'Of course. I shall be glad to go.'

She shook the last grains from her flat basket, and the hens rushed about, pecking the ground at her feet.

'Away with you!' she said, as one seized the lace of her shoe, perhaps mistaking it for a worm. It received a firm push in the rear, propelling it toward the scattered grain.

'I shall just wash my hands and take off my apron. She is at the Cross Inn, you say?'

'Aye.'

She tucked a loose strand of hair into her wimple. 'Will I do? Am I respectable enough?'

I smiled. Amongst her own, Margaret had the confidence of a queen, but she was not always so sure of herself amongst strangers.

'Quite respectable enough. You will like her, Mistress Farringdon. And they are our kind of folk. Not grand. There is a girl as well, Juliana. About thirteen. She has taken her brother's death very hard, but I would say that she has a mind of her own, for all that.'

I left her debating whether it would be acceptable to take the Farringdons some of her baking, and I went into the shop to collect Widow Preston's bestiary. Turning over the leaves again, I was even more impressed with its quality. Like all works of this type, it portrayed a number of beasts no man had ever seen. Or at any rate, no man who had not travelled the silk road or gone on pilgrimage to the Holy Land or ventured into Barbary. Whether the artist had even seen them, I could not tell you, so I had no knowledge of their accuracy. However, with the common animals of England the artist showed himself to be a careful observer. The fox, the wolf, the badger, the boar, the otter, the squirrel – all seemed to leap alive off the page. The parchment was of excellent quality and the binding was of polished calfskin, tinted maroon, over boards. The edges of the pages were gilded, with no sign of rubbing.

The moralising texts which accompanied each illustration were the usual rather limping efforts, but one does not buy a bestiary for the texts. It is the pictures which are important. I wrapped the book carefully in a soft cloth and slid it into my stiffened satchel. I was not greatly looking forward to my encounter with Philip Olney, but whatever other worries occupied my mind, I must keep up my business so that my family could eat.

The day had started dull after the previous afternoon's storm, but at least the rain had laid the dust in the streets. Now the sun was shining through a thin veil of cloud and behind it the sky was a delicate blue. Elizabeth had worn a gown of that very shade the day we were married. It was folded away now, in a coffer under the eaves. One day, Alysoun might like to wear it.

Past University College, I turned down Magpie Lane to Merton. There was building work in progress in the first quad of Merton – the college seemed forever to be adding a wing here, a new floor there, though there was still no sign of that promised library. Once it was built, they would need to fill it with books, so I had high hopes of them, in the way of increased business. What would Philip Olney do then? Could he guard access to the books as jealously as he did at present? It would be more difficult to keep a watch on a whole library instead of simply two adjacent rooms. And surely the purpose of the library would be to provide books for all the Fellows of the college to peruse. Well, I would watch with interest, if the library was made manifest in my own lifetime.

As usual, the porter made no impediment to my entering the college, and as I crossed the quad I nodded to a few of the Fellows I knew. Most were customers of my shop. Some of the younger ones had been fellow students with me in the past. Had my life taken another course, I too would be sharing this tranquil peace – tranquil but for the hammering of the builders. A life devoted to study, the day-to-day worries of getting a living lifted from my shoulders. A mind devoted to intellectual study. Oh, it had its temptations! But that would have meant no precious years with Elizabeth, however tragic their end. No Alysoun. No Rafe. No pride in making my bookshop the finest in Oxford, which I knew, without modesty, it was.

The scholar's life was in many ways enviable, but was it not also a sort of prolonged childhood? The college enfolded you and became a kind of parent, provided you with a home and companions, fed you, kept you safe, shielded you from the harsher realities of life outside these tranquil quadrangles.

I was still turning over these thoughts as I climbed the staircase to the book rooms. Philip Olney answered my knock with a peremptory 'Come!' He was sitting in shadow, with the shutters half closed, although this was one of the rooms to have glass in the windows, so that light could be provided without the risk of draughts disturbing precious papers within. For once, he did not have a book in his hands, but was sitting hunched up, seemingly doing nothing.

Even in the partial light, I was shocked at the change in him, just since I had seen him a few days ago. He looked ill. He had always the pasty complexion of a man who spends most of his life indoors, but now his skin showed an almost yellow tinge, like old parchment which has been left exposed to too much harsh sunlight. There were dark shadows under his eyes as though he had not slept, and his hands, which were gripping the arms of the heavy oak chair he favoured, were trembling.

Best not to show that I was disconcerted by this unexpected sign of weakness in my old adversary. I was here, after all, purely on a matter of business.

'Good day to you, Master Olney,' I said, in a cheerful voice. 'I have brought this very fine bestiary, as I promised, but I fear you must make your decision today, for Master Caundish of Gloucester College has already got wind of it, and is hot on the trail. I cannot deny him, if you do not wish to purchase it for Merton.'

I walked toward the window. 'You will not be able to examine it properly without light.'

Not asking for permission, I drew open the shutters and allowed the strengthening afternoon sunlight to stream in. He raised a hand to shield his eyes.

'The bestiary?' he said vaguely. 'Ah, the bestiary.'

He seemed to recall himself from some way off and stirred in his chair. I laid my satchel on his desk, unbuckled the straps, and carefully drew out the book. Olney became a little more animated and leaned forward as I unwrapped the bestiary from the cloth and laid it before him.

As he picked it up and stroked the binding with the true connoisseur's touch, he seemed more like his usual self, though I noticed that his hands still had a slight tremor. Carefully he began to turn over the pages. He was not a man to be rushed. He would examine every page for damage or flaws, as well as assessing the quality of the workmanship. I knew he would be unable to find any fault, but I was not sure whether he – or Merton – would be prepared to pay the price I intended to ask.

Olney's assessment would, I knew, take some time and there was no point in trying to hurry him, so I found myself a stool and sat down, prepared to wait. I took care to place it fairly close to the shelf reserved for the Irish Psalter, but not so close as to arouse suspicion, even in Olney's strange mood. What ailed him? Something was clearly worrying him. In fact, he looked sick with nerves, like a man about to undergo some great ordeal, or to endure a punishment. Had someone discovered that the Irish book was missing? I had found it strange that when I was last here, Olney had claimed that Master Basset had given instructions about the handling of the book. Then there had been that curious visit of Basset to my shop (where he had never set foot before), when he had warned me off taking an interest in that same book.

It all pointed to Basset himself being aware that something was amiss with the book, so it could not be fear of him that left Olney looking sick. Perhaps he dreaded discovery by the warden of Merton, Warden William

Durant. Less easy going than his predecessor, Robert Trenge, Durant might well inflict serious disciplinary measures on a *librarius* who allowed the college's greatest literary treasure to be stolen. Olney might lose his position as guardian of the book collection. Might he even lose his Fellowship? That would be enough to turn any man sick.

At last Olney closed the book and laid it on his desk, keeping his hands possessively cupped around it, a promising sign.

'I can find no damage,' he said grudgingly.

'Indeed you will not,' I said crisply. 'Not only is it in perfect condition, it is an exceptionally fine specimen. I do not believe I have had a better one through my hands. I must, therefore, charge accordingly. And you will understand that Master Caundish is also most anxious to obtain it for the specialised collection he is amassing.'

'How much?'

I named a figure about half as much again as I was hoping to get.

He shook his head. 'Too much.'

I shrugged. 'Very well. I quite understand if you do not have the funds to buy it.'

I got up and went over, reaching out to wrap the book and return it to my satchel. He snatched it away and held it close to his chest.

'Wait! I am not sure... I must speak to Master Basset... he may have funds...'

With that he rose to his feet and hurried out of the room. I was astonished. In all my previous dealings with Olney, he had the authority to make such decisions for himself. Basset was a keen bibliophile and a collector of books himself, although he never dealt with me directly, only sometimes through intermediaries. His consent was not normally required before the purchase of a book for the college. Perhaps changes had taken place at Merton.

But now was my chance, during the brief time Olney was out of the room. Basset's set was in the same quadrangle but up a different staircase. As I heard Olney clatter to the bottom of the stairs, I ran to the box which should hold the Irish book. It was inlaid with Bible scenes in carved ivory and it had a lock. I had no need for a key. I picked up the box and weighted it in my hand. The Psalter, a little larger than the common size, filled with whole page illuminations, was quite heavy. There was no doubt about it. The box weighed of nothing but itself.

It was empty.

When Olney returned, I was standing at the window, my hands resting on the sill, looking out at the stretch of greensward which reached to the town wall. No doubt the college would build there eventually, but for the present, some of the Fellows were enjoying the sun on this Saturday afternoon, lectures finished until Monday. Several benches had been placed for them to take their ease – some in the shade of a few old and lichened apple trees, some in the sun.

I wondered about those apple trees. Perhaps this had once been some wealthy burgess's holding, with an extensive garden and a fine orchard on its south side. Merton was not a new college, like Queen's. It had been founded nearly a hundred years ago, so the land would have been purchased then. Established shortly before the pestilence struck the town, Queen's College – named for our popular Queen Philippa – had been able, like many other colleges of the university, to take advantage of whole families wiped out, with properties within the town fallen vacant and going cheap. The colleges and the abbeys now owned the greater portion of the town, even where they had not yet built, but had shops and houses let out to tenants. I was grateful that my father-in-law had had the foresight to buy the freehold of our shop and house outright.

Olney came in, still showing the signs of worry on his face, but more decisive than he had appeared when I arrived.

'Master Basset has agreed to your price,' he said curtly, 'though in my opinion it is too high. If you present your bill to the bursar, he will see that you are paid.'

He laid the bestiary on his desk, but kept his hand on it.

As a matter of business, I have learned to keep a blank face, so I was careful not to show my astonishment that they had accepted my demand. Perhaps they were both too distracted by the matter of the Irish book to give any energy to haggling over the price of the bestiary. It would certainly be an ornament to their collection.

'Very well,' I said pleasantly.

I removed the book firmly from under Olney's hand, wrapped it, and returned it to my satchel. I was not such a fool as to leave it here, unpaid for.

'I will call on the bursar on Monday with the account made out, and if it is paid then, I shall hand the book to him.'

That would stop any deceitful delays on their part. They should not have the book until I received payment. I had grown tired of their prevarications.

Olney opened his mouth to protest, but I could see that he had not the heart for it. 'Very well,' he said abruptly, sitting in his chair and picking up some papers by way of dismissal. I crossed to the door, smiling to myself. He might assume a superior air, but I had won that round. I would have an ample profit on the book, and if the bursar paid me on Monday, I could take a little extra with me when I rode out to pay the Widow Preston in Banbury the same day. And not only had I secured far more than I had expected for the bestiary. I had now established beyond doubt that the Irish Psaltery was no longer in Merton.

I was halfway through the door when Olney spoke again.

'That student you mentioned before, Master Elyot, found in the river.'

I turned back. 'Aye? William Farringdon. You would know him. He was to take up a Fellowship here in the autumn.'

He blenched at my mention of the name.

'He drowned, did he not?'

'Nay.' I paused. 'He did not drown. He was murdered. Stabbed in the back.'

He made no reply, but he had no need. I could read on his face that he already knew.

—

I spent the rest of the afternoon in the garden with the children. The days of the week were generally so busy, especially during the university terms, that I hardly saw them save at meal times and when I put them to bed, but I tried to keep the afternoon on Saturdays for them. This was also the time when they had their lessons, though I tried to intersperse these with play.

The puppy was still a novelty, and they were full of news about the rest of the litter.

'The miller from Trill's Mill is a friend of Jonathan's,' Alysoun said. 'And he took the biggest puppy. He also said he knew someone who might take the last one, the one Miller Wooton did not want. 'Tis a widow who lives down Grandpont, near Denchworth Bow. I think he said she is his aunt. She lives alone, and there's always strangers passing, coming to Oxford. He thinks she would like a dog for company and to keep her safe.'

'That is good news,' I said. 'I am sure the puppy will be happier there than out at Holywell Mill.'

She wrinkled her nose. 'I do not like Miller Wooton.'

I glanced down at her in surprise. We were sitting on the bench under the pear tree, with her Latin book between us.

'I did not know that you had met Miller Wooton.'

She flushed guiltily, and began to chew her thumbnail, a sure sign that she had been caught out in some misdemeanour.

'I am not cross, Alysoun, but it is best you tell me.'

'He was horrid to Jonathan, Papa! Last harvest time, Jonathan took just a few of the miller's apples. They had fallen on the ground, because he never bothers to pick them all. Not having a family, I suppose there are too many of them for him. Anyway, he would never have missed these, just left them to be eaten by the blackbirds and the field mice or rot away. But he caught Jonathan and gave him such a beating! His back was covered with red stripes. He dared not let his father see, so I borrowed some of Aunt Margaret's salve and dressed them for him.'

'Did you tell Aunt Margaret?'

She wriggled. 'It was only the smallest little bit of salve, Papa, and Jonathan did not want anyone to know but me.'

'So you have not seen Miller Wooton yourself?'

She bit her thumbnail so furiously that a piece broke off and she spat it out.

'Well—'

'Aye?'

'I was picking up apples too, and when we saw the miller, we both ran, but Jonathan tripped. I got away, but the miller saw me. Afterwards, I went back and helped Jonathan come home. He was really hurt, Papa, but the miller did not want those apples. He just wanted to stop us having them.'

'Nevertheless, it was stealing,' I said firmly. 'And I do not know why you did it. We have plenty of apples.'

'They were not for us, they were for Jonathan and his father. They only have one apple tree and it is dying.'

'Next apple-picking time,' I said, 'we will give the Bakers a big basket of apples. Remind me.'

'Thank you, Papa!' She stood up and kissed me on the cheek.

'Enough of apples,' I said. 'Sit down now. Rafe has read his horn book for me. Have you prepared your Latin reading?'

'Aye.' She picked up the book and found the place, marked with a grass stem. She pushed her hair behind her ears and began, reading each sentence first in Latin, then translating it. After half a dozen sentences she stopped.

'Papa, why is Caesar always withdrawing to winter quarters?'

'It is what soldiers do, my pet.' I remembered thinking the same at her age. 'It would be too cold for them to stay out in the field. They were very good at building forts very quickly, so they could be snug for the winter. I expect they spent the time sitting by the fire, polishing their boots and telling stories.'

'Like Walter?'

'Aye, just like Walter.'

Probably the same stories, I thought, though with Roman variations. Jestyn was probably called Julius and had to steal the *lares* and *penates* from some rich man's house.

When Margaret returned from her visit to the Cross Inn, the children were trying to persuade Rowan to fetch a stick they were throwing for her, but she simply sat down and looked puzzled, or else wandered away to rootle amongst the long grass near our garden wall. I was dozing, off and on, for to tell the truth, my head still ached from the blow I had taken.

Margaret sank down beside me and eased off her shoes. 'The right one pinches.'

'Get the cordwainer to look at it.'

'I will.'

She picked up a scrap of paper I had left lying on top of Alysoun's Latin book.

'What is this? It looks like magical symbols. What have you been teaching the child?'

'The Greek alphabet. We were writing out all the family names in Greek letters. That is Margaret.' I pointed. 'And that is Rowan.'

She looked disapproving. 'Almost as bad as magical symbols. What does the child want with learning Greek?'

'It was only the letters. She asked me about them. I do not know whether I shall teach her the language. For now, Latin is enough.'

'So I should think. She is only six, and only a girl.'

'A girl with a bright mind. I would hate to see that mind caged, like a singing bird which cannot take flight.' I paused for a moment before venturing on a difficult subject.

'I would not have her married off when she is scarcely more than a child.'

'I was fourteen.'

'As I said, scarcely more than a child.'

'I managed. So will she.'

'Not at that age,' I said decisively, patting her hand. 'How did you find the Farringdons?'

'Still in great distress. I think they understand now that William had become tangled in something underhand and criminal. So distant from the boy's true nature. I always found him a decent, honest lad. And to add to their distress, they know now that he was doing it to relieve them of their poverty, so they feel in a sense responsible, both for his actions and his death.'

I sighed. 'I suppose it is to be expected. A mother will always feel responsible for her child, and the girl was clearly devoted to her brother.'

'She is a good wench, concerned for her mother as well as for her brother. She is the sort of girl who would make a better companion for our Alysoun than that idle scamp Jonathan Baker.'

'Juliana is a mite too old for Alysoun. Twice her age and mature beyond her years. Besides,' I said mildly, 'Jonathan is a good lad. He needs a woman's care, but he is kind and loyal. Alysoun could do worse for a playmate.'

Margaret shook her head. 'As she grows older you must look for better companions for her. Girls of her own state in life. And – if you must have your way – literate.'

'Time enough,' I said. 'Did you sit with the Farringdons all this time?'

'Nay, I persuaded them to walk about the town a little with me. There were some longing looks at our shops, but nothing bought. I am sure they are truly without means.'

'Since the father's death and the loss of the pension, that is certainly the case. Little wonder that William was so desperate to help them. It is hard to know how to give them any assistance now. If William had but taken up his Fellowship at Merton, the college might have been moved to do somewhat for them, but he was not to have been admitted until the Michaelmas Term. I know that Jordain is doing all he can – the funeral mass, their stay at the Cross Inn – but he has little enough himself. He has no family money, only what he earns from his teaching. He makes a pretence that Hart Hall is paying, but it is a myth. The only money Hart Hall has is the fees from the students for their lodging, and the better part of that goes to Stapledon's Exeter College, which owns the property and charges an exorbitant rent.'

'Can we help?'

'A little, perhaps, but you know that there is never a great deal left when I have paid for my materials and given Walter and Roger their wages. Our family also has to eat. The children are growing and forever needing new clothes and shoes. I know that you make most of their clothes, but the cloth must be bought, and shoes, even for children, do not come cheap.'

'Aye, Rafe's feet seem to grow a size every month. I think he will have big feet like our father.'

We both laughed. It was an old family joke.

'But, Nicholas, there is always my widow's dower.'

'That we must not touch,' I said emphatically. 'I will see what I can do, but I have another widow with a daughter in Banbury awaiting money from me.'

'With the Death and the French wars, the world is full of widows and orphans these days,' she said sadly.

On Sunday morning the students from Hart Hall processed solemnly down Hammer Hall Lane to attend Mass at St Peter-in-the-East. They must have been thinking, as I was, that last Sunday William had been among them. I wondered whether he had made his confession that day, as the students often did, for before the next day was done, he was dead. I shivered at the thought of him going into the next life unshriven.

Jordain did not, as he usually did, lead this procession of his students, but arrived shortly afterwards, escorting Mistress Farringdon and Juliana. Both were veiled, for I suppose they had no mourning garments and there was little else they could do to mark their grief for William. Juliana's hair had been loose when I had seen her at the inn, but now it was pulled into plaits so tight, wound round her head, that her eyebrows were drawn upwards. Both mother and daughter held themselves severely under control, however. There would be no weeping during the service.

Margaret went to join them, taking Rafe with her, and Alysoun, who had me by the hand, followed. I was not sure how much she understood of their plight, but she knew they were William's mother and sister. Earlier in the morning I had decided that I must explain to her that William was dead, though not that he was murdered, and that his family was here in Oxford. When we reached the Farringdons, Alysoun slipped her other hand into Juliana's. The girl looked startled for a moment, then smiled down at Alysoun.

'I am Juliana,' she whispered.

'I'm Alysoun.'

As we stood all through the long service, watching the priest and his acolytes up by the altar, separated from us by the rood screen, the two girls clung together. I let the familiar Latin wash over me, with its mysteries and awe, and wondered, as I often did, what the lay parishioners made of it all. Apart from members of the university, at least half the congregation was made up of townsfolk, most of whom would not understand a word of the service. Did they find some comfort in the familiarity of the ritual, even if the words passed incomprehensibly over their heads?

There was a fellow student of ours who had often argued this point with us. Nowadays he was a Regent Master of Arts, like Jordain, and in fact he was the very man whose lectures on rhetoric William and Peter de Wallingford had attended. John Wycliffe had argued – and indeed very persuasively – that the Bible should be translated into English, so that any man might read its words for himself. It was a dangerous and radical idea, verging on heresy. As students we had urged him to be careful who heard him put forth such ideas. I had not seen much of him of late, being taken up with my secular life, but I reckoned that he probably still held his radical views. You cannot often turn a fanatic from the path on which he has set his foot, whatever the catastrophe that lies ahead.

The congregation seemed larger than usual that day, and with the weather improved again, it grew stifling in the church. I knew most of the parishioners, but there were a few unfamiliar faces. A group of three women clung together near the west door, by their clothes – cheap and provocative – they were whores from the warren of half derelict cottages further up the lane. They did not usually show themselves here, but word of William's death would have spread throughout the parish. The violent death of one so young is bound to force folk to confront a fear of mortality which can normally be thrust aside in the daily business of living. The whores were young, no older than William. One, indeed, looked no older than Juliana.

As the service drew to an end and the crowd eased cramped limbs and stirred, I noticed another unexpected face. Standing well back in the south aisle, where he would be all but hidden when the door to the churchyard was opened, was Philip Olney. This was not his parish. Indeed, Merton had its own chapel, where services were held for the members of the college. It was strange for him to attend Mass here. It was clear, however, that he had no wish to be seen, so I allowed my glance to pass over him without giving any indication that I had noticed him. Perhaps in the nervous state I had noticed the previous day, he was unwilling to worship amongst his colleagues.

The rector moved down through the congregation and stood by the south door, smiling and greeting people as they drifted out into the sunshine. Those who wished to make confession remained behind, including Mistress Farringdon and Juliana. The whores, too, I saw, felt in need of penance and absolution.

Margaret and I, with the children, converged on Jordain in the churchyard, where he hovered, clearly waiting for his charges to join him.

'Will you come and dine with us, Jordain?' Margaret said. 'And bring Mistress Farringdon and the girl? It is a sad business for them, taking all their meals at an inn in a strange town. It might be some comfort to come to a family meal.'

Jordain hesitated. 'I have promised to show them Hart Hall. They wished to see William's room, and where he studied. They were to come there to dine.'

'Jordain,' Margaret said decisively, 'you cannot possibly provide them with the kind of meal you and the students eat. What is it today? More boiled cabbage and stale bread? Or do you rise to the glories of pease pudding?'

'I like pease pudding,' Jordain said with a mulish look. Then he laughed. 'Perhaps you are right, though I believe there was to be a little bacon with the cabbage today. Extravagance! But have you enough to feed three extra?'

'Ample. I spent yesterday evening baking. I have a custard tart and an apple pie to follow a beef pottage, and today's new bread. You cannot refuse the poor women a decent meal. You may take them to see William's room after you have eaten.'

'Very well, and my thanks to you. I will wait until they have made confession, but you need not stay. The children will want to be away home.'

'Rowan cries when we leave her,' Rafe confided.

'Rowan? Oh, the puppy. I expect she thinks you have abandoned her,' Jordain said. 'We cannot have Rowan crying. Away with you, Rafe, and let her into the garden.'

As we came down the lane, I saw Philip Olney ahead of us, scuttling along in an oddly furtive manner. When we reached the High, I expected to see him heading right, in the direction of Merton, but instead he was hurrying the opposite way, toward the East Bridge. I could not imagine what business he could have in that part of Oxford, and on a Sunday too. Altogether, he had been behaving strangely in the last two days. However, I could not imagine that it had any bearing on the disappearance of the Irish Psalter and the murder of William Farringdon, so I dismissed Philip Olney from my mind.

Tomorrow I would deliver the bestiary to Merton and collect the payment, then I would ride out to Banbury and hand over Widow Preston's money, no doubt to her great relief. I did not keep a horse myself, rarely having need of one, but I could hire one for the day from one of the inns. It occurred to me that it would be possible to turn aside to Godstow nunnery on my way back, provided I was not too late. If I was admitted as a visitor, I would call upon William's cousin, Emma Thorgold, or rather Sister Benedicta. It was unlikely that she had yet heard of her cousin's fate. Since, according to Juliana, she and William had been as close as brother and sister, it was an unkindness to keep her any longer in ignorance of his death.

I wondered whether the fondness between them had been more than that of brother and sister, which might partly account for Emma's reluctance to enter the convent. Still, even if it had been closer, nothing could have come of it, for they were too close in degrees of kinship. The church would never have permitted their union. All this was nothing but pure speculation. The two young people were probably no more than affectionate cousins. However, it would be interesting to meet the girl, even if she could throw no light on what scheme William had been involved in. If he visited her regularly, as Juliana had said, it was possible that she might know why he was making a copy of the Psalter and what his plans for his family might have been.

Jordain followed us within the half hour, and because I am sure that we were all determined to make no mention of William's death, we had a pleasant meal. Margaret had made a particular effort, for she felt great sympathy for

Mistress Farringdon, having lost sons herself. Both mother and daughter had shed their veils after leaving church, so that if one closed one's mind firmly on the reason why they were here, it might have been any pleasant neighbourly visit. The two women were already on terms of friendship. Juliana set herself to amuse the children and took them out into the garden as soon as we had finished eating. There was nothing left for Jordain and me to do but to chat idly about the end of year debates, and which of his students he expected to acquit themselves well.

At last, however, it was time for Jordain to take the Farringdons to see William's room, which cast a sadness over us all, although Margaret had extracted a promise from Mistress Farringdon – whose name, it appeared was Maud – that she would come to spend the next day at our house, though I would not see them, since my trip to Banbury would occupy the entire day.

I walked with Jordain and the Farringdons as far as Catte Street, then carried on to the Mitre, to bespeak myself a horse for early the following morning. Somewhat to my shame, I was looking forward to my day away from the shop. I rarely had the cause or opportunity to leave Oxford, so that it felt already like a kind of holiday. The weather looked set to remain fair, I enjoyed riding, and the road to Banbury lay through beautiful country. It would be good to escape the worries over William's murder and the missing book, not to mention the attack I had suffered. Altogether, it would make a pleasant diversion.

Chapter Ten

In order to ride all the way to Banbury and back in the day, I would need to make a very early start on Monday, so I asked Margaret to wake me when she rose to bake the day's bread. With a grey pre-dawn light in the sky, I came down to the kitchen yawning, but already the air was filled with the warm, heart-lifting smell of bread in the oven beside the kitchen hearth.

'You must make do with yesterday's bread to break your fast,' she said by way of greeting. 'Unless you want to wait for this batch.'

I shook my head as I pulled up a stool to the table. 'Even your day-old bread is good, Margaret. And I must be away as soon as possible, if I am to be home before dark.'

'There is a mouthful of last night's custard tart you may have as well. And I will pack you some cheese and cold bacon in your scrip, that you need not stop for a meal at an inn. For,' she said darkly, 'who knows what those inns in Banbury may serve?'

I laughed. 'I daresay the people of Banbury do not die of it. But I thank you, it will save me time. If I am not too late on the return journey, I shall call at Godstow. I do not know whether they will admit me to see William's cousin, but I shall try for it.'

'I have heard that Godstow is not so strict as some nunneries. They give house room to noble ladies who wish to withdraw from the world for a time, without taking the veil, but whether they will allow a man who is not a relative to visit a novice – that might be asking too much.'

'Well, I shall try. Someone should tell her of her cousin's death, and it may be that she will know something that will throw light on this scheme to copy the Psalter.'

She looked dubious. 'I cannot think that she will know anything, but you are right. The lad has been dead a week now. The novice should be told. Maud Farringdon agrees that William used to visit his cousin regularly, as much as once a week, so she will be wondering why he has not come. Poor maid! She was forced into that life much against her will. I do not hold with such things. Man or woman, either should have a true vocation before giving themselves up to the religious life. Any other way is pure hypocrisy, and can lead to nothing but misery and despair.'

'That is very true. I know the girl was hostile to it from the start, but that was nearly a year ago,' I said. 'Perhaps by now she may be reconciled. It cannot be so terrible a life. Not very different from becoming an Oxford Fellow.'

'Which you, very properly, refused.' She passed me my scrip, loaded with food for my journey.

'Aye. Very true. Now I must away. I have left a note for Walter about today's tasks for them both.'

'Do you go to Merton first? You said last night that you would deliver the bestiary.'

'It is here.' I picked up my satchel. 'I will collect my horse first, to give the bursar of Merton a little more time to leave his bed, though I know he is an early riser. I want the price of the book in my purse before they change their minds.'

Very few people were yet abroad as I walked up the High. It was more than another hour before lectures began, and some students would scramble out of their beds just in time, obliged to forego even the meagre breakfast provided by their halls. At the Mitre I found my horse ready saddled, as I had requested the previous day, and led him to the block so I could mount. I had chosen a sturdy gelding, a bright chestnut bay called Rufus. I had hired him before and knew that he had the stamina for a long day's riding, even though he had no great turn of speed.

By the time I had ridden him down to Merton there was more activity in the streets. Oxford was waking up as the church bells sounded five o'the clock. The porter was surprised to see me mounted, but made no objection to my hitching Rufus to the ring beside the gate before I stepped through the wicket.

'Do you know if the bursar has gone to his office yet?' I asked the man.

'Aye, Master Elyot. Just this minute. You will catch him now.'

I cannot say that the bursar was pleased to see me, or at all willing to part with the college's money, but clearly he had been given his instructions, either by Philip Olney or Allard Basset. The transaction took but a few minutes. I placed the very substantial sum in my purse and stowed it, together with the purse for Widow Preston, inside the neck of my shirt for safety. The bestiary I drew out of my satchel and laid on the bursar's desk. As I fear often happens, I was very reluctant to part with it, however good the price.

'That seems little enough for so much money.' The bursar gave a disapproving sniff. No doubt he was thinking of the building works, and all that might be done for the same sum.

'It is a very valuable book,' I said coldly. 'See to it that you handle it with care and deliver it to Master Olney as soon as possible.'

'I will, when I can. He did not spend last night in college.'

This was astonishing information, but I believe I was able to conceal my surprise, for the bursar was not looking at me, continuing instead to regard the book with dislike. I bade him good-day, and returned to my horse. Why had Olney stayed away from college overnight? As far as I knew, he had no family to speak of, only some distant cousins down in the West Country. And he certainly had few if any friends amongst the townsmen of Oxford. Well, it was not my affair, though I remembered Olney hurrying away furtively from St Peter's after Mass yesterday.

My way took me to Carfax, then up Northgate Street to the town gate. Beyond, past the church of St Mary Magdalen, the road opened out into the wide expanse of St Giles, where St Frideswide's Fair is held every autumn. St Giles church stands at the far end of this long tree-lined triangular space. Strictly speaking, Oxford ends at the North Gate, but the houses and workshops that run along both sides of St Giles were built before ever I came to Oxford. They are without the security of the town wall in time of trouble, but they make up for it in the size of each messuage here, where extensive land at the back provides enough room to keep a cow and a pig, as well as an orchard and vegetable garden, more than enough for a family. Beyond the houses on my right lay

Durham College, beyond those on my left, the Carmelite Friary, both occupying sites much larger than those of the colleges within the town walls. Gloucester College also lay outside the walls, further away past the Carmelite Friary. It would not be long, I suspected, before more colleges burst out beyond the wall.

When I reached St Giles church at the north end of the fair ground, the road forked and returned to normal size. The left fork led to Woodstock, where earlier kings had a hunting lodge, grown into a palace some two centuries ago. That on the right was my road to Banbury. On my journey back to Oxford I would need to turn aside to the other road, for leading off the road to Woodstock lay the lane to the villages of Wytham and Wolvercote, and between them, Godstow Abbey.

It was nearly thirty miles to Banbury, so I took it steadily, alternating stretches at a brisk canter with a quarter of an hour or so at a walk, to pace Rufus and not tire him. When I reckoned I was about halfway, just past the village of Middleton Stoney, the horse and I had a rest under a broad oak, barely into leaf yet. We both drank from a clear stream, and I ate some of the provisions Margaret had stowed in my scrip. I also took the opportunity to transfer some of the Merton coin to the purse for Mistress Preston, so that she might share in my good fortune in securing a better than expected price for the bestiary.

When I thought Rufus was sufficiently rested, I mounted again and headed for Banbury. There were few people on the road, mostly farmers and villeins about their daily work, for it was not market day in either Oxford or Banbury. The villages I passed through had all the sad, half deserted appearance that was to be seen everywhere in England since the pestilence. In one there seemed to be not a soul left alive, doors hanging open on cottages where no smoke rose from cookfires, and birds nesting in the thatch, where they were busily wearing away the roofs. A few gaunt dogs scavenged amongst the abandoned homes.

Yet for all that, it was a pleasant ride, if one looked away from the signs of human desolation. The hedgerows on either side of the road were alive with bird song, newborn lambs frolicked in the fields, and when, from time to time, we forded the shallow streams that crossed our path, plump trout, gleaming with opalescent sides like jewels, darted away, then hung in the quietly flowing water, waiting for us to pass.

By the sun it was not yet midday when I reached Banbury. I found an inn where I could stable Rufus, paying an ostler to feed and water him, then I went in search of Mistress Preston. Since she was newly moved to the town, I feared it might take me some time to find her, but I started by enquiring from a baker in the main street of shops. Everyone must have bread and I thought it unlikely that, in a rented cottage, the widow would have the means to bake her own bread. Like most townsfolk she would buy this daily necessity from a baker.

I had chosen well. The baker knew the widow, not only since she had come to live in Banbury but from earlier years, when she had brought produce from the family farm to market.

'A good woman,' he said, arranging a fresh batch of loaves on the counter. 'Always worked hard and tried to keep the farm going. That husband of hers, they say he was a clever man, but he was a poor farmer. She is better off without him, her and the girl. They've taken a cottage just a step from here.'

I doubted that the widow would agree with him about the loss of her husband, but I held my peace.

He came out into the street and pointed ahead. 'You see that tavern there, sign of the Black Bull? There's a turn down to the left, just beyond. Three houses down, that's where she's living.'

He was clearly curious about why I wanted her, so I enlightened him.

'I am a bookseller from Oxford. She has sold me some books of her husband's, and I have brought the money for them.'

He blew out a great breath and smiled. 'So the man was good for something after all! She'll be that glad of the coin. That is good news to hear. That daughter of hers has little to hope for in the future, poor wench. As a child she could chatter away with the best. Now she lives in a world of silence.'

With the smell of his fresh bread enticing me, I could not walk away but bought a loaf, too big for my scrip, so I stowed it in my satchel, which was empty now that the bestiary had been delivered.

The lane past the Black Bull Inn was barely wide enough for a horse to pass, and the cottages here were tiny, though they seemed clean and well kept. My tap on the door was answered at once by Mistress Preston herself.

'Master Elyot!' she exclaimed. 'I did not look to see you here in Banbury. I thought to come with the carter next Oxford market, to see whether…' Her voice trailed away. I thought she would probably have said, 'to see whether you had any money for me', but was too well mannered to do so.

'Come away in,' she said, motioning me into a room which seemed to form the only accommodation on the ground floor of the cottage, though a door at the back led to what must be a scrap of a garden, perhaps room enough to keep a few hens.

The daughter was sitting by the hearth, working at lace laid over a cushion. She smiled and bobbed her head, but her fingers never ceased throwing the lace bobbins in some complicated pattern. I had noticed a rough chimney projecting from the roof, as though it had been added after the cottage had been built, for the building looked old, the timbers sagging a little and the daub walls bulging like a fat alderman's paunch. There was a hook on a hinged arm for a pot and a three-legged vessel standing close to the fire, so this was where they both cooked and lived. A ladder led up to the roof space above, a garret where they must sleep. From the height of the cottage I doubted whether they would be able to stand up there. It was a far cry from the farm house where they must have lived before, but it was spotless, their few possessions arranged on shelves. A coffer, which had probably come with them, must hold their clothes, while a small table and a few stools provided a place to prepare food and eat.

'Please sit, Master Elyot. I am afraid we have only stools.'

She blushed and I realised that it shamed her to receive me in the circumstances to which they had been reduced.

'I have here the payment for the books you brought me, mistress,' I said, taking out the purse for her. 'And I have already sold the bestiary for a better price than I expected, so I have added a little extra.'

'The bestiary? Oh, was that the book with all the animal pictures? Sissy always loved to look at those.' She cast a fond glance at her daughter.

'Well,' I said, 'it has gone to Merton College, and they are very pleased to have it.'

Privately, I thought it a pity that it could not have remained here, to give pleasure to the deaf girl, rather than lie on a shelf in a book room, occasionally fingered by dour-faced scholars. However, I supposed the money would bring them comfort and some security.

'You are so kind to come all this way to bring the money,' she said, and there were tears in her eyes, which I pretended not to see. 'Will you have something to eat, Master Elyot?'

She had taken a seat opposite me, but now sprang to her feet. I could see her calculating how she might offer me whatever she had put aside for their supper. Her gaze had lingered on the fat purse, but she had too much sensitive pride to tip out the contents.

'Nay, that is very kind of you, mistress,' I said, 'but I have the long road to ride back to Oxford before nightfall and I must be on my way. I left my horse at an inn by the town gate. I'll collect him and be off.'

I got to my feet, but paused a moment to admire the girl's work, fine as a cobweb, but much more intricate.

'Beautiful,' I said, smiling at her. I think she could understand some words, remembered from the past, when she could hear like anyone else. Or at any rate she under-stood my meaning. I laid my hand for a moment on her shoulder, then turned to her mother.

'She is very skilled,' I said. 'I have never seen it made before. Where did she learn the art?'

'When I was a girl, we had a Flemish woman as a neighbour, and she taught me, then I taught Sissy. It is a craft hardly known in England, but is becoming familiar in the Low Countries. We also make decorative braids, but they are best done with some thread of gold in them. Now I have the money from the books, I shall be able to buy some.'

'I hope you will bring your lace and braids sometime to Oxford market. I think you would get a better price for them there than here in Banbury.'

'Perhaps.' She bobbed a small curtsey by way of thanks. 'At least we may come to St Frideswide's Fair this autumn. They say merchants from London buy there.'

'Aye, they do. And folk come from miles away, keen to buy what they cannot make themselves or buy in their own neighbourhoods. If you are in Oxford, come to visit us, my sister will always be glad to make you welcome.'

She was still thanking me as I left, but I hoped she would not take too long before examining the contents of the purse. It would provide for them comfortably until they could make their living from lace and braid, and would still leave some over to help the girl. Unlike that other girl of a like age, Emma Thorgold, Sissy Preston might choose to enter a nunnery, where she could be safer and happier than in the world outside. A postulant must bring a dower with her when she entered, and the money from her father's books would do that.

Rufus looked well fed and cared for when I collected him, and quite willing to set off again. On this return journey I reckoned we could canter rather more and walk rather less, for when we reached Oxford he could rest in his stall, without a further journey ahead of him. It was barely past midday as we set off on the Oxford road, so I would have time to call at Godstow. The sun was setting later these days, now that we were near the end of May. If all went well, I could see Sister Benedicta and still reach home before dark.

Rufus went well and seemed tireless, but nevertheless I decided to stop halfway again, and while he grazed I ate the rest of the food Margaret had given me, together with nearly half the loaf I had bought from the baker in Banbury. Despite Margaret's dire warnings, the bread was excellent.

Once we were on our way, I found myself growing impatient to reach Godstow, and kept Rufus moving briskly along, dodging the occasional farmer's cart, and having to draw into the verge once to allow a fine and heedless gentleman with half a dozen armed attendants the full width of the road. I had become very curious about this cousin of William's. His young sister had declared passionately that Emma Thorgold had been forced into the convent against her will by an uncaring stepfather. It sounded like the opening of one of Walter's tales – a forlorn orphaned maiden, a cruel step-parent, a forced imprisonment. All it needed was for a prince to ride up, break down the convent walls, and set her free.

But this was no fairy tale. The girl was probably much happier amongst the nuns than she could ever have been had she remained in her stepfather's house after the death of her mother. By now she had probably realised just how lucky she was. The peace and serenity of Godstow, the rhythm of the monastic hours, the tranquil life – all these would almost certainly have reconciled her to her future within the convent. Her aunt and cousin did not believe she had yet taken her final vows, but they might be mistaken. I was not sure, but I thought the novitiate, for a girl who would now be about eighteen, was unlikely to last more than a year. I did not know whether it would be more difficult for me to obtain permission to visit her if she was already a full nun and not merely a novice. Well, I should soon see.

When we were but a few miles from Oxford I found a side road heading west, which would enable me to cut across to the Woodstock road, and so approach the town from the direction in which the village of Wolvercote lay. Godstow Abbey was nearby, built on an island in the Thames north of Oxford and reached by a bridge from Wolvercote or Godstow village, I was not quite certain which, but I was sure it would be clear once I came near, for I knew that Godstow Abbey was large and well endowed.

I found the turn easily enough, for it had been pointed out to me before, although I had never visited the abbey. The country lane, winding through a wood newly in leaf, passed through a string of tiny villages, none of them more than hamlets. Godstow itself was but a cluster of cottages which probably served to house the lay servants of the abbey. At Wolvercote the first glimpse of the Thames had become visible through the trees, and at Godstow a stout wooden bridge led across to the large island on which the abbey was built. As I reached the bridge, I reckoned that there would still be about two hours of daylight left. Time enough to carry out my final errand of the day and be home in time for supper.

At the far end of the bridge stood a substantial gate-house, two storeys high. With most of the day's work finished, the large gate for carts was closed, but the wicket stood open. From the outside, the abbey resembled an Oxford college and I thought my analogy to Margaret was not far off the mark. Surely many women must find fulfilment in such a place, where they could assume the sort of responsibilities never allowed them in the secular world. And for those who might face unwanted forced marriages and the endless danger of child-bearing, it must offer a welcome refuge. I was inclined to be sceptical about Emma Thorgold's perceived misfortune in finding herself lodged here.

Dismounted, I gave a tug at the iron bell-pull, and heard it clang sweetly within the gatehouse, bringing a lay porter trotting smartly out of his room. Beyond him I could see a large court, very like a college quadrangle. All very neat and well maintained. They kept the Benedictine order here, which values useful labour as much as prayer.

'I am here to call on the novice, Sister Benedicta,' I explained, hoping that she was indeed still a novice. 'I come with messages from her family, in especial her aunt, Mistress Farringdon.' I had decided that this approach was most likely to gain me admittance. 'I am Nicholas Elyot, Master of Arts, from Oxford.'

I rarely claimed my title, but I was prepared to use anything which might sway the abbess to give me permission to see the girl.

'Certainly, master,' the porter said respectfully. 'Will you step inside the gatehouse while I speak to Abbess de Streteley? You may tether your horse there.'

He pointed to a ring secured in the wall of the gatehouse. Once I had Rufus hitched, I followed him through the wicket and into the gatehouse. He paused only for the courtesy of pouring me a cup of ale, before setting off briskly for the abbess's house. I was glad of the ale, for my throat was dry from the dust of the road, but I did not remain inside the gatehouse. The porter had lit a small fire against the cooler air of the evening and I found the small room stuffy. I did not venture far until I had permission, but I stepped just beyond the threshold and studied the place while I sipped the ale. It was cool and good, flavoured with rosemary and bay, and something else that I could not identify.

Godstow Abbey was a prosperous place. Founded originally with ample lands, then further endowed nearly two hundred years ago by the second King Henry, when his much loved mistress, Rosamund, daughter of Lord Walter de Clifford, was buried here. That was an old scandal, with many lurid tales attached to the affair and the jealousy of Queen Eleanor, but who knew the truth, so long afterwards?

What was undeniable was the prosperity to be seen here. All the buildings were of stone, even the stables and outbuildings, the local limestone, glowing like honey as the sun sank toward the west. There was a fine abbey church and the usual convent buildings – refectory, dortoir, chapter house, infirmary – all connected by elegant arched cloisters. Set a little apart was a large guest house, for Godstow accommodated not only travellers but also those more permanent guests of whom Margaret had spoken. The other large, separate building must be the abbess's private dwelling, for I saw the porter knock before being admitted there. I could not determine at first what the small building beside the gatehouse might be, until I noticed a middle-aged man in clerical garb vigorously wielding a spade in the adjoining garden. This must be the nuns' priest. Nuns may conduct simple services and manage all the secular requirements of their community, but they cannot take confession or administer the sacraments. Where a nunnery is close to another religious establishment, the nuns have the pastoral care of a neighbouring priest. In this remote place they were provided with their own spiritual guide.

The porter soon made his way back across the courtyard, and I could tell from his smile that my request had been successful.

'The Lady Abbess is willing for you to speak to Sister Benedicta. She is sending her clerk, Sister Clemence, to conduct you to the visitors' room. She will be here shortly.'

'I thank you,' I said, handing him my empty cup, 'and for the ale also. I have ridden to Banbury and back today, and my throat was as parched as week-old bread! Tell me, I can see the abbey church there beside the main monastic buildings, but is that not also a church?'

I pointed to what looked like a tiny chapel, just beyond the priest's house, not a quarter the size of the abbey church.

'Oh, that is St Thomas's chapel,' he said. 'We lay servants worship there, not with the sisters. And anyone else from Godstow or Wolvercote may come, though there is little room.'

Little enough, I thought, for the many servants, compared with the ample space provided for the nuns, but perhaps the seculars preferred to worship apart. They must spend all their working lives under the strictly devout eyes of the nuns.

'Here is Sister Clemence,' he said. 'She will show you where to go.'

Sister Clemence proved to be a brisk, competent woman of middle years, with an ugly, intelligent face, and a gait which suggested that under the ample folds of her habit she was all bony elbows and knees.

'This way, if you please, Master Elyot,' she said, setting off smartly across the courtyard without looking to see whether I was following.

We passed the cloisters, where I noticed several nuns working in the carrels. In the space between the monastic buildings and the guesthouse there was a postern gate standing ajar in the abbey wall, and beyond it a large walled kitchen garden where both nuns and lay servants were working.

'Our room for visits is here in the guesthouse,' Sister Clemence said, opening the door and ushering me through. 'We do not permit outsiders to set foot in the monastic buildings. I have sent for Sister Benedicta and she should be with you shortly. You may have half an hour.'

She gave me a sharp, assessing look.

'You must leave this door ajar at all times.'

She opened the door to a small parlour, nodded me through, then strode away.

It was a pleasant room, no doubt normally used by the abbey's guests, for it provided some chairs made comfortable with cushions, a luxury I doubted the nuns enjoyed. Someone had left a piece of half-finished embroidery on the deep window seat. The building must be let into the rear abbey wall, for this window looked out beyond the wall, over another part of the extensive grounds. Between rows of carefully tended apple trees I caught the sparkle and flash of the river. Blossom was still abundant, but it had also begun to fall, so that each tree stood with its feet in a skirt of white and pink petals.

'You wished to see me, sir?'

She had moved so softly I had not heard her come in. I turned swiftly to see nothing but a silhouette outlined in the open doorway, my eyes stilled dazed from the reflection of the moving waters.

'Sister Benedicta?' I said.

'That is what they call me.' Her tone was colourless and reserved.

'Please,' I said, unaccountably disconcerted, 'will you not sit?'

She moved forward and took her place on one of the chairs, sitting rigidly upright, her hands tightly clasped on her lap. I thought, Does she know already of her cousin's death?

As I moved away from the window to take a chair near her, the sun flooded in and I could see her fully for the first time. I caught my breath, and felt myself unaccountably colouring. I had expected an awkward, possibly sullen girl. What I saw before me was a young woman of remarkable beauty. Every hair was concealed by the tightly bound wimple of her order, but her skin was pale as cream and her eyes a deep violet blue, which suggested that her hair would be fair. But of course, did they not shave the heads of novices? I felt a rush of disgust at such mutilation of so lovely a creature. Her figure was carefully hidden by the bulky habit, but those clasped hands were delicately boned. To my surprise, I noticed that several fingers of her right hand bore ink stains. There were also spots of coloured inks or paint on both hands – rich scarlet and the precious lapis, used for the Virgin's robe.

She must have caught me staring at her too long, for a faint flush rose in her cheeks.

'You wished to see me, Master Elyot?' she said again, this time with a slight loss of composure.

'Aye,' I said, clearing my throat to cover the fact that I had nearly called her 'Mistress Thorbold'. 'Aye, Sister Benedicta. I come with word from your aunt, Mistress Farringdon. I fear I am the bearer of sad news.'

'It is William,' she said. Her voice was calm, but a convulsive movement of those hands betrayed her. 'Some ill has befallen William.'

'I am afraid that is true,' I said, 'but how did you know?'

'He did not come on Friday. He always walks out here on a Friday afternoon, when he has no lectures. If he cannot come, he sends word by one of the carters who deliver to the abbey. On Friday, there was nothing. Is he hurt?'

I leaned forward. I longed to take her hand, to offer some comfort, but I must not touch a woman of the cloth.

'I am afraid he is dead, Sister Benedicta.'

She flinched, and her eyes filled with tears, but she struggled to contain them and they did not fall.

'How? He was not ill.'

'Nay, he was not ill.' I hesitated. Foolishly I had not planned beforehand how I would break the news. This girl looked as delicate as ivory, but I was sure it was deceptive. Underneath she was iron strong.

'He was stabbed in the back and thrown into the Cherwell,' I said bluntly. 'Murdered.'

She looked away, and her fingers began to pleat the stuff of her habit until I heard a nail catch on the rough cloth.

'I was afraid it might be so.' She looked at me directly. 'Has he been taken, the man who did this evil thing?'

I shook my head, for I was speechless. What did she mean?

'You suspected he was in danger?' My half-formed thoughts had been right after all. This girl might know something which could throw light on the death of her cousin.

She threw aside her disciplined monastic pose and sprang to her feet, crossing to the window and leaning out, as if she needed to breathe the air outside these confining walls. With her back still turned to me, she began to speak.

'When William came back to Oxford after he had visited his home at Christmastide, he was full of concern for his mother and sister. He knew that most of his father's pension would be stopped, but hoped that, out of compassion, some might continue to be paid. It seems, however, that the royal coffers have been emptied by the French wars and by the fall in taxes since the Death. The royal clerks cut off all funds as soon as news of my uncle's death reached them.'

She turned around and leaned back in the window embrasure. The swirl of her habit clung to her, revealing a slender form beneath all that thick cloth.

'Perhaps if the king had heard of it, he might have continued the payments, for he valued my uncle, but no doubt kings have more important matters on their minds than the fate of one widow and two girls.'

Two? I wondered. Then I remembered that there was also a small child, left in the care of neighbours.

'William realised that once the rent on the farm ran out on Lady Day, his family could only remain at the good will of their lord, and I know their lord. He is not a man of generous spirit. William knew that once he took up his Fellowship he would be able to provide for his family, but what to do until then?'

She began to prowl restlessly about the room. 'I do not know quite how it happened, but it seemed he was overheard one evening in the Swindlestock Tavern, speaking of his need to earn some money quickly. He was thinking of coming to ask you for work. Did he?'

She gave me a sharp, accusing look.

'Nay,' I said. 'I wish he had done.'

'However it fell out,' she said, 'it seems that someone at Merton wanted a scribe to carry out some work. Word reached him – again I do not know how – that William had the skills and needed money. This man wanted a personal copy made for him of some book owned by the college, and William agreed to do it. The money offered was generous, although the conditions were strange, and he found them worrying. He was to do the work, not at Merton as he had expected, but in some old deserted building, and he was not to speak of it to anyone.'

'A derelict mill,' I said, 'up a branch of the Cherwell.'

'Aye.' She flashed me a surprised glance. 'William did not like the secrecy, but urgently wanted the money for his mother. He made a start. Did you know that?'

'We found some pages hidden under his mattress.'

She nodded. 'Then somehow he discovered – though he never told me how – that he had not been told the truth.'

Ceasing her prowling, she sat down again opposite me. 'The last time he came to see me – that would be the Friday before last – he said that he had overheard some conversation, though not between whom. It became clear that his copy of this valuable book was not meant for the man who had ordered the work. It would be placed in the box where the old book was kept, and the man who was paying for the copy would keep the original. It was clear theft! William was being made a party to stealing the ancient book, and he would not do it. He had very few dealings with the Merton Fellow himself. There were two men who found the mill and provided all his materials. On the Monday after he was here, he planned to tell them that he would not carry on.'

She pressed her fingers to her mouth, and her voice, which she had kept steady all this time, suddenly broke. 'He had such principles! He swore he would tell them that he was going to report them all to the Warden of Merton, though I begged him to say nothing. I feared for him! And they killed him!'

Now the tears did well up again and ran down her face. She ignored them.

'They did,' I said. 'So that is why they killed him. We could not understand why they should do it, when they needed him. But if he refused to carry on and threatened them—'

'Aye, that is just what he would do. He would be blind to the danger from such men, angry and justified in his anger.'

'Sister Benedicta,' I began.

'Please do not call me that. My name is Emma, and I have not taken final vows.'

'Emma.' I felt uncomfortable saying it, and glanced over my shoulder in case Sister Clemence had returned to end our interview. 'Did William ever tell you *who* was the man at Merton?'

She shook her head. 'Only that it was a man obsessed with books.'

Olney, I thought, but did not speak it aloud.

I thought I could hear footsteps in the distance, crossing toward the guest house. Quickly I said, 'Do you know what he did with the Irish book? It has not been found.'

She gave a wan smile. 'That Friday, the last time I saw him, he brought it with him. I have it in safekeeping.

There is a hidden shelf at the back of my *prie-dieu*. It is there. Shall I fetch it for you?'

I was flooded with an overwhelming sense of relief. The book was safe, not sunk to the bottom of the Cherwell.

'Nay, continue to keep it with you for the present, until the men who killed William are caught and handed over to the sheriff. It will be much safer here than in Oxford.'

The footsteps were drawing near. I stood up and moved away from her, so that we should not be seen so close together.

'Tell me,' I said, 'the ink on your fingers—' I spread my hand, so she could see the identical stains on mine.

She gave a wry laugh. 'I am lettered. They make use of me.'

'I think, by traces of the Virgin's lapis, that you are also an artist.'

She inclined her head.

'It was you!' I exclaimed. 'You made the book of hours that I saw at the bookbinders! With all the creatures in the margins. It is beautiful.'

Embarrassed, she flushed. 'William and I have always loved to draw, ever since we were children. I shall miss him so much.' There was an ache in her voice, but before I could say more, Sister Clemence was at the door.

'You have had your half hour and more, Master Elyot,' she said.

'Master Elyot has brought me news of my cousin's death, Sister Clemence,' the girl said with steady composure. 'It was kind of him to come all the way out to Godstow.'

'I am sorry it was on such a sad errand,' I said. 'When William's affairs are settled, may I call again?' I addressed my remarks to Sister Clemence.

The nun was clearly a strict woman, but not unkind. 'Certainly, if there is further news of her family, you may call. I am sorry to hear of the young man's death. He was to take up a position at Merton College, I believe?'

She was guiding me towards the door and I knew I could have no more speech with Emma Thorgold now. I had failed to ask her when she would be obliged to take her final vows. It was cruel to think of the cage snapping closed on that bright, restless spirit.

'Sister Benedicta,' Sister Clemence called over her shoulder, 'it is nearly time for Vespers. Try to remove some of that ink from yours hands before you attend service.'

I glanced back. The girl was standing with a submissively bowed head. 'I will, sister,' she said. A quick flash of her eyes showed that she knew, as I did, that she could not so easily shed the stigmata of her vocation. Truly, from what I had seen of her work, it *was* her true vocation, and not this forced monasticism.

Sister Clemence saw me all the way out of the wicket gate, as if she suspected me of trying to linger within the sacred walls. Before I was even in the saddle, the wicket was closed and bolted.

—

Rufus seemed not at all tired after his long journey. Refreshed by his rest at Godstow, he sensed he was nearing home and set off eagerly, ignoring my attempts to give him an easy time for these last few miles. We followed the lane up to the Woodstock road at a brisk trot, and once on the broader highway he broke into a canter. I let him have his head, for my mind was whirling with all I had learned at Godstow.

It was now clear not only why William had taken on the work of copying the Irish Psalter, but how it had come about, although his cousin had not known exactly how word had reached the man at Merton. Perhaps William himself had not known. The man at Merton. It must surely be Olney, coveting the Irish book for himself, and arranging to substitute a copy. And he was clearly frightened. Allard Basset must somehow have discovered what was afoot, or at any rate he had discovered that the book was missing from its box. However, he cannot have reported Olney to the Warden but agreed to cover up the fact that the book was missing. Why should he do that? I shook my head. I could see no reason for it, but perhaps it would become clear in time.

And William, in his righteous anger at being made a party to this theft, had gone to meet the two men a week ago at the old mill. Despite Emma's warning to be careful, he must have threatened them with exposure, so that the bigger man, the one of known violence, had stabbed him when he turned his back. With a body on their hands, they had tipped him in the river, no doubt hoping he would drift away under cover of dark, but the current had been flowing faster than they realised, and I happened to be crossing the East Bridge just at the wrong moment. There had been few people about. Had I not been there, they might have been successful.

I slowed Rufus as we reached St Giles and walked him quietly into Oxford and along to the stables of the Mitre in the High.

'Here's a little extra to give him a good feed,' I said, handing sixpence to the ostler. 'He has gone very well for me today.'

I gave the horse a final pat on the neck, then made my way down the High. I had one more thing to do before I went home. As I walked up Catte Street in the gathering dusk, I realised just how tired I was. I was not in the habit of riding so far. Tomorrow I would have the aching muscles to prove it.

There was light shining from the windows of Hart Hall, which were open to the warm spring evening. I could hear laughter and the chatter of young voices, which made me suddenly sad. It was just a week since I had found William's body, and already his fellow students seemed to have forgotten him. I stepped through the door without knocking. Jordain and the students were seated round the table, eating their supper, but Jordain looked up and must have seen something in my face, for he swung his leg over the bench and came to meet me. I beckoned him outside.

'I have found the book,' I said.

Chapter Eleven

Jordain seized my arm as soon as we were out of the students' hearing. 'You have it here?' he said. 'The Irish Psalter?'

I shook my head. 'I did not in fact see it or handle it, but I know where it is. In a place so safe those scoundrels will never find it.'

He shook my arm impatiently. 'Then *where*?'

'In a hidden shelf, in a novice's *prie-dieu*, in Godstow Abbey.'

He rocked back on his heels and let out a gust of breath. 'You have seen William's cousin.'

'Aye, I have. It was not too far out of my way, returning from Banbury. They made no quibble about allowing me to see her, and without a chaperone, though the door must be left open at all times!'

I gave a wry smile. 'As if they expected an old widowed bookseller to deflower one of their novices.'

'Old? You are only five and twenty. Granted, of course, that you have not the protection of the tonsure, as I have. Perhaps I should be the one to visit her next time, vowed, as I am, to the celibate life.' He gave a knowing smile. 'Pretty, is she?'

'Beautiful,' I said curtly. I found I did not want to discuss Emma Thorgold with Jordain when he was in this teasing mood. 'She had a great deal to tell me, and it does at last make clear why those men killed William. He threatened them.'

As quickly as I could, I recounted everything Emma had told me about William's agreement to copy the book, and his revulsion when he discovered that his copy was to be used to replace the stolen original.

'So we now understand better what happened,' Jordain said, 'but we are no nearer finding these two men, foxy hair and the man with the knife. And we have no name for the man at Merton, who is the one behind it all.'

'It must be Olney,' I said. 'He had access to the book whenever he chose. He lives and breathes books. I can imagine that he would covet that book above all others, to own for himself. He is clearly frightened of Allard Basset, who must have discovered that the book is missing. And if word reaches the Warden – as it would have done, if William had exposed him – then he would certainly lose his Fellowship.'

'You are probably right,' Jordain said. 'I do not know Olney as you do. Would he condone murder?'

I hesitated. It was the one thing I was not sure about.

'He does not seem to me a man who would condone violence of any kind. He is a sharp-tongued, mean-minded fellow, but I would not have said he was violent, though I suppose any man might be driven to violent measures if his future was about to be destroyed. Of course, we do not know whether he was present at the mill last Monday afternoon. It should be easy enough to find out if he was in college then.'

'So these hired ruffians – we must assume they are hired ruffians – might well have acted from their own fear of exposure, without Olney's knowledge.'

'That seems very possible.'

I gave a huge, jaw-cracking yawn. 'I must away home. I have had a long hard day, though a profitable one, and I am weak with hunger. I shall see you sometime tomorrow and we shall think what to do.'

'Aye. I dine with the Farringdons, but I will come afterwards. You saw the widow in Banbury too?'

'I did. It pleased me to put that purse in her hands. It should prove a help to her and the deaf girl. Sissy, she is called. I wonder whether it was the pestilence that struck her down. Those scars, and deafness – I think it might have been the pox, or the mumps. The scars do not look to me like the scars of the plague. Whatever it was, she has suffered for it.' I yawned again. 'I must bid you good-night, Jordain.'

'God go with 'ee, Nicholas.'

I headed away down Catte Street. It was only as I turned the corner by St Mary's into the High that I realised that I had not told Jordain that Emma Thorgold, or more properly Sister Benedicta, had made the beautiful little book of hours I had seen in Henry Stalbroke's book-bindery. Well, he had no need to know. I smiled to myself at the thought of those delicate, ink-stained hands.

Margaret had kept a substantial supper hot for me, and I fell on it hungrily, for the unaccustomed long ride and the fresh air, with very little to eat during the day, had given me an appetite. When she discovered the remains of the loaf protruding from my satchel, she held it up accusingly.

'What is this?'

'Bought from a baker in Banbury,' I admitted. 'He pointed out Mistress Preston's home to me, and I felt obliged.'

She gave me a withering look and bore it away. Later, I found she had given it to Rowan, soaked in milk. I dared not tell her that the bread had been excellent.

When I had finished eating, I looked in on the children, who were in bed, but not quite asleep. Rafe was on the point of it, but Alysoun was sitting up, wide-eyed, watching the doorway.

'Not asleep, my maid?' I said, kissing the top of her head as she slid down under the feather bed.

'I wanted to be sure that you had come safely home, Papa.'

I leaned down and tucked the covers round Rafe, curled up in his truckle cot, then I sat on the end of Alysoun's bed.

'Of course I am come safe home. Why should I not?'

'Jonathan says there are bad men roaming the highways. Outlaws and wild men of the woods. It is a long way to Banbury. They might have attacked you, he said.'

'Sometimes I think Jonathan likes to scare himself, and you as well, by making up such stories. On the road I believe I saw eight – nay, perhaps it was nine – farmers, busy about their work. And there was one fine gentleman with his attendants. Banbury is a small town, smaller than Oxford and with no university. It has bakers like Jonathan's father, and blacksmiths, and butchers, and tailors, and shops like the Oxford shops, and all sorts of folk, but I saw never an outlaw or a wild man.'

'Still,' she said, yawning, 'I am glad you are come back.'

I patted the lump under the covers that was her shoulder. 'So am I.'

When I went back to the kitchen, Margaret looked up from her sewing. 'Are they settled?'

'Aye, Alysoun was waiting up for me, but she will sleep.'

I decided not to mention Jonathan's fears of wild men, it would only turn her more against him.

'And so how did you fare in Banbury?'

I sat down opposite her and peeled off my boots. I was ready for my own bed, but she deserved some account of my day, so I told her briefly about Mistress Preston.

'You are right to advise her to sell her lace and braid here in Oxford,' she said. 'I cannot imagine it will fetch much in a small place like Banbury. And did you then come straight back?'

'Nay, I called at Godstow Abbey, to see William's cousin, the novice Sister Benedicta.'

She shook her head. 'That is a bad business, from what Maud Farringdon tells me. Is the girl resigned to the cloister?'

'Nay,' I said slowly, 'I should say that she is not. However, she has made a great deal clear that we did not understand about William.'

I repeated again all that I had told Jordain of what Emma Thorgold had explained to me.

'And the missing book is safely hidden away in Godstow Abbey!' Margaret said. 'No one would think to look there. But what shall you do? Can you return it to Merton?'

'Jordain and I will discuss that tomorrow, but I am uncertain. If I return it quietly to Merton, it will fall, certainly, into Olney's hands, as keeper of their books. What is to stop the whole fraud being undertaken once again? If I deliver it to Allard Basset, he will probably accuse me of having stolen it. I could give it directly into the Warden's hands, that might be best, but it would leave the question of William's murder still unsolved. I am too tired to think tonight.'

I got up and stretched. 'I can feel my unaccustomed riding muscles seizing up already. Was all well in the shop today?'

'Aye. I believe Mistress Lapley came calling again, to ask about her book.'

I groaned. 'Her custom is welcome, but she is surely the most tiresome of my customers. Anything else?'

'The Fellow of Gloucester College came asking about the bestiary, but Walter told him it was already sold to Merton. I believe he was quite angry.'

'I am sure Walter was able to deal with him. Let Master Caundish take it up with Olney. I am off, before I fall asleep standing up, like a horse.'

She rolled up her sewing and set it aside. 'I have only to cover the fire. The bread is already proving. God give you goodnight, Nicholas.'

'And you, Meg.'

–

The following morning, as I had feared, I was stiff from my long ride, but I could make no excuses. My accounts, begun a week ago, would not wait any longer. It was not only Merton which owed me money. However, Roger was making good progress with his collection of tales, and the three of us spent some time discussing what full-page illuminations each tale should have. I knew that Roger's illustrations would be competent, if a little stiff, and I could not help wondering what Emma Thorgold would have drawn. She had a freedom and skill Roger would never match. With a few lines she could catch the likeness of a leaping hare or the infant Jesus sleeping in his mother's arms.

Walter too had made progress, writing down his first attempt at two more of his mother's tales, so I sat with him, going through each and making nothing but small suggestions. As he gained in confidence his pen flowed more freely. Altogether I managed to avoid my accounts until nearly dinner time, although I wrote out two more overdue stationery bills, one for Queen's College, and one for Durham College. I was annoyed with myself, for I had been close to Durham yesterday and might have saved myself an extra journey.

Just as we were closing the shop for dinner, one of Henry Stalbroke's apprentices put his head through the open window.

'Maister says your book be ready, Maister Elyot,' he said. 'You may collect it any time you wish.'

I thanked him, and Roger jumped to his feet. 'I can fetch it, Master Elyot. Anything, to send Mistress Lapley on her way!'

'I think I will go myself, Roger, for I have other business on Bookbinders Island, and it will leave you free to copy more of the collection of tales. I am eager to see it finished. However, you may have the pleasure of delivering the completed book of Robin Hood to the lady yourself. I would not deny you that satisfaction.'

Roger laughed. It was a rare occurrence, and transformed him.

When the men had left for Tackley's Inn to dine, I joined the rest of the family in the kitchen.

'Jordain has promised to take dinner with the Farringdons at the Cross Inn today,' I said, after I had spoken the blessing over our meal. 'Afterwards, he will come here and we will confer on what is best to do.'

'Best to do about what, Papa?' Alysoun asked, speaking round a hearty spoonful of braised mutton.

'Mind your manners,' Margaret said. 'Do not speak with your mouth full.'

Rafe was concentrating on eating as rapidly as possible, in case there was a chance of a second helping. He had put on a spurt of growth lately.

Alysoun chewed and swallowed, then repeated her question. 'What must you and Cousin Jordain confer about? You are never in the shop these days.'

'Nothing that you need worry about, my maid,' I said. 'Some business we have in hand. We must decide on the best way to proceed.'

'You are not going away again are you?' There was a slight note of panic in her voice, so I reached across the table and squeezed her hand.

'I am going nowhere. Or at least nowhere further than Godstow Abbey, but that will not be for some time yet. I shall not need to go to Banbury again.'

'Did you ride to Banbury, Papa?' Rafe asked, chasing the last drop of gravy round his bowl with his spoon.

'Indeed I did. I could never have walked there and back in a day.'

'Will you teach me to ride soon?'

'Aye, you must learn, and Alysoun must practice, but it is not so easy in Oxford. When next we visit Grandmama at the farm will be best.'

We were finishing our dinner, with small sweet pastries that Margaret had made with the currants she dried last summer and some of the dried apple rings, when Jordain arrived and I took him out into the garden where we would not be overheard.

'Alysoun is beginning to take a little too much interest in this business of ours,' I said. 'I want to keep her well away from it all.'

'Oh, I am sure she will be safe enough,' Jordain said, sitting on the bench and stretching out his legs. 'The Cross Inn was put on its mettle today, for one of the Bishop of Lincoln's canons is staying there. They produced a very acceptable dinner.'

He closed his eyes and looked as though he might be about to fall asleep after his acceptable dinner, but I poked him in the ribs.

'I have a possible plan,' I said.

He opened one eye. 'You have thought how we might return the Psalter to Merton?'

'Not yet. I have a mind to set a trap for our two rogues.'

He sat up. 'Since we do not know who they are, or where they are, I cannot see how we can trap them.'

'If you were a shepherd, whose flock had been worried by a wolf,' I said, 'and you did not know where to find him, what would you do? You could scour the whole countryside, but you could not be sure you would find him, so what then?'

'I am in no mood for riddles, Nicholas.'

'You would tether a lamb in some convenient spot to tempt the wolf to come to you, then you would lie in wait, with your bow strung, and shoot him when he arrived.'

'If he did not kill the lamb first. What meaning does your riddle have for our two-legged wolves?'

'Now that I know where the Psalter is, I can trail that information, like the baited lamb, and see whether it draws the wolves.'

'You'll not reveal its whereabouts!'

'Nay, merely let it be known that I know where to lay my hands on it. No need to mention Godstow at all.'

He looked dubious. 'It might draw in the wolves, but with yourself as bait, you might be slaughtered like the unfortunate lamb.'

'They would not kill me until they had discovered what I know.'

'I do not think I like the sound of this, Nicholas. It could be very dangerous. They have killed once already.'

'Only when their plans went awry and they were threatened. And I have more to the plan than this. They need the book, but they also need a new copyist. Who better than an accomplished scrivener with a grudge against his master for not paying him well enough?'

'This may all be very clear to you,' he said, 'but I find it very opaque.'

'Roger has the very face of a disgruntled man,' I said, warming to my plan, now that I was making it clear even to myself. 'How if he were to complain – in his cups, say, at one or two taverns – that he is in urgent need of money? If word spreads, our rogues are bound to hear of it. Oxford is not such a large town. Sister Benedicta believes William was approached after he had been heard talking about his urgent need for money.'

'At the Swindlestock Tavern. Was that not what she thought?'

'Aye, exactly. A large tavern at the very centre of Oxford, on Carfax,' I said. 'Perfect for spreading the word. A perfect place to tether our lamb. One of our lambs.'

'Do you think Roger would do it?'

'I am sure of it. He is thirsty for action. Remember how he broke his wrist playing football? Fortunately his left wrist, so not a permanent impediment to his work. He often grows restless.'

'Even if you were to trail your bait, both yourself with your knowledge of the Psalter's hiding place and Roger as a scribe eager to earn an illicit fee, how would that serve to catch the two rogues?'

'I have not quite thought that through yet,' I admitted. 'Should we take this to the sheriff and bespeak his assistance in catching these men?'

'Do you even think he would heed you? A knight? A king's officer? And you a bookish Oxford tradesman? I am not being unkind, Nicholas, but I think he would laugh in your face.'

'Perhaps you are right,' I said gloomily, slumping down with my elbows on my knees and my chin on my fists.

'I suppose,' he said slowly, 'we could recruit my students. Some of them come from gentry families and know how to handle a sword. They could be at hand whenever these wolves made an approach either to you or to Roger. But I should fail in my responsibility to them if I put them in danger.'

'Aye.' I sighed. 'I must think on it further. But these men must be feeling some desperation. They now have neither the Psalter nor the first pages of William's copy. Sooner or later, the disappearance of the Psalter from Merton will be discovered.'

'Why do we not simply go to the Warden of Merton and hand him the Psalter? It would be safely returned, and the man Olney's part in it exposed.'

'Somehow Olney must be exposed, I agree. But if we were to follow that course, the two men who killed William would slip away, unpunished. We cannot let that happen. We set our feet on this path to find justice for

William, not to recover a book Merton has been careless enough to mislay. Let us not lose sight of that.'

'You are right, of course,' he said. 'Well, let us give your plan more thought before we act. Did you not say that you were going to see Dafydd Hewlyn this afternoon?'

'Aye. I want to make sure that the parchment I found at the old mill was indeed part of the same quarter ream he sold those men. It must be. I cannot imagine that it is not, but I should look a fool should it turn out *not* to be the same.'

'I am sure it comes from the same batch, but you are right to speak to Dafydd. Though it's a long walk after your exertions yesterday!'

I laughed. 'I must also collect a book from the binder and pay him. And it is a perfect excuse to avoid spending any more time today on my accounts.'

'My accounts are simple enough,' he said ruefully. 'I have a small box of coin at the beginning of term containing the students' fees for their keep. When I have paid the rent, all I must do is divide the rest by the weeks of the term, and that is the money I have for buying food. Very simple.'

—

I set off for Bookbinders Island as soon as Jordain had left, and went first to Dafydd Hewlyn.

'Aye, that is part of the same batch,' he said, hardly needing to glance at it, 'the parchment I sold to those two men. Where did you find this?'

'In the place where I believe the copying was being done,' I said. 'I thought it was the same, but I have not your expert eye.'

'Have you found those scoundrels yet?'

'Not yet.'

'My journeyman,' he said, jerking his head toward the drying green, 'thinks he saw them in the Swindlestock Tavern, Saturday evening.'

'Did he indeed! That is useful to know. Men are creatures of habit and tend to have their favourite drinking places.'

'If you catch them, I'd be glad to hear of it. I do not spend long hours making parchment for it to be misused.'

'I will certainly send you word.'

At the bookbinder's workshop, Henry Stalbroke handed me the neat little book his journeyman Thomas Needham had made of Roger's pages. He had tooled the cover, front and back, with a pattern of swirling lines, and imprinted the title on front and spine in gilt letters. The edges of the pages were delicately tinted crimson, and the binding was firm, but not too stiff for a woman's hands.

'Excellent work, Thomas,' I said. 'Henry must keep a watch, or you'll be setting up to rival him.'

I handed him a half noble on top of the fee, in thanks. He smiled modestly.

'I have a lot still to learn, Master Elyot. Master Stalbroke has nothing to fear from me.'

I turned to Henry Stalbroke. 'Do you still have the book of hours you showed me when last I was here? The one from Godstow?'

'Aye,' he said. 'They have not yet collected it or sent for it.'

'May I look at it again? I thought the illuminations were very fine.'

'The novice has a good eye,' he agreed, and handed down the small book from a shelf.

I examined it more closely this time, having met the artist.

The text was written in an elegant hand. When you work with scriveners as closely as I do, men who must master a number of different letter forms and be able to lay out a page of text that is not only clear and legible but elegant to look upon, you learn to judge how easily they write. This was the hand of someone who wrote swiftly but with the lightest of touches, so that the words flowed across the page as smoothly as the lines of her drawings.

Above all, these drawings were worth a careful examination. I had been struck by their skill before, but I now saw more of the humour. A little dog lay at the Virgin's feet in the annunciation scene, ignoring the angel and rolling on his back, asking to be petted. During the flight into Egypt, the Holy Family passed a coney warren, whose inhabitants grazed and frolicked, all except one, who had hopped on to the back of the donkey and joined the journey.

In one of the interleaved pages, which stood for the month of April, signalled by a very English downpour, the artist had enjoyed herself depicting the procession of animals into the Ark. I particularly liked the unicorn hesitating at the base of the ramp and looking anxiously over his shoulder at his mate, who was frolicking in a flowery meadow and was clearly about to be left behind.

I handed the book back to Henry. 'I suppose this is for the use of the sisters at Godstow.'

'They have not said. As you know, some monasteries augment their income by making books for secular buyers. Godstow has not done so before, but now that they have this talent, they may do so.'

'If they wish to sell this book, I might buy it,' I said, feigning a carelessness which did not deceive Henry for a moment.

'I will ask,' he said.

By walking briskly I reached home before Walter had closed the shop, and handed the French Robin Hood to Roger. Like any lover of books, he caressed the smooth leather of the binding.

'They have made a fine job of it,' he said.

I smiled. 'It is always good – is it not? – when all that hard work of writing pages is turned into a solid book which will last for generations. You can be proud of that. Now, off with you and take it to the impatient Mistress Lapley, but do not let it out of your hands until either she or Master Lapley has paid for it. I have spent a great deal on it already.'

Roger hurried off, looking contented for once, and Walter and I exchanged smiles.

'It has taken time,' Walter said, 'but I think at last he is learning to take a pride in his work, instead of seeing it as drudgery.'

'You have the right of it,' I said. 'We must find him interesting tasks, though he must still take his share of writing out *peciae*, and not leave it all to you.'

I was glad of a quiet evening after my long journey of the previous day, and I needed time to think how to implement my plan for tempting the two scoundrels out into the open. If Dafydd Hewlyn's journeyman had indeed seen them in the Swindlestock Tavern on Saturday, that seemed a good place to make a start. Tomorrow I would test Roger's reaction to playing the disgruntled scribe in a tavern or two. I was less sure how I was to spread word that I knew the whereabouts of the Irish Psalter, or how we might apprehend the men if they did show their faces. I would sleep on it.

—

In the event, it was Roger himself who came up with a suggestion. He was delighted at the prospect of spending time (at my expense), visiting the taverns of Oxford to moan about his need for money, in the hope of securing an offer of work from the two men who had dealt with William. As far as we had been able to discover, it had been these two who had employed William and provided him with the Psalter and the writing materials. The man from Merton, whoever he was, had rarely or never appeared, although he must be providing the money.

Of course it had been necessary to tell Roger everything we knew. Jordain had joined us after his morning lecture and between us we gave a full account of all that we had learned, from the time I had pulled William's body from the Cherwell until my visit to Godstow Abbey and my meeting with Sister Benedicta. From time to time Walter joined in. There was always a lull in the shop before the students came in after their lectures, so we were left undisturbed. It was clear Roger had guessed a little of what had been happening, but he was taken aback at the audacity of the plot to replace the original book with a copy.

'Surely no one would be fooled for a moment,' he objected. 'I have never seen this Psalter, but any book which is hundreds of years old, no matter how carefully kept, will show its age. No one could mistake a newly bound book for an old one. It would not even smell the same.'

'That is very true,' I said. 'The book I fetched from the binder's yesterday, it still smelled of freshly dressed leather.'

'And glue,' Walter said.

'And the feel of the parchment in your fingers is different,' Roger said. 'Some of those old books we have had here to sell, their pages feel different. I do not know whether it is age, or whether they used to cure the skins in some other way.'

'Nay,' said Walter, 'I think parchment makers have used the same methods for centuries. Even the Romans—'

He broke off when Jordain laughed.

'It is very instructive,' he said, 'listening to the three of you on the fine details of the book trade, but the fact remains that this was the plan. It is no concern of ours whether it would have succeeded or not. It is our aim to prevent it happening at all.'

'So you are content to start this afternoon, Roger?' I said. 'Though I am still uncertain how I am to spread the word that I know the whereabouts of the book – which these men must find before they can employ you.'

'But, Master Elyot,' Roger said, bright eyed, 'I can do both. While I am grumbling about how miserly you are in paying your hardworking scriveners, I can also say that you have found a most wonderful ancient Psalter, probably Irish, a veritable treasure, which will no doubt make your own fortune. Not that we poor scribes will see any benefit from it.'

'You know,' Jordain said slowly, 'I think that might be the answer. It would look very suspicious were you to talk about it yourself, Nicholas, but if your discontented scrivener let the information slip out while in his cups, that would have the ring of truth about it.'

'I think you might be right,' I said.

'You must not overplay your hand, lad,' Walter said. 'Don't be too eager about telling folk everything.'

'I know just how to let it out, a little at a time,' Roger said scornfully. 'You may trust me.'

'But there is one thing you must *not* do,' I said. 'You must not let your listeners believe that I have the book here. I do not want those ruffians breaking into my home and endangering my family.'

'I shall say that you have it hidden away, not anywhere about the shop or house, for I have searched for it. Only you know where it is.'

'Aye, that's best,' I said.

Jordain frowned. 'I do not like this. You could be putting yourself in great danger, Nicholas. If these men are desperate enough to lay hands on the Psalter again – which they must be, as will be the man who is behind it all – what might they not do to extract its whereabouts from you? Men who do not scruple at murder will not, I think, scruple at torture.'

Despite putting on a brave face, I shivered involuntarily. 'Then I must take care not to walk alone down any dark alleys, or wander about Oxford at night.'

'I wonder how quickly they will act,' Walter said. 'For a few days, we could make sure there is always someone with you.'

'That would arouse their suspicions, I think,' I said, 'if I were to be seen always in company with any of you.'

'I have a couple of stout lads amongst my students,' Jordain said. 'Both of them from good families, only spending time in Oxford to get a little of the new learning, not in order to take holy orders or to become scholars. Both have been brought up to handle arms. Yesterday evening I raised with them the possibility of the need for some lads with such training, although I did not say why or for what purpose. They were, I am sad to say, only too eager. Any excuse to neglect their studies! They could stay near you, within shouting distance. They would not be recognised as having anything to do with you.'

'Perhaps,' I said reluctantly. I was not sure just what kind of hare I had started running. 'Let us try this for a day or two, and see what comes of it. Today is Wednesday. We will attempt our scheme until Monday. If we have not enticed the wolf to the tethered lamb by then, I think we may assume that the rogues have abandoned Oxford, and I shall return the Psalter to the Warden of Merton. Let Olney take the consequences.'

This we all agreed. Roger would leave work early that very afternoon, and begin haunting the taverns. By now I had started to feel that it was a foolish plan, no one would be taken in, and much time would be lost for no gain. And I should look a very fool.

—

Roger returned much later that evening, long after the children were abed, looking remarkably pleased with himself. I brought him through to the kitchen, where Margaret plied him with oatmeal porridge laced with honey.

'Clearly you have taken too much drink, Roger,' she said sternly. 'You reek like a spilt barrel. This will soak up some of it and steady your stomach.'

'I thank you kindly, Mistress Makepeace,' he said meekly. Margaret could subdue even Roger.

Once he had made a start on his porridge, I could contain myself no longer. His complacent air must have some cause.

'Well?' I said.

'I started first at Tackley's,' he said. 'I'm well known, taking my dinner there most days. No point in playing the downtrodden scribe there, else how could I afford my dinners? But I did know that some of the servants from Merton drink there of an evening, and I was in luck. Three arrived soon after I was sitting with my mug of ale before me, and they came to join me at my table. I let them chatter for a while, but I managed to slip in a hint about you finding a valuable ancient book. I hadn't seen it myself, but I thought it might be a Psalter. Two of them were not interested, but I saw one prick up his ears. If what you think is true, that they've concealed the loss, he'll know nothing of that, but it could be that he's heard of Merton's Psalter.'

I nodded. 'That all sounds like good strategy. Word may not get back to the college, but it is worth the attempt.'

'From there I went on to the Mitre, but I stayed only a short while. I think it is too grand a place for our villains, so I went on to the Swindlestock.'

His eyes were gleaming, and he was clearly containing his news with difficulty.

'It was here that I became the misused, underpaid scrivener who works long hours for a miserly master, who pays him barely enough to live on. I became quite drunk, weeping into my ale.'

He gave Margaret a startled look. 'I was not really drunk, mistress! Indeed, I think I have missed my calling. I should be one of these travelling players who can become an angel or a devil at will.'

'So,' I said, 'you were drunk and maudlin in your cups, and too poor to eat. How did you pay for your ale?'

'It was my last farthing, maister,' he whined. Then he laughed. 'I was bought two more pots out of charity, and the second of them by a red-haired man with a small beard and a pock-marked face.'

I gave a gasp. I had not expected my ill-made plan to work at all, certainly not so soon.

'It must be the man,' I said. 'It was in the Swindle-stock that William was overheard speaking of his need for money. And it was there that Dafydd Hewlyn's journeyman saw them last Saturday. Surely it is their regular drinking place.'

'It is more than that.' Roger looked smug. 'They have been lodging there for the last two months, and I had their names before I came away, from one of the potboys I know. He's the son of my landlady. They are Robert Frowike and Pierson Gidney. Robert Frowike it was who bought me ale, and drew out from me my tale of woe, how I have worked for you these four years, but still paid barely enough to live on. And there is my master, living in comfort, buying books and selling them at a great profit. And now he has found some wonderful old Psalter which is worth more than his whole shop together. Will I see any of the great fortune he will make when he sells it to some nobleman? Not I!'

I drew a deep breath. I hoped that Roger had not overdone his pose and caused the man to suspect he was being deceived. It was almost too much to hope that the wolf had been drawn to the bait.

'And this fellow, Robert Frowike,' I said, 'what was his reaction to your sorry tale?'

'Patted me on the shoulder, bought me another ale, told me to be of good cheer. He needed to speak to someone, but I am to meet him there on Friday after I have finished the day's labour for my thankless master. He might have work for me, which would be well paid, but I must bring him a page of my writing and illuminations, as evidence of my skills.'

'You have done remarkably well, Roger,' I said. 'I never expected that you would find any trace of the men so soon, or that they would approach you at once. Clearly they are growing worried.'

'I think it was the mention of your find, Master Elyot, that really drew him in. Without the book, they cannot offer me work, can they? That was a ruse to keep me satisfied. Or else he thinks he will be able to secure the book from you by Friday. You had best watch your step.'

'Aye.' I was troubled. 'This fellow did not follow you, and see that you came back here to report?'

'Nay, I thought of that. I waited until he had gone off himself, then slipped away.'

Gone off to Merton, I thought, to make his own report.

'I am surprised,' Margaret said austerely, 'that you were able to walk straight after so much ale.'

Roger laughed. 'I gave that last tankard to my friend, the potboy. It's thirsty work serving in an Oxford tavern all evening.'

'Well, now we have the names,' I said, 'we could report them to the sheriff, though I would prefer to catch them in the midst of some illegal act. It will be difficult to prove them William's murderers. I wish now that I had not taken the ink well from the mill. If it had been found in their possession, it would have been proof clear of their connection with him. Still, too late to grieve over that.'

'I'll away home now,' Roger said, getting up. 'I thank you for the supper, mistress.'

'Are you sure you will be safe in the dark streets?' Margaret said. She might deplore the drinking, but she cared for his safety.

'Aye, 'tis but a five minute walk.' And he went off, whistling jauntily.

'I do not think he understands the risks you are all running,' Margaret said.

She frowned. She was right, of course.

'I truly had no real hope that they would take the bait,' I said apologetically. 'It was a wild scheme.'

'Well, tomorrow Jordain's students will be here, to keep a close watch on you,' she said.

'Then I must lead them a merry dance. I have bills to deliver to Queen's and Durham. That should stretch their legs for them.

–

The following morning I made much of going in and out of the shop. I called on Master Crowmer to buy a small flagon of wine, but I did not tell him anything of what we had discovered. Like the coroners he seemed happy to forget the case, yet one more Oxford killing, with nothing to indicate who the culprit might be.

When Margaret set off for the market, I walked with her as far as the Mitre, then turned back to take my reckoning to Queen's College. I hoped that by turning sharp about I would be able to see whether there was anyone following me. I saw nothing but Jordain's two students keeping close. They were two lads I recognised from my visits to Hart Hall. They were far from inconspicuous, being unmistakably students who should have been attending lectures. However, it should ensure that our two scoundrels would not attack me in broad daylight in the middle of Oxford.

After my visit to Queen's, I decided I would go myself to Durham College. I could have sent Roger, but if we were to maintain the story of the ill-used servant, I would hardly be entrusting him to fetch home the substantial sum owed to me. Besides, it was a pleasant spring day, and I would enjoy the walk. Up Catte Street I led my faithful attendants, past the turn to their hall and out through Smith Gate. It was as far again to Durham College, but it was a delightful place, with exceptionally large grounds, something only possible for colleges outside the town wall. The bursar there was a good fellow, not a mean penny-pincher like his counterpart at Merton. If he paid late it was because he was as disorganised in keeping his accounts as I was. He invited me to take a glass of wine sitting in the garden, which I accepted.

'It would be a kindness, however,' I said, 'if you were to tell the porter to serve a stoup of ale to those two students waiting outside. They are providing me with a kind of bodyguard.'

He sent word to the porter, but said in astonishment, 'Bodyguard, Nicholas? What devilment have you been about?'

'I shall tell you all when it is over,' I promised.

Having enjoyed the wine and half an hour's conversation, I took my purse of coin, collected the students, and made my way leisurely back home. There was no sign of either Robert Frowike or Pierson Gidney.

It was only when I entered the shop that I found I had been playing a foolish game. Walter and Roger had abandoned their desks, Margaret was in the shop, her hair escaping in disarray from her wimple, her cheeks pale and streaked with tears.

I seized her hands. 'Meg! What has happened!'

She gulped and mastered herself, freeing one hand to wipe away her tears.

'I went on from the market to call on Mistress Farringdon at the Cross Inn. We sat talking for a time. It was as I was coming away. There was a crowd in Northgate Street.'

She gripped my hand hard.

'Please, Meg!' I said.

'Someone grabbed me about the waist. For a moment I thought it was a cut-purse, but then he clamped his hand over my mouth so I could not cry out. He said he had a knife and if I looked back or made a sound, I would regret it.'

Her voice trembled. I have never known Margaret so afraid, except during the Death.

'He said that if you did not deliver up the Psalter by tomorrow midday, to the innkeeper at the Swindlestock, then you would regret it.'

'He was bluffing,' I said, with more conviction than I felt. 'He cannot touch me.'

My foolish plan was working itself out rather more rapidly than I had expected.

'I am sorry he has given you such a fright, Meg, but he hopes to frighten me through you, and I refuse to play his game.'

She looked at me unsmiling.

'This is no game, Nicholas. He meant every word he said.'

Chapter Twelve

Walter and Roger were clearly shaken, as well as Margaret, and although I did my best to keep up a calm front, I was beginning to be frightened. Blithely setting afoot this gamble, this wolf trap, I had thought I might take some risks myself, should the previously nameless villains try to discover from me the whereabouts of the Irish Psalter. With a bodyguard, however inexperienced, I thought myself safe enough. And I had warned Roger to make it clear that the book was not to be found here, so that there should be no danger to my family. I had never expected that one of the men would seize Margaret in the middle of one of Oxford's busiest streets and threaten her.

'Did no one come to your aid, Meg? There must have been dozens of people about of a morning.'

She shook her head. 'Since the Death, I think folk have become more careful of their own skins. All that matters now is to survive. Let others fend for themselves. Things have changed. It was never thus, before. People must have seen, but they turned away. There is a kind of hardness of heart amongst us now. We have seen too much, lost too much. 'Tis as if we all wear a kind of armour of indifference.'

'I hope it may not be so,' I cried, 'for what kind of world would that be in store for the children?'

'I wish I had never gone to Swindlestock Tavern,' Roger said bitterly. He was pale, and looked as though he might be sick at any moment. 'This is my doing. If I had never blabbed about that b'yer lady book, this would never have happened.'

It was a mark of Margaret's fright that she did not reprimand him for swearing.

''Tis not your fault, Roger,' I said, 'it is mine. This whole misguided scheme was mine, you were but doing as you were asked. I think there is nothing much that we can do today. We'll stay quiet, not let them see that they have frightened us. But before tomorrow we must think what is best to do. And I must speak to Jordain.'

I knew I was babbling, for I could not see my way ahead without either courting danger or sacrificing the very book William had died to protect.

'Perhaps it is time to call in the sheriff,' I said. 'A threat of violence has been made against my sister. We know it stems from these men. And we know their names. And where they lodge.'

I turned to Margaret. 'Were you able to see the man, Meg? I know you say that he warned you not to look round, but did you gain any impression of him?'

She was a little calmer now, tucking her hair into her wimple.

'I did not see his face, but he felt like a big man, strong.' She thought a moment. 'The hand he clamped over my mouth sprouted black hairs.'

'You are sure? Black hairs?'

'I am sure.'

'Then it was not the foxy haired one,' I said, 'he would not have had any black hairs.'

'Pierson Gidney,' Roger said, 'not Robert Frowike.'

'He does appear to be the one more given to violence,' I agreed, 'though it was the other who clouted me over the head.'

'To your advantage,' Walter said dryly. 'Pierson Gidney might have thrust his knife between your ribs.'

'For the rest of today,' I said, 'I think we should go about our work as normal. In the meantime, I will send a message to the sheriff, to say that we have found the murderers of William Farringdon, who have also mistreated my sister and made threats against me. He must at least pay some heed to that. We have until tomorrow midday before they carry out their threats against me.'

'You are very trusting,' said Margaret. 'These are hardly men of honour. Who is to say that they will wait until then?'

'I do not know what else to do,' I said simply. I realised that I was impossibly out of my depth in this affair.

'You will not hand over the book to them?' Walter said anxiously.

'Never.'

Margaret went through to the house and I told the men to shut the shop and go for their dinner as if nothing had happened. If the rogues believed Roger's tale that he was an ill-used servant, they would not expect Margaret to have told him of the threats made to her. They must give every appearance of behaving normally.

As soon as they were gone, I sat down with paper and pen to write to the sheriff. I would have preferred to talk to Jordain first, but there was no time to lose. I kept my message short, saying that I had discovered the identity of the two men who had attacked and killed William Farringdon, giving their names and where they lodged, and explained further that they were involved in a plot to steal a valuable book from Merton College, with the connivance of a Fellow of that college, although I baulked at naming Olney. I concluded by saying that my sister had been assaulted and threats made against me, so that I sought his help urgently. After dinner I would take my letter to Edric Crowmer, who would know how to reach the sheriff quickly. It was most likely that he was resident in the castle, but for all I knew he might be at his town house, or at his manor in the north of the county.

After dinner, as the men returned to open the shop and I was about to go along the street to the vintner's shop, Alysoun called out to me.

'Papa, may I go to Jonathan's to show him how well Rowan is walking on her lead now? We practised in the garden all day yesterday and she is very good and obedient. Jonathan is supposed to be training the terrier pup, but he has not even put a collar on him yet.'

'Aye, you may go. What of Rafe?'

'He is coming too. *We* will show Jonathan how to train his puppy.' When she was so sure of herself, she reminded me of my sister.

So Jonathan had claimed the terrier pup for his own. Well, let Alysoun busy herself with puppy training, it would keep her well away from our shop and house, and prevent her from becoming too interested it these dangerous affairs. Together Alysoun and Rafe ran off across the street toward the bakeshop, Rowan dodging about and nearly tripping Alysoun up. Perhaps she was not quite so well trained to the lead as Alysoun supposed. All for the best. It would keep her occupied all afternoon in the Bakers' garden.

My student guards were leaning against the trunk of a spindly ash tree which had taken root at the side of the street and somehow managed to survive. As I set off for Crowmer's shop, they sauntered after me at a discreet distance. I wondered whether I should set one of them to guarding Margaret, but she had promised me that she would not venture out again today.

I was kept waiting a good half hour on Crowmer's threshold, but at length he returned and unlocked the door of his shop, his journeyman following behind and pushing a handcart. The journeyman lowered the counter in front of the window, ready for the afternoon's business, while I followed Crowmer inside.

'I need to send an urgent message to the sheriff,' I said, plunging in without preliminaries. 'I thought that, as the current parish constable, you would know where he is at present.'

Crowmer was lifting a large jar on to a table, ready to decant the contents into smaller flasks. He straightened with a groan, and scratched his head.

'The sheriff? Why, he's away at his manor these two weeks. What would you be wanting him for?'

'An urgent matter, concerning the murder of the student William Farringdon. You remember the body I found in the river just last week?'

My tone was sarcastic, for I did not think he took his duties as seriously as he should, except when they gave him the opportunity to lord it over others.

'Of course I remember,' he said irritably. 'What concern is it of yours? You fished the body out of the river, and there's an end to it.'

I strove to keep my temper. 'I knew the boy, and the Warden of his hall is a long-time friend of mine. We have been looking into the circumstances. I now know a great deal about what lies behind the killing, and the names of the men who did it. Then this morning one of them assaulted my sister in Northgate Street and uttered threats against me. It is time the sheriff acted.'

Crowmer regarded me with a superior smile. 'I think you take too much upon yourself, Nicholas. Leave these matters to those in authority. We will see to all that concerns the fellow's death. You, on the other hand, have no authority at all.'

This was intolerable, but I bit down on my caustic reply.

'Even those in authority should pay heed when they are offered important information. If the sheriff is away at his manor, how can I reach him? And does he have a deputy here in town?'

Crowmer shrugged. Two customers had appeared at the window and he had lost interest in me. He turned away, but threw over his shoulder, 'You could try the castle.'

There was nothing else for it. I would get no help from Crowmer. I set off in the direction of Carfax, with Jordain's two students shadowing me behind. By the look of them, they were growing bored. It had seemed at first an exciting diversion from the dull round of daily lectures – for two lads who were not serious students – but it was fast becoming a tiresome trek back and forth across Oxford. I considering sending them home to Hart Hall, but then I remembered Meg's words, that Gidney and Frowike might not wait until tomorrow's noon. If they could catch me before then, they would try to force me to reveal the whereabouts of the Irish Psalter.

When I reached the castle at last, the guards at the gatehouse were in no hurry to let me through.

'The sheriff is not here,' one of them said, a super-cilious young fellow, who clearly looked down his long aristocratic nose as a mere tradesman from the town.

'So I have been told,' I said patiently. 'I would like to see his deputy.'

'Have you any authority?'

The word was beginning to annoy me.

'I have information for him,' I said.

'Hark,' he said, turning an amused face to his companion, 'our little shopkeeper here has *information* for Deputy Sheriff Walden. Do you suppose he weighs it out by the pound, and charges per weight?'

The other guard sniggered at this supreme piece of wit, and they both stood, hands on hips, barring the entrance.

'It concerns a recent case of murder, tried before the coroners last week, and you would do well not to impede any information which may be of considerable value to the deputy sheriff in preventing further bloodshed.'

I was growing increasingly angry, which was reflected in the arrogant tone of my own voice. Surprisingly, this had some effect. I suppose these fellows responded auto-matically to the voice of authority, like well trained dogs.

'Oh, very well.' The man who regarded himself as in charge stepped slightly to one side. 'Across the bailey. Guardhouse on the right before you reach the keep. Deputy sheriff is away till tomorrow, but the captain of the guard is there.'

I edged past them, since they barely allowed me room. The students were left outside, no doubt drumming their heels. So neither sheriff nor deputy sheriff was in Oxford. Perhaps the captain of the guard would have the authority to arrest Gidney and Frowike. If not, the deputy sheriff would be back tomorrow. I could only hope it would be before midday. Once the two men were arrested, surely they could be forced to reveal which Fellow of Merton was behind the plot. If not, I would be obliged to reveal all I had deduced about Olney. Somehow, it stuck in my throat. I did not like the man, but he was a poor miserable creature, with nothing to love but his books. Driving him away from them would be like another kind of killing.

The captain of the guard seemed a competent enough man. One who would carry out his orders scrupulously, but he did not look like one who could take the initiative himself. As soon as I saw him, I had misgivings, but I explained in detail why I was there.

'I have set it all out in this letter to the sheriff,' I said, 'but I am told that he is away at his manor, and his deputy out of Oxford until tomorrow.'

'Aye, that's so.'

'You had better read this for yourself, then,' I said, handing him the letter.

He peered at it. 'But this is addressed to the sheriff.'

'Aye. It is the letter I wrote to the sheriff before I learned that he was not here.'

'I can't open a letter to the sheriff.'

'I say that you may. I wrote the letter.'

He shook his head, and laid the letter down. 'Can't do it. More than my position is worth.'

'Heaven preserve me from fools!' I said. 'If this is the protection the castle offers to the town, why is it here at all?'

I seized the letter, flipped off the wax with my thumb-nail, and set it before him. He was so astonished at my behaviour he took up the sheet and peered at it again. His lips moved as he struggled to read it. Clearly he was not a lettered man. When he was finished, he looked at me, baffled.

'What do you expect me to do?'

'I expect you to arrest those two men,' I said, hoping I was making some progress at last. 'Pierson Gidney and Robert Frowike. They are lodged at Swindlestock's Tavern. Go cautiously, for they are armed.'

'I cannot do it.' There was a certain smug satisfaction in his tone. 'Not until the deputy sheriff comes back tomorrow and orders it.'

I had run my head against the stone wall of military command.

'Very well,' I said, through gritted teeth. 'Have your men ready to go at once, and hand that letter to the deputy sheriff the moment he sets foot in the castle.'

There was nothing more I could do.

Drearily I tramped back into town. I must have worn out more shoe leather in the last two weeks than in the previous six months. I would be heartily glad to become a little shopkeeper again. What I must do now, before all else, was to tell Jordain all that had happened since I had last seen him. He did not even know that Roger had discovered the men's names.

When I reached Hart Hall, I nodded to the students to follow me inside. It would be perfectly natural, should anyone be watching, for them to return to their own hall. Indeed I was beginning to have an uneasy feeling that I was being watched, and anyone watching must have noticed my two shadows. It would be best to dispense with them, but that would be risky.

Jordain was relieved to see me. 'I have been to the shop, but Walter said you had gone off to see the constable directly after dinner and never come back.'

'Crowmer was as useful as a plate of wet fish,' I said, sitting down and easing my feet out of my shoes. I hoped I should be able to put them on again. 'I thought he would direct me to the sheriff, but the sheriff is away. All he could tell me was to visit the castle, where I wasted my time. Did Walter tell you what Roger discovered last night?'

'Aye. And what happened to Margaret this morning. 'Tis as well that she has such a stout heart. Many a woman would have fainted with the terror of it, a hand clamped over her mouth and threatened with a knife.'

'She was badly frightened, even so.'

'What happened at the castle?'

I gave him a brief account of my tussle with the gate-keepers and the ineptitude of their captain.

'I can only hope that the deputy sheriff returns before I am due to hand over the Psalter at the Swindlestock Tavern.'

'What shall you do if he does not?'

'I have had a thought of something which might win us some delay,' I said. 'I have in stock an old book – not a Psalter but a copy of Aquinas's *Meditations* – which is much the same size and shape as Merton's Psalter. My feeling is that Gidney and Frowike are barely literate. I may be wrong, but I think to them one old book may look much like another. I thought I would wrap the *Meditations* carefully in several layers of cloth, tie it around and about firmly with well knotted tape, and present that to the innkeeper at the tavern. I doubt whether they will even unpack it, but will take it at once, just as it is, to the man who is employing them. By the time the substitution has been discovered, surely the deputy sheriff will have returned.'

'That should certainly buy us some time,' he said slowly. 'Though once they have discovered the deception, I should not like to be in your place.'

'I will not give up the Psalter to them. Once it is safe to do so, I will retrieve it from Godstow and put it in the hands of the Warden of Merton.'

'Lads!' Jordain called to the two students, who had made off to the kitchen, no doubt hungry after their exercise. 'Bring us a stoup of ale here.' He lowered his voice. 'They have kept you safely under their eye?'

'They have, but anyone watching me will have noticed them by now. They had better stay here when I leave.'

One of the students brought us a flagon and two beakers, then returned to the kitchen. Jordain poured us each a generous measure.

'After this, I must go back to the shop,' I said, 'and hunt out that copy of the *Meditations*. Have you seen Mistress Farringdon today? Margaret visited her this morning, just before she was grabbed in the street.'

I took a long drink of my ale, which was welcome after the walk back from the castle.

'You know,' I added, before he answered, 'I wonder whether they were watching the Farringdons, on the chance one of us might call on them.'

'Perhaps,' he said. 'But it would not be difficult for them to discover that Margaret is your sister, and you are their means of recovering the book. I did call at the Cross Inn after dinner. The Farringdons knew nothing of what happened to Margaret, any more than I did, then. They go home tomorrow. I would have given them William's ink well along with the rest of his belongings, but we had better keep it for the sheriff.'

'Aye.' My mind was on other things. 'Do you know, Jordain, in all that crowd in Northgate Street, not a soul came to Margaret's aid? She could have been stabbed and left for dead. No one would have cared.'

'Men have grown skins as thick as ox hides, these last years. It is that or go mad with despair.'

I sighed. 'I wish I had been the one given the warning, not my sister, but I had my stout bodyguards. For the rest, I must keep my family safe.'

I donned my shoes again and got to my feet. 'I'm off home. Will you come with me and sup with us? I should like you to see whether you think my substitute book will pass muster, for a short time at least.'

'Aye, I'll come with you. Best if you do not walk alone, even in daylight. I'll just leave word where I shall be, if I am needed.'

When we set out down Catte Street, Jordain suddenly chuckled. 'There is a certain irony in it, is there not? Their plot was to substitute William's copy for the Psalter. Now you hope to deceive them by substituting the *Meditations* for the Psalter.'

I gave a wry laugh. 'Indeed, there is something very satisfying in that.'

As we walked slowly down the High toward my shop, I noticed a familiar hunched figure in front of us, heading past the shop and on toward the East Gate. I caught Jordain by the sleeve.

'That is Philip Olney! It's strange, that is the second time I have seen him heading that way. What business can he have at that end of the town?' I racked my brains, trying to remember. 'It was after Mass on Sunday. I thought it odd, that he should come to St Peter's. Merton is not even in our parish, and besides, they have their own chapel and their own priest to celebrate Mass. Then afterwards I saw him scurrying away furtively like this. I had forgotten, but it surprised me at the time.'

'Well, why do we not follow, discreetly, and discover the answer?' Jordain said. 'Anything that might be connected with William's murder is worth investigating.'

Olney hurried ahead of us along the High and we followed at a distance. As usual there were plenty of people passing to and fro, since the High is one of the main thoroughfares of Oxford, so that it was not difficult to seem to be merely walking in the same direction.

'He is not wearing his academic gown,' Jordain said. 'That too is odd.'

By the time we reached the East Gate, Olney was already through it, walking more confidently now, as though he did not expect anyone who knew him to notice him out here, beyond the bounds of the town. We paused on the far side of the gate and saw him turn in at the third of the cottages which lay on the left hand between the East Gate and the hospital of St John. These houses were set a little back from the road, with a patch of ground in front, each one put to a different purpose. One held a stall for selling vegetables. One sold eggs. Another had allowed a carpenter's workshop to overflow into the space, with stacked timber, half-finished stools, and a heap of wood shavings. Olney's destination was a house which sat back behind a well-stocked herb garden, bisected by a narrow path laid with flat stones. The cottage too looked neat and tidy.

Before Olney had reached the door, it was flung open and a pretty young woman flew down the path and into Olney's arms.

'His sister?' Jordain said, bemused.

'I think not,' I said dryly. 'I do not think any man kisses his sister like that.'

Olney and the girl clung together passionately, heedless of the world around them. Every line of their bodies betrayed them as lovers.

The two were still intertwined when a small boy appeared in the doorway. He was about Alysoun's age, but he did not run down the path, as she would have done. One leg was withered, and he hobbled along painfully with a crutch under his armpit. The lovers both turned, then Olney lifted the child gently and held him high in the air for a moment, before carrying him into the cottage. The door closed behind them.

I looked at Jordain, stunned.

'Did you see the child?'

'Aye,' he said, and without a word we turned back to the East Gate, both of us, I know, feeling the same sense of shame at prying where we should not have done.

'He is the image of Philip Olney,' I said at last. 'Olney, vowed to celibacy, has a woman and a son.'

–

Once back in the shop, I tried to thrust from my mind that image of Olney in close embrace with a very fair young woman, and then lifting his crippled son in his arms. We must prepare our substitute book and give our minds to the next few dangerous hours, but it was impossible to forget what we had seen. Could it have any bearing on the plot to steal the Psalter? Perhaps Olney needed money for the woman and child, and planned to sell the Psalter for enough to provide for them lifelong.

What made me most ashamed was that in spying upon Olney I had seen him for once happy. And why should he not be happy? Yet the rules were strict. He could not keep his Fellowship, remain a senior member of the university, and marry. Of course, he was probably *not* married, although it was clearly a long established liaison, not a brief interlude with a prostitute, to which his college would probably have turned a blind eye. Such a liaison was tantamount to marriage, in the view of the university. He would not be permitted to have both – his Fellowship and his woman. The whole thing had shaken me, so that I was distracted as Jordain and I, with the two scriveners, packed up the old copy of the *Meditations* to look as convincing as possible in its role as the stolen book.

Neither Jordain nor I mentioned what we had seen, but I was sure he was also pondering whether it might have any bearing on this other matter. Nevertheless, the substitute book was prepared and Walter and Roger were told about my visit to the castle.

We were still discussing how best to prepare for the next day, whether or not the deputy sheriff returned before midday, and Roger had just closed the shutters, when the shop door opened, and Rafe wandered disconsolately in. His face was grubby and tear-stained.

'What is the matter, my fine man?' I said, laying the wrapped book aside and lifting him up. I gave thanks that all his limbs were straight and strong.

He buried his head in my shoulder and muttered something into the cloth of my cotte that I could not make out.

'What is that you say? Have you and Alysoun quarrelled? Is she playing with Jonathan and won't let you join them?'

He heaved away from my shoulder and shook his head vigorously.

'Nay! She went off walking Rowan up the street, to show Jonathan how well she is taught. And she said she would come straight back. And that was hours and *hours* ago, and she didn't come back. She just left me there and didn't come back.'

'What do you say?' At first I could not follow what he was saying, my mind still on Olney.

'She didn't come back!' he wailed, and burst into tears.

I sat down with him on my lap and tried to soothe him, for I would get no sense out of him in this state. What did he mean – hours and hours? My heart was beginning to pound, but I told myself that small children have no understanding of time. Probably Alysoun had walked no further than the Mitre and was now back at the bakehouse. Still, best to make sure.

'Walter,' I said, as Rafe's tears subsided into gasps and hiccups. 'Will you run over to John Baker and find out what is afoot? Perhaps the older children have played a game with Rafe.'

I made my voice as convincing as possible, but I do not think any of them were deceived.

'Rafe,' I said, 'run along and wash your face. Then tell Aunt Margaret I said you were to have some bread and honey.' His distress forgotten in the prospect of honey, he trotted off. Jordain, Roger and I waited in a strained silence until Walter returned, accompanied by both John and Jonathan Baker.

'Is the maid not with you, then?' John said. 'The children were all playing in the garden the afternoon long, then Jonathan comes in and says both of yours were gone. I was sure they were back home. Speak up, son.'

I thought that Jonathan looked too frightened to speak.

'Rafe tells us you were trying to train the puppies on the lead,' I said, to give him encouragement. I wanted to shout out, *Where is she?* Yet that would but send him tongue-tied.

'Aye, that's right, maister.'

'When would that be?'

He looked vague. 'From when she came to mine, until, maybe, three o'the clock? I heard St Mary's bell. I think it was three. It might have been four.'

It was now nearly six. Dear God, where was she?

'And then?' I prompted.

'Well, we got Digger to wear a collar, but he wouldn't take to the lead. Alysoun was walking Rowan up and down, showing how biddable she was, and I said—'

He broke off and turned pale, twisting one leg around the other.

'What did you say, Jonathan? I am not angry. I just need to know what happened.'

'I said it was one thing to walk Rowan in the garden, but I'd wager she'd not be so biddable in the street.' He got the words out in a rush.

I clenched my fists but willed myself to stay calm until he had told all.

He gulped and went on. 'And then we left Rafe in the garden, saying we'd be back. And we left Digger with him. And me and Alysoun took Rowan out into the High Street.'

I turned to his father. 'You must have seen them come through the shop. What time would it be?'

He shook his head. 'I would have been kneading the dough for tomorrow's bread by then, over at the troughs, with my back to them. The door was open to let out the heat. I would not even hear the door.'

No help there.

'So you were in the High Street, Jonathan. Which way did you go?'

'Toward Carfax. And I was right!' he said, in a glow of self-justification. 'Once she was in the street, with all the crowds, Rowan took off like an arrow, Alysoun running to keep up with her. Then she pulled the lead out of Alysoun's hand. And Alysoun went running after her.'

'And you?'

He shuffled his feet and would not meet my eye. 'I let them go. I *said* she wouldn't stay biddable in the street. I let them go. Why should I chase after? I came back to Rafe and Digger, and we waited. When she didn't come back, I thought she'd gone home, in a sulk with me. I told Rafe he should go home.'

I drew a deep breath. Just children heedlessly playing. And Alysoun knew her way around Oxford, she had often walked with me. She would have been trying to catch the dog. But it had been at least two hours. I tried to keep calm, but my head was beginning to pound. I looked at Jordain, and it was clear what he was thinking.

No! I thought, *No!* She is just hunting for the puppy.

'Never worry about the maid,' John Baker said comfortably. 'She'll be chasing after that dog.'

He gave his son a cuff to the ear, but only a gentle one. 'You should have helped her, lad, not left her to hunt for the dog on her own.'

'I thought she would be back in a few minutes,' he mumbled. He was red from collar to brow. 'When she wasn't, it was too late to go after.'

'Well,' said Walter, 'let us not sit about here raking it over. Let us all go and search for the maid and the dog. There are six of us here, if Master Baker and his son come too. Between us, we'll surely find them.'

I jumped up. He was right, with so many looking we would soon find her. She had the sense not to go near the rivers. There would be another two hours of daylight.

'I had best tell my sister what we are about,' I said.

To Margaret, I tried to sound reassuring, but she turned white with shock, pressing her fingers to her lips.

'He warned us,' she whispered.

I put an arm around her shoulders and gave her a quick hug.

'We don't know that those men had anything to do with it. Alysoun loves that dog. She will search until she finds her, never thinking about how long she has been gone or how worried we will be. You and Rafe stay here in case she comes back before we do. Oxford is not such a big place. With six of us searching—'

She nodded, and made a valiant attempt to smile. 'Off you go, then, and start searching. A dog might make for a butcher's stall.'

Back in the shop, we looked somewhat helplessly at one another. Where to begin? Although Jordain and I had lived in the town since we were boys, the others had been born here and knew every street and alleyway far better than we did. It was natural that John Baker took charge, setting out for us which areas we should each search.

'We must hope neither the maid nor the dog will have gone outside the walls,' he said. 'Let us keep to the town. We'll all return here at dusk, with or without the maid.'

It was fortunate that Oxford is laid out on so simple a plan, with its four main streets meeting at Carfax, and

the line of Catte Street and Magpie Lane at right angles
to the High, so that the whole town falls naturally into
six segments, the two below the castle little populated.
He assigned me the area south of the High Street, from
the edge of Oriel west to Fish Street, then down as far
as the South Gate. That included St Frideswide's Priory
and Canterbury College, neither of which Alysoun could
have entered, but there was also a maze of small lanes lined
with houses. The dog might have found her way into any
of the holdings.

Before we set off, Jordain took me aside.

'I do not like this. It looks too much like your wolf trap
turned on its head, with Alysoun as the lamb. You should
not go into those narrow lanes on your own, with dusk
coming on.'

'I do not care if it is a trap,' I said wildly. 'Let them take
me. I'll gladly change places with my daughter.'

'Take care,' he said, 'and keep your eyes open behind
as well as before.'

I nodded, hardly heeding him. They could not have
taken Alysoun. They could not. I had until midday
tomorrow.

We hurried out into the street and dispersed in our
separate directions. I found myself running up the High
until I was past St Mary's, then I slowed down and started
along the north end of my allotted area, calling out to
Alysoun, but with little hope she would be anywhere here.
It was along this stretch of the street that she had gone
in pursuit of Rowan two hours ago. Little likelihood,
then, that she would be near here now. On the opposite
side of the street John Baker was searching. He had set
himself one of the most densely inhabited areas of the
town, which also contained a number of butchers' shops.

283

Like Margaret he believed in following the likely route of the dog. I saw him disappear into the Mitre to ask if any had seen Alysoun.

On my side of the street the houses were tightly packed together, although here and there a narrow alley led through a further maze of houses. I followed one of them which passed St Edward's church, where a churchwarden was sweeping the porch.

'My daughter is lost,' I said to him, 'running after her dog. Red gold hair. Six years old, but well grown for her age. Have you seen her?'

He shook his head regretfully. 'I am sorry, I've seen no such child. May God aid your search.'

I thanked him and hurried on. At Canterbury College I asked the same of the porter and received the same answer. I turned my back on the college and looked to right and left. There was no systematic way to search the area. I cut back along a lane to Fish Street and ran up it in the direction of Carfax, but stopped at the Guildhall. In all the houses, people would now be making supper or sitting down to eat it, and there seemed little point in knocking on their doors. Alysoun would not be inside. If she had found Rowan, she would be on her way home. If she had not, she would still be searching the streets and any open area where the dog might have gone. There were few such open areas in this part of town. I would not let myself think about the third possibility.

At the Guildhall I knew there would be someone about, for the town officers often worked late, but here again the doorkeeper shook his head. It was already nearing dusk when I retraced my steps back down Fish Street and all the way to St Michael's-at-the-South-Gate.

There was a large churchyard here, the sort of place where the dog might have gone chasing after cats or rodents. I walked through it, calling, so that from two of the houses overlooking the churchyard heads peered out and I was asked what I thought I was doing.

'My little girl is lost,' I said. By now I could no longer keep the despair from my voice. I found I was weeping and rubbed my face with my shirt sleeve.

They were sympathetic, but no one had seen a little girl looking for a dog.

Past St Frideswide's Priory, around the back of Canterbury College, and up past Oriel to the High. I had stopped calling now. I knew in my heart it was useless.

I was the last to return to the shop but for Walter, hard on my heels after searching the area below the castle, the furthest away. Gathered again we looked at each other and shook our heads. Jonathan had been crying.

'Send the boy home to his bed,' I told John. 'There is nothing more he can do tonight.'

Jonathan crept away, his shoulders hunched, wiping his nose on the back of his hand.

I sank down on to the chair behind the counter.

'No word anywhere?' I asked, though I knew the answer.

They shook their heads.

'We must give up for tonight,' I said. 'We have tried, and I thank you.' My voice cracked, but I could not prevent.

'I shall speak to the Watch,' John Baker said. 'Best if they keep an eye open as they go about. They'll have their lanterns. And their dogs may smell out another dog. I'll warn them that it's a part spaniel puppy, probably still wearing a collar and lead, not a stray. And I'll describe

Alysoun to them. Keep your heart up, Nicholas. She must be somewhere in the town. Perhaps she grew tired hunting for the puppy and has fallen asleep somewhere.'

I nodded my thanks, but could not find words. When he was gone, Jordain fetched Margaret through to where we sat in the shop, and she brought ale with her, with bread and cheese. I was thirsty, but I could not eat, my stomach turned sick with fear. My little maid, she would be helpless in their hands. What would they do to her? Even short of killing, they could ruin her for life.

As we were making our sorry little supper, there came a scratching at the door. I flew to open it. Perhaps Alysoun was too tired to knock.

The light from within fell on the creature upon the doorstep. Muddy, bedraggled, apologetic, Rowan squirmed at my feet. I ran out, shouting.

'Alysoun! Alysoun! Are you there?'

But the street was deserted.

By the time I returned, Jordain was on his knees examining the dog.

'She's dirty and tired but has come to no harm. She's not been in the river.'

That was one consolation. Alysoun had not tried to rescue the dog and been swept away. Somehow the dog had found her way home alone.

I dropped down into my chair and clenched my trembling hands together.

'We all know what this means,' I said. 'Margaret brought a warning from the man Gidney. They have carried out their threat. They mean to make me talk.'

'But you had until midday tomorrow!' Jordain objected.

'I do not think they are men of their word,' I said drearily. 'Besides, that was the word of one of the underlings. Perhaps he has been ordered by the chief instigator to raise the level of the threat.'

'I would have thought,' Jordain said slowly, 'that Olney was otherwise occupied.'

We exchanged a glance. We had not mentioned what we had seen out beyond the East Gate.

'I do not think there is anything else to be done tonight,' Margaret said. 'If the Watch keep a lookout for Alysoun, that is the best that can be done during the dark. Walter and Roger, you had best go home. And you too, Jordain.'

'I shall stay here tonight,' Jordain said.

'We can stay too,' Walter said, and Roger nodded.

I was about to send them off, when there was another noise at the door, a furtive rustle, then running footsteps fading away down the street.

'It is a note pushed under the door,' I cried, springing to retrieve it.

I was half expecting this. It was at least better than nothing at all. I carried the note over to the candle standing on the counter. It was merely a folded paper, unsealed. I unfolded it, though my hands shook so much that I dropped it and had to grope under the counter for it. Written boldly on a scrap of good parchment, it was brief and to the point:

> *If you want to see your daughter alive again, bring the Psalter as instructed, without fail. Try any trickery, and her throat will be cut.*

I felt the room dip and swoop around me, as if I had been struck again on the head. Jordain seized the note from my hand and read it.

'Well,' he said grimly, 'this is what we expected.'

'Nay,' I said, when I could get the words out. 'Not quite. I know that hand.'

'Can you be sure?' Margaret said.

'It is my business to know a man's hand, whether he tries to disguise it or not,' I said.

'That is the hand not of Philip Olney, but of Allard Basset.'

Chapter Thirteen

The discovery of Basset's hand on the note changed everything. For a long moment we all stood in silence as the pieces of the puzzle fell apart, then came together in an entirely new shape.

'Not Olney after all,' Jordain said slowly. 'We thought Olney was afraid because Basset had discovered that he was behind the theft of the Psalter.'

'He was afraid of Basset, certainly,' I said, 'but for quite another reason.'

We looked at each other, but by unspoken consent we knew we should not reveal to anyone else what we had discovered by a shameful act of spying.

'Basset has had a hold over Olney,' I said. 'If he revealed everything to the Warden, Olney would have lost not only his livelihood but his beloved books. Basset took the Irish Psalter and Olney kept his mouth closed. No wonder he sweated with fear when I wanted to see it.'

'And Basset wanted that book for himself,' Jordain said, 'enough to hire Frowike and Gidney to act as his go-betweens, for he could not be seen himself buying parchment from Dafydd Hewlyn, or hunting out a scribe to do the copying. He is far too well known in Oxford.'

'Aye,' I said wryly. 'Far too well known. One of our greatest scholars. Yet he forgot himself so far as to come to my shop and warn me off.'

'It must have been a moment of panic, since you were showing too much interest in the book. Since then he has kept well out of sight. If the Psalter was discovered to be missing before the copy was ready, it was Olney who would be blamed.'

'A very successful plan. We were convinced it was Olney behind it all.'

'William's cousin,' Margaret said, 'Sister Benedicta. She said that William had discovered that the copy would be placed in the box, and the Merton man who had devised the plot would keep the original for himself. How could he expect to succeed? Would no one have noticed?'

'He could never have succeeded,' Walter said emphatically. 'Anyone who knows books would recognise it at once as a fraud. It was madness.'

'Aye,' I said, slowly and fearfully. 'There is a kind of madness at the root of this. And this madman has Alysoun in his hands.'

They looked at me in shocked silence. A madman might do anything. Madness is unpredictable.

'Surely,' Margaret said, twisting the stuff of her skirt in her hands, 'surely he cannot be mad? He is a respected scholar. A Fellow of Merton. A senior man in the university.'

'Not mad as the wild men of the woods are mad, Meg,' I said. 'Gibbering and foaming at the mouth and running naked. Mad with an obsession to possess some beautiful object. Some men will run mad to possess a beautiful woman, seeing that woman as an object they must own. And if they cannot, they would rather kill her than let any other man possess her. Men have run mad to possess great jewels – the largest pearl ever found, the most perfect ruby. To such a man, anything that stands in his way will be swept aside. It is a mote in his eye. A hindrance to his perfect vision.'

'So William was murdered,' Jordain said. 'We thought that those two ruffians acted on their own, in a moment of panic. Now I am not so sure.'

'I think now that Basset, too, was there,' I said. 'Out at the old mill, where William met his death.' I swallowed with difficulty. 'And now this man has Alysoun.'

A stifled cry broke from Meg, though she pressed her fists against her mouth.

I felt cold. So cold. Yet at last I was thinking clearly. I knew what I must do.

'At dawn tomorrow – or is it today? – I shall ride out to Godstow and fetch the Irish Psalter from Sister Benedicta. I should be back in Oxford well before midday. I shall then go to the castle in the hope that the deputy sheriff has returned. With his help, Frowike and Gidney may still be captured, but only *after* Alysoun is safe. He must not arrest them before, for that will endanger her life. I do not trust that thick-headed captain to understand the need to hold back from the arrest. I have already given him their names and lodging.'

'You will exchange the Psalter for Alysoun?' Jordain said.

'If I must. My girl's life is more precious than any book, even that book, but I will deceive them if I can. Once she is safe, I shall go to Warden Durant and tell him of Allard Basset's treachery.' I pointed to the scrap of parchment. 'This alone is proof. Durant may not know the man's hand as well as I do, but there will be plenty of examples for comparison. Basset has a particular flourish that he gives to the tails of the letters that fall below the line. It is unmistakable. See.'

They all leaned over the note to study it.

'In his arrogance, he has not even attempted to disguise his hand. I was his student for many years. He must know that I would recognise it. Because he holds my child, he thinks he is invincible.'

'Perhaps he is,' Margaret whispered.

'He shall not be.'

I was sure of myself now, filled with a cold anger which sustained me.

'I will write a note to these villains,' I said, 'which I want Walter to take to the innkeeper of the Swindlestock at eleven o'the clock, and bid him make sure they receive it at once. They must bring Alysoun with them, to the small back parlour of the tavern, and at midday I will come with the Psalter. I will not hand over the Psalter until I have Alysoun. They are desperate for the book, and what use is a dead child to them? I will say in my message that if any harm comes to her, I will throw the Psalter on the fire.'

'Will you?' Jordain asked.

'Oh, you may be sure I will.'

Margaret gave a great sigh. 'It might succeed.'

'It will. One other thing. Have we more of that cloth that we used to wrap the *Meditations*? And the tape? Once I have the Psalter, I shall wrap it so that the two will look as much alike as possible.'

Roger had been listening to all of this in silence, but now he spoke. 'Will you be able to tell them apart, if they are wrapped identically?'

'Aye, the bands on the spine of the *Meditations* are not nearly as thick as those on the Psalter. I shall be able to feel them through the wrapping.'

'You still hope to pass off the *Meditations*?' Jordain said.

'If I can. I would not endanger the Psalter unless I must, nor will I hesitate to burn it if they harm my child.'

It had grown very late, but none of us could sleep. Walter found me more of the cloth and tape, which I stored in my satchel with the wrapped *Meditations*. I was impatient to be away, but I could not hire my horse until dawn brought the stable lads at the Mitre from their beds.

Margaret had disappeared into the kitchen, but now she called all of us to come through.

'You may think you do not wish to eat, but the day will demand strength from you and you will do no good, any of you, fainting from hunger.'

We followed her obediently to find that she had laid out a great spread, half supper, half breakfast – soup and bread and cold bacon and porridge and the remains of an apple pie, with a jug of thick cream. Roger looked shy to be sitting at table to eat with us, but Walter pulled him down on to a bench next to him. Jordain carried the great pot of soup over to the table. Rowan, subdued and penitent, was pushing her empty bowl across the floor.

I had thought I could not face food, but found suddenly that I was ravenous. Margaret was right. Strength would be needed for all that I must achieve this coming day. And now I knew who was my enemy.

–

As I rode out of the North Gate on Rufus, the sky was gradually flooding with a curious grass-green light of dawn. Most of the world was still asleep, so that I seemed to pass through a kind of dream world, where the horse and I were the only living creatures, apart from the birds who filled the air with morning song which sounded more intense than usual, while the strange light gave the buildings the flat appearance of shapes cut from paper.

I had hoped to hire a horse with a greater turn of speed than Rufus, but none was to be had today at the Mitre and I could not spare the time to hunt round the other stables. At least Rufus knew me and would do as I bid. Once we were through the gate and into the wide expanse of St Giles, I gave him his head, urging him first to a canter, then a gallop. The rain of the previous week had laid the dust of the road and the surface had now dried firm, the best for riding, so we made good time, although every moment seemed to fly past, as the sun rose. By the time it was overhead I would have Alysoun safe, or I would have failed.

The distance to Godstow must be about six miles, but parts of the road to Woodstock were in poor repair, forcing me to slow the horse to a walk, so that we could pick our way around holes and fallen branches. It was worse when we turned off down the lane and through the woods to Wolvercote. I had not noticed the poor state of the lane before, but I had not been in a hurry then. Every delay was maddening. And what if I reached the abbey, only to find that I would not be allowed to see Sister Benedicta?

It was worse. I arrived just as the bell was ringing for Terce. I would be forced to wait until the service was finished. Now I would barely reach Oxford in time.

The lay porter recognised me and greeted me pleasantly.

'Will you not come into the gatehouse, sir? You may wait here until the sisters have finished their devotions.'

'I thank you,' I said resignedly, and joined him in his little room.

'I am here on most urgent business,' I explained. 'Sister Benedicta has been caring for a book which is the property of Merton College, and it must be returned by midday today. No blame to her. Her cousin rescued it from the thieves. But now, if it is not returned in time, a life will be in danger.'

The man stared at me, mouth agape. No such alarm surely ever disturbed this tranquil place. I wondered whether he would believe me, but he appeared sympathetic.

'I do not even need to visit Sister Benedicta,' I said, 'if a message could reach her, to bring the book to me here, as soon as the service is over?'

'I will do my best for you,' he said. 'It is not a long service.'

It felt long, sitting there, with the time slipping away, but at last he seemed to recognise the end of the service in the music and the nuns' voices raised in song, for he gave me a cheerful smile and walked away briskly across the courtyard to the church. I watched as he approached one of the senior nuns, who came first out of the church, perhaps the abbess herself. She stopped and looked across at me. She must have given her consent, for he waited until the novices emerged at the end of the procession and spoke to one. From this distance they were difficult to tell apart in their habits, but Emma Thorgold was tall, almost as tall as I, and this girl was tall. She inclined her head, left the procession and moved slowly toward the dortoir.

Hurry, hurry, I urged her silently, but I understood that she would not be permitted to run, at any rate within sight of the senior nuns. However, she must have run once she was out of sight, for she reappeared quickly, and she was carrying something. With a glance over her shoulder to make certain that all her sisters were now within doors, she flew across to the gatehouse, her habit billowing out behind her.

'I was as quick as I could be,' she said, pressing the book into my hands. 'The porter said someone's life is in danger.'

'My daughter. She is six years old and these villains have taken her.'

'You have a daughter?'

Her expression was difficult to read, and I knew I must leave at once, but I said, 'A daughter of six and a son of four. My wife died in the pestilence.'

She laid her hand lightly on my arm. 'I am sorry. So many died.'

I nodded. What words were there that could be spoken?

'I must go.' Yet I lingered.

'Go, go. May God keep your daughter safe. But please,' she hesitated, 'will you come to see me, and tell me how it all ends?'

'I will. We know who killed your cousin.'

She nodded, then she was gone, walking demurely the way the other women had gone, into the refectory.

I barely glanced at the Psalter before slipping it into my satchel to join the *Meditations*, then I mounted Rufus, called my thanks to the porter, and headed back across the bridge and through the woods.

Shortly past the village of Wolvercote I reached a clearing, where I dismounted and threw the reins over a branch. I needed to wrap the Psalter before I returned to Oxford. When I drew it out of my satchel, I turned it over in my hands, and opened it to look again at the illuminations which I had not seen since a few weeks before I married Elizabeth. In the soft green light of the woods the pictures glowed as brightly as ever. The pages were unmarked, the binding firm. It had taken no harm from the time it had spent away from its ivory inlaid casket. It was beautiful, but it was only a book. William had died for it. Olney had suffered for it. And Alysoun?

I found a fallen tree to sit on, drew out the piece of cloth and the tape, and did my best to wrap it as much like the other book as I could. Running my thumb down the spine of each, I could detect a distinct difference.

My heart was pounding faster as I stowed the two books in my satchel and mounted again. If only I could reach the tavern in time!

The ride back to Oxford was torment. Every fallen branch, every broken hole, meant more delays. At last, nearer the town, the road improved, and I set Rufus flying down St Giles, past market stalls and angry customers, nearly crashing into a flock of geese but swerving and slowing to a slithering halt at the North Gate. Rufus snorted, as if baulked of entertainment, and danced sideways as I tried to coax him through the gate. Only the length of Northgate Street now, and there was the tower of St Martin's church rising ahead of us, across the street from the Swindlestock Tavern.

Then I realised what had caused Rufus to hesitate. Directly in front of me was a solid group of horsemen, clad in half armour. At their head, Cedric Walden, the deputy sheriff. Perhaps at last God was looking favourably on what had seemed like a hopeless task. I edged Rufus round the group of soldiers and drew in next to Walden. There must have been twenty men with him and by the look of them they had been putting down trouble somewhere in the shire. I had thought I had been left with no time to go to the castle for help, but now help was delivered into my hand.

'Sheriff Walden,' I said, reaching out to touch his arm. 'I am in urgent need of assistance from you and your men, in a case of murder. And now a child's life is at stake.'

He turned to me courteously, a man of a very different calibre from his captain of the guard or the pompous fools guarding the castle gate.

He reined in. 'A case of murder?'

'The murder of William Farringdon. The inquest was held last week.'

'I know of the case.'

'The men who committed it will be in the Swindle-stock Tavern at midday. I am to meet them there, to hand over a valuable book in exchange for a child. My daughter, whom they have seized and hold as hostage.'

As quickly as I could, mindful of the minutes slipping away, I explained what was afoot.

'If you are right that they will be there,' he said, 'then we can surround the tavern and arrest them. From your descriptions, they should not be difficult to pick out.'

'But you must wait until I have my daughter safe!' I had him by the arm and was shaking it.

'Aye, we'll proceed with caution.' He gave a small smile, and I thought that he was enjoying himself. He did not have a child caught up in this dangerous game.

'Best if we are not seen approaching the tavern,' he said, 'or our birds will be flown before ever you reach it. Go you on ahead. I will hold back my men, then come around by the back alleys to Great Bailey and approach that way. We will stay out of sight, but cover all the ways in and out. Once you have your daughter safe, go to the door of St Martin's and wait there. I will watch for you. When you are clear, we will move in.'

I nodded. 'I understand. Should they slip past you, they will almost certainly be making for Merton.'

His lips tightened in a grim smile above his beard. 'They will not slip past us.'

He signalled with his hand to the men, and they began to melt away to the right. I turned back down Northgate Street. Some precious minutes had been lost, but a great deal gained. As fast as I could, in despite of the crowds, I headed toward the square tower which showed above the other buildings. Past the Cross Inn, past a row of shops, with customers impeding my passage, and then I was at Carfax. I drew a deep breath and slid from Rufus's back, hitching him to one of the rings in the wall of the tavern and gripping the strap of my satchel tight against my side. After his final gallop he needed to be walked and rubbed down, but he would have to wait. As I opened the tavern door and stepped through, St Martin's bell struck midday.

I had chosen the small back parlour of the tavern for our meeting partly because I knew that they would not transact any business with me in the public room, and partly because I knew that the innkeeper always had a small fire burning there so that guests who wished could mull their wine. I wanted a fire, so that I could make it quite clear that I intended to carry out my threat to burn the Psalter if they harmed Alysoun.

There was a sharp pain in my chest as I threw open the door to the small parlour. There was no one there. I left the door open, but stayed close to it, half hidden. As I hoped, there was a small fire lit on the hearth, no more than two yards away. Feeling sick, I wondered what I should do if they did not come. They might not have received my message with the meeting place and my terms. Or Alysoun – I must face it – might already be dead.

Then I heard footsteps approaching along the passage from the public parlour and two men entered, with the small figure of Alysoun between them. Her gown was torn and muddy, there was a bruise on her cheek, but she was not crying. She looked defiant. She saw me before they did, and I pressed one finger quickly to my lips. She understood at once and looked away.

The men swung round and saw me. The dark-haired one, Pierson Gidney, clamped his great fist over Alysoun's thin arm. She winced, but did not cry out. I saw that the backs of his hands were indeed covered with thick black hairs. I moved a step or two closer to the fire as the other man, the ginger-haired Robert Frowike, rubbed his hands together and smiled, showing small sharp teeth, which gave him even more the appearance of a fox. I saw why Dafydd had not mentioned the beard. It was a pathetic wisp of a thing, the sort young boys try to grow in the hope that it will give them the appearance of men, while it only serves to make them look feeble. Somehow that sparse fringe of hair gave me a boost of courage.

'So, Master Elyot,' Frowike said, 'you have seen the advisability of handing over our property.'

'Not your property, I think, but the property of Merton College.'

He shrugged, not bothering to reply.

'I have it here.' I patted my satchel. 'However, you know my terms. I will give it to you only once my daughter is handed over safely to me. She can be of no use to you, a child of six. Give me the child and I will give you the book. Fair exchange. But if you try any trickery, there is a fire there.'

I drew the book out of my satchel and held it up so they could see it.

'Any trickery, and the book flies straight into the heart of the fire.'

'You would not dare.' Frowike tried to sound convinced, but there was a nervous tick in his left eyelid. 'You bookmen, these things are too precious to you to be destroyed.'

'Do you want to try me? What will your master, Allard Basset, have to say to you if you present him with nothing but a heap of ashes? I would not value your necks too highly in that case.'

I was aware that a solid volume of parchment does not burn so easily, but I was counting on their not knowing that.

They looked startled when I mentioned Basset's name and exchanged a worried glance. I hoped I was starting to rattle them, but not too much, not too soon. Alysoun stood absolutely still, her eyes fixed on me. *Good girl*, I said to her silently. *Keep still and don't provoke them.*

Clearly it was Frowike who made the decisions. He had not quite made up his mind. I decided to show him that I was serious. I leaned over the fire and trailed the end of the knotted tape over the burning logs. It caught almost at once and a red bud of flame glowed, before beginning to move slowly up the tape toward the wrapped book.

'No!' Frowike shouted. 'Give him the brat, Pierson!'

Gidney shoved Alysoun toward me. She stumbled and almost fell, but I grabbed her in the curve of my left arm, then flung the book, with the tape catching fully aflame, to the far side of the room. Both men leapt after it. I scooped up Alysoun and ran.

Down the passage, out of the door onto Carfax, then into the doorway of St Martin's.

'Oh, Papa!' Alysoun wound her arms round my neck and her legs about my waist, clinging to me like some small terrified animal. She was weeping now, great wrenching sobs. I held her close and pressed my cheek against hers.

'It's over, my pet, no need to weep now. Such a brave girl you have been. Now watch. See what will happen to the bad men.'

I eased her round on to my hip, so that we could both watch the tavern. Walden's men were closing round it in a tight circle.

'Are those soldiers?' Alysoun whispered, her breath tickling my ear.

'They are. They will catch the men, but I needed to get you away first.'

It was neatly done. As Gidney and Frowike came out of the tavern smirking in triumph, Walden's men simply closed around them, but not before I had seen a thin wisp of smoke still rising from the book.

'That is my horse over there,' I said to Alysoun, 'wondering what is happening. As soon as we can reach him, we shall ride him home.'

'Ride? Through Oxford?' Her eyes glowed. I knew she was hoping she would be seen in such splendour.

'All the way down the High Street to home,' I promised.

The two men fought their captors, but must soon have realised it was hopeless. Before they were marched away to the castle, I spoke to Sheriff Walden.

'I will come to the castle tomorrow, with Master Brinkylsworth of Hart Hall, and bring all the evidence we have of the men's guilt. And might I have my book?'

'Here, take it,' he said. 'It seems to have had a singeing, but no serious harm. I will see you tomorrow.'

As the ruffians and their escort headed away down Great Bailey, I lifted Alysoun on to Rufus's back and mounted behind her. We were halfway down the High when she squirmed around in my arms.

'I'm sorry, Papa, it was all my fault. I should not have taken Rowan into the street. Those bad men caught me when I went chasing after her.' Tears welled up in her eyes again. 'And now Rowan is lost. Everything is my fault!'

'Nothing is your fault, my pet. And as for Rowan, at this very minute she is making up to Aunt Margaret, saying that it is long past her dinner time.'

'You found her!'

'Nay, she found her own way home herself. I think she is an exceptionally intelligent dog. But no more walking in the street until she is thoroughly trained.'

'I promise.'

Suddenly she yawned. By the time we reached the end of her triumphant ride down the High Street, Alysoun was asleep.

Jonathan was lurking across the street and came running when he saw me ride up. He stared up at Alysoun, slumped against my chest.

'Alysoun, is she—?'

'She is asleep. No harm done.'

I hoped that was true. I slid down from Rufus, still with Alysoun in my arms. She stirred, but did not wake.

'Hold the horse for me, Jonathan. I shall be back shortly.'

He grabbed the reins eagerly. It was not often that he was able to come so close to fine horse flesh.

I found Margaret, Jordain, and my two scriveners in the kitchen, their faces turned to me, drawn with worry and anxiety. Rafe was sitting on the floor, cradling Rowan. He knew that something was amiss, but I do not think he understood. At least I hoped he did not.

'All's well,' I said softly. 'I am just going to take her upstairs.'

I set Alysoun gently down on her bed, just as she was in her torn and dirty gown, only removing her shoes and pulling the feather bed over her. Back down in the kitchen I laid my satchel on the table and smiled round at them. One speaks of a burden being lifted from one's shoulders, but it is no empty metaphor. I felt suddenly light, as if I might spring from the floor and take flight.

'We'll let her sleep as much as she needs. I doubt whether she had any rest last night. When she wakes, Margaret, she will need a wash and food, but apart from a fright, she seems unharmed. All she was worried about was losing Rowan.'

'I said from the start that the dog would be trouble,' Margaret said with severity, and Rafe looked up, clutching the puppy protectively. 'Nay,' she added, 'now the pup is here I suppose she must stay. From the way she found us again last night, she has decided this is her home.'

Jordain smiled at me across Margaret, as she bent to fondle the puppy, giving the lie to her words.

I unbuckled my satchel and drew out the book with the singed tape. Walter gasped.

'You did set it to the fire, then!'

'Only the end of the tape.' I untied the tape and the charred end fell onto the floor, then I carefully removed the cloth wrapper, and drew out Aquinas's *Meditations*.

'You schemer!' Jordain said admiringly. 'So even *in extremis* you dared to trick them!'

'It was a gamble, but by then I had the support of Sheriff Walden and his men surrounding the tavern. I took both books with me, but I managed to bring Alysoun away without risking the Psalter.'

I gave them a brief account of how I had met Walden returning to Oxford and so had avoided the need to go to the castle.

'Which I would have had no time to do, in any case,' I said.

I got up. 'I must go.'

'Go?' Margaret said. 'Where must you go? I thought we had you safely home at last.'

'I still have the Mitre's horse. Jonathan is holding him for me. And I want to return this to Merton.'

I drew the other wrapped book from my satchel to show them, then returned it. 'I shall not be long.'

On my way out, I picked up Basset's threatening note and dropped it into my scrip.

Having retrieved Rufus and sent Jonathan to tell his father that Alysoun was safely home, I mounted and rode to Merton.

'The Warden?' the porter said. 'He'll be in his lodgings, I'd say. Do you know the way?'

'Aye,' I said, setting off across the quad. I had been shown around the entire college by Allard Basset when I was about to join as a junior Fellow. I averted my eyes from the staircase to his rooms as I made for the Warden's lodgings.

It took some time to explain to William Durant why I was there and what had been happening under his very nose within his college. He had heard some mention that the Irish Psalter was in poor condition and not to be handled, but that was all. Initially, he was inclined to disbelieve my story, but when I unwrapped the Psalter and laid it before him in all its undiminished glory, he grew thoughtful.

'The two hired villains are now imprisoned in the castle,' I said, 'in the custody of Sheriff Walden, who will corroborate all I have told you about how my daughter was taken hostage. There is other evidence to link them to the murder of William Farringdon, who was to have come here in the Michaelmas term. Whichever way you look, I am afraid Merton is entangled in this affair. I am sure that, under questioning by the sheriff, these two men will be only too ready to claim that they were merely hired to act for another, the man who wanted to replace the Psalter with a copy and keep the ancient book for himself. He is a Merton man.'

The Warden leaned forward, frowning. He had said little during my explanation, but I could read from his expression that he now accepted it. This last remark, however, went too far.

'I cannot believe that is true.'

I sighed. 'I am sure Sheriff Walden will call on you tomorrow, but since I wanted to see the Psalter safely into your hands, I thought I should also show you this. Do you recognise the hand?'

I drew Basset's note from my scrip and laid it on top of the Psalter. It curled a little, and Durant smoothed it flat. His face changed from disbelief to shock. He knew the writing at once. Those trailing letters gave it away.

'I am afraid that Allard Basset is the man behind this plot,' I said, 'which has seen the theft of a valuable book, the murder of a gifted young man, an attack on my sister, and the kidnapping of my six-year-old daughter. I do not doubt that he meant what he threatens in that note. He would have killed her without a qualm.'

Picking up my empty satchel, I got to my feet. 'I will leave the matter with you. The university prefers to judge its own.'

If he detected any sarcasm in my voice, he showed no sign, for he was still too shocked. I let myself out of the Warden's lodgings and crossed to the staircase leading up to the book rooms. As usual, Olney was poring over some tome and gave me an unfriendly look. I did not sit down, but remained standing by the door, gazing down at him.

'I have found and brought back the Irish Psalter,' I said. 'William had hidden it in a safe place, where it could not be stolen again. I have handed it to the Warden.'

He had blanched white and dropped his quill, which left a great smear of ink on his sheaf of notes.

'The Warden now knows who was behind it all, so you need have no fear any longer of Allard Basset. I know your secret and so does Jordain Brinkylsworth.'

He staggered to his feet, clutching the edge of the desk or he might have fallen.

'You have told the Warden?'

I shook my head. 'He shall never hear it from me, or from Jordain. Why should a man, even if he be a scholar, not have the love of a family? I made my choice. You have chosen a more tortuous path, but I wish you well.'

In the doorway, I turned and looked back at him, small, hunched, perhaps still afraid, but with the light of hope in his eyes. I smiled at him.

'She is very pretty, your woman. And the boy favours you.'

–

By the time I had returned Rufus to the Mitre and walked home, I was very tired, but it was a satisfied tiredness. It was still early afternoon, but I sent the two journeymen home, and Jordain went back to Hart Hall.

'My students will either believe I have deserted them,' he said, 'or they will have eaten the whole week's supply of food. Or both.'

Alysoun woke long enough to eat an early supper and to fall asleep again over it.

Once the children were both abed, Margaret and I were sitting in the kitchen, she with her interminable sewing, I with my restored *Meditations* open on my lap, pretending to read, but doing no such thing, when there came a tentative tap on the street door. I walked through to see who would be calling at this hour. It was twilight, but not yet dark.

When I opened the door, I was astonished to see Philip Olney standing there, without his academic gown, in nothing more than a simple cotte and hose.

'Philip!' I said, 'come within.'

He shook his head. 'I'll not come in, Nicholas.'

We had both been surprised into such intimate terms by the events of the day and the dimming of the light.

'I want to apologise,' he said, 'for not thanking you, for—' He could not get the words out. 'I have not always treated you with courtesy, yet what you did seven years ago was more honest than what I have done, and you would have every right to report me to the Warden. I am grateful for your silence.'

'Philip,' I said, 'I hope you can find the happiness that I found with Elizabeth. It was God's will to cut it short, but I have never regretted my choice.'

He nodded, and half turned away. 'There is something else,' he said so quietly I could barely hear him. 'Half an hour ago, a fisherman drew Allard Basset's body from the Thames, not far down from our boundary wall. He had strapped to his chest a satchel full of stones.'

It was my turn to be shocked. 'What a tragic waste of a gifted man!' I said. 'I admired him beyond all others when I was a student. He was my hero. Dear God, I wanted to be like him! Now my evidence has destroyed him.'

'But he never forgave you for the choice you made,' Olney said, turning back to me. 'And do not think the blame lies with you. He brought his own destruction upon himself.'

He held out his hand to me and I took it.

'God go with 'ee, Philip,' I said.

'And with you, Nicholas.'

I gave a wicked grin. 'And give my regards to your lady.'

Perhaps I was mistaken, but I thought I heard him laugh as he walked away.

The street door locked and bolted, I walked through to the house. Margaret had fallen asleep, her hands resting on her sewing, which I slid away carefully and laid aside, lest she stab herself on the needle. None of us had had any sleep the previous night, yet I felt curiously wakeful.

The garden lay in silver and grey under a clear starlit sky, with the moon just rising, but not yet usurping the glory of the stars. I thought I had never seen so many, a bounty of God's jewels cast over a velvet black sky, which most of us never witness, tucked up asleep in our beds.

There was a strong, richly pungent scent of vegetable growth to my left, and the sweet and aromatic perfume of the herbs to my right. Why does the night bring out such scents so powerfully? A rustling came from the hen house as I passed, as one of the birds shifted in her sleep. Down in our small orchard even the bee skep was quiet. The fruit trees had mostly shed their blossoms now, and tiny fruits would be forming, no larger than the nail of my little finger. All that promise of the future, coiled tight within stem and bud and infant fruit.

The bench was a little damp with the night dew, but what did I care? I sat down and stretched out my legs. When I threw back my head I could see a wisp of cloud no bigger than a lady's veil drift across the sky from west to east, so thin that the stars shone through it.

I was enveloped in tranquillity and silence. Tomorrow I would ride out again to Godstow, peacefully and content, and I would tell Emma Thorgold all that had happened. I thought of those long, fine hands, ink-stained. And I smiled.

Historical Note

For those who know Oxford, there will be much here that is familiar, but also some oddities. The university structure had not yet taken on its later form, so that in 1353 undergraduate students were not admitted to the colleges. They lived in 'halls', or sometimes in town lodgings, and would only join a college if they proceeded to advanced study after completing the Trivium and Quadrivium.

It would be another century before the invention of printing replaced the handwritten book, but nevertheless booksellers did exist and in university towns they could be licensed to provide the *peciae*, extracts from essential texts. Students would hire and copy these, in order to have their own versions of the study texts, and the system provided booksellers (who were also stationers) with a regular income.

Only a handful of colleges existed at the time, and not all are extant. Gloucester became Worcester, Canterbury was replaced by Christ Church, much of Durham was taken over by St. John's College. Hart Hall has become Hertford College. You will not find the Hospital of St John, it has vanished under Magdalen. The monastic establishments were suppressed at the Reformation.

The area of dirty hovels north of St-Peter-in-the-East, inhabited by thieves and prostitutes, was swept away later in the fourteenth century and replaced by New College.

The main street plan survives, although the Broad now lies over the line of much of the filthy Canditch, and very little of the town wall can still be seen. Hammer Hall Lane is New College and Queens Lane. Even now the maze of waterways encompasses the town and the water meadows are still at risk of flooding.

A curious personal note. A later building replaced the medieval Holywell Mill, but as a first year student I cycled there once a week for a tutorial. Miller Wooton, I'm glad to say, no longer lives there.